6-

Pierce the Veil

By Bob Adamov

Other Emerson Moore adventures by Bob Adamov

Rainbow's End

The following publication provided reference material:

Jimisms by Vanita Oelschlager, Copyright 1999 by
Ultimate Acorn, Inc.

The poem, *Pink Velvet Ladies*, is used with the permission
of its writer, Jimmy Van Hoose from Jimmy's Café.

ISBN: 1-929774-33-8

Library of Congress Control Number: 2004104174

Cover art by John Joyce, red inc.

Perry's Monument photo by ©Kelly Faris Photography

Layout by Francine Smith

Submit all requests for reprinting to:
Greenleaf Book Group LLC
8227 Washington St. #2
Chagrin Falls, OH 44025

Published in the United States by:
Greenleaf Book Group LLC, Cleveland, Ohio
and
Packard Island Publishing, Cuyahoga Falls, Ohio

www.greenleafbookgroup.com
www.packardislandpublishing.com·

First Edition—May 2004

Printed in the United States

Acknowledgements

This book is dedicated to the memory of the real Mr. Cassidy, Louis "Hook" Cassidy, the master spinner of humorous stories. It's also dedicated to those wonderful people who are courageously fighting MS. Never give up!

My gratitude for the support and encouragement provided by Jim Oelschlager, "a hero in my eyes"; Clint Greenleaf at Greenleaf Book Group, who believed in me; and my friends in Put-in-Bay and at Jimmy's Café.

A special thank you to my team of editors and advisors: Hank Inman from Goldfinch Communications, Joe Weinstein, Kryste Stone, Ron Fields, Nicole Hirsh, and Greg Hite.

And I'd also like to extend a special thank you to so many of you readers who tracked me down by e-mail or in person at other book signings after reading *Rainbow's End* to let me know how much you enjoyed the first book in the series.

Mom, thank you for your encouragement!

The National Multiple Sclerosis Society will receive a portion of the proceeds from the sale of this book.

They that wait upon the Lord shall renew their strength; they shall mount up with wings as eagles; they shall run, and not be weary; and they shall walk, and not faint. – Isaiah 40:31

WESTERN LAKE ERIE

PUT-IN-BAY
SOUTH BASS ISLAND

PERRY'S MONUMENT

PEACH POINT

GIBRALTAR ISLAND

AUNT ANNE'S

BUCKEYE POINT

CHAPMAN'S POINT

Mike's Dr.

Massie's Dr.

Columbus Ave.

Lakeview Dr.

East Point Blvd.

Chapman

Delaware

Toledo Ave.

Hartford

Bayview Ave.

Victory

Erie St.

Sybil

Doller

Ibis

Concord Ave.

Portsmouth

Lakeview

Conlan

Thompson Road

Langram Road

Tri-Motor

New Colony

Mitchell Road

West Shore Blvd.

Catawba Ave.

Meechen

Trenton Ave.

AIRPORT

Niagra

South Bass Island
State Park

Put-In-Bay Road

BEACH

Birkman Investments
New York City

~

Alex Birkman slowly ran his 74-year-old hand through his thinning hair as he looked out of his Broad Street office window. It was late on a rainy November night.

He cleared his desk just as he had at the end of every day since founding his successful investment company 40 years ago. Being organized and able to find a file at a moment's notice when a client called was important to him.

Birkman liked routine. That way you didn't have to think twice about the trivial matters.

He walked across his office to his coat tree and placed the black fedora on his head. Slipping into his overcoat, he grabbed his umbrella and closed his office door behind him as he stepped out.

He paused to look at his staff who were completing the paperwork from the day's stock trading activities and for the required reporting. Birkman was a stickler for following the rules and reporting on schedule to the SEC and his clients—not that he ever worried about an investigation from the Securities and Exchange Commission. He ran a clean investment house.

Max Ratek glanced at Birkman as Birkman passed his desk. Ratek smiled. "Have a nice evening, Alex. It looks like a wet and dreary one out there tonight." Ratek pushed back from his desk and allowed his 6 foot 5 inch frame to stretch to its full length. Ratek's height combined with his ability to radiate energy immediately differentiated him from other people.

What a change in disposition from earlier in the day, Birkman thought to himself.

Ratek must have recovered from Birkman's harsh and very direct lecture. Birkman had sternly delivered his lecture because of an illegal approach Ratek had proposed regarding an insider-trading scheme—although the firm could have benefited lucratively if Birkman had permitted it.

Ratek and his close associate, Simon Grimes, had stormed out of Birkman's office following Birkman's lecture regarding ethics. Since the morning's meeting, Ratek had not spoken to Birkman unless it was necessary.

"Yes, yes. It does appear to be a bit gloomy," Birkman replied.

Birkman had his eye on the 23-year-old Ratek as a possible successor to him whenever he decided to retire. He felt that he owed it to Ratek since his father had been a close friend and junior partner in the firm. Following the death of Ratek's father from cancer four years ago, Birkman had taken Ratek under his wing and had tried to help with his professional growth.

Ratek had worked for the investment firm while he attended classes at NYU. Even at his young age, he had shown initiative and financial prowess rivaling senior financial professionals at the firm. His shrewd investing techniques resulted in garnering the best returns in the firm. Each quarter, Ratek had been assigned increasingly larger amounts of cash to invest and continued to amass substantial returns for his clients.

Ratek was shrewd like his father, but had a tendency toward crossing ethical boundaries with the schemes he proposed. He was unlike his father in his choice of friends. Birkman couldn't understand why Ratek established the close association with sleazy Simon Grimes whom he had met at NYU. Ratek had paid off several gambling debts for Grimes when Grimes had been involved with some loan sharks who were threatening Grimes with physical harm. As a result, Grimes grew very close to Ratek.

The slim, short, powerfully built Grimes seemed more like a street fighter than an investment analyst. But then again, Grimes did have a knack for coming across interesting bits of investment tips that he'd pick up. Nevertheless, Birkman was not comfortable with him and left him to Ratek to manage.

Birkman felt, at times, that he and Ratek had too much of a father-and-son relationship. Birkman had high expectations of Ratek and would become very disappointed in the young man's unethical approaches and attempts to circumvent stock trading regulations. Ratek always was looking for a short cut, a way to beat the system. Birkman sensed that Ratek wanted him to retire and transfer the daily management of the firm to him. However, Birkman felt that Ratek wasn't ready to head the firm. He was only a 23-year-old young buck.

Birkman opened the outer office door, pulled it shut as he stepped through and walked to the railing at the edge of the rectangular, sky lit atrium. Glancing down, he could see the deep red African marble floor in the courtyard six floors below.

He looked up at the skylight 16 floors above and the darkened sky. He smiled as he thought about his inner struggle between frugality and displays of success. He had coveted the office suite on the 20th floor, especially the spacious corner office with its private skylight.

On several occasions when the office suite had become available, the building's leasing agent had tried to convince him to lease it.

But at his age, he thought to himself, why should I spend the extra money? He was reluctant to move up to some suite that was a bit pretentious. After all, his clients were focused on the return on investment that he could deliver for them and not a spacious office suite. And Birkman was content to invest his profits rather than waste them frivously. The firm's overall returns weren't outstanding, but they were steady—avoiding the rollercoaster rides of some of the other investment houses.

Birkman resumed his walk to the elevator. He was pleased that the car was awaiting him when he pressed the down button and the Gothic-trimmed doors opened.

As he exited the elevator on the first floor, Birkman's footsteps echoed as he strode across the lobby's marble floor. He stepped through the revolving doors and paused under the brass portico so he could open his umbrella.

The wind had turned Broad Street into a wind tunnel and was driving sheets of rain like pointed daggers.

Birkman clutched his portfolio close to his body, gripped his umbrella firmly and began walking toward Water Street to catch a taxi.

With weather like this it could be especially tough finding a cab, he thought. He should have called one of the car services; but then again, it would have cost more money.

Birkman crossed Pearl Street and struggled against the wind and rain to the intersection of Broad and Water Street. He turned the corner at Water Street and sought refuge in a doorway 20 feet down from the intersection.

After catching his breath, Birkman eased himself from the doorway and crossed the sidewalk to the shelter of a large truck parked along the curb. Birkman stepped from behind the truck to see if any cabs were coming and slipped as he stepped back. He grabbed the rear of the truck to regain his balance.

Not as spry as I used to be. Maybe I should have called the car service, he mused to himself.

Waiting a few minutes, Birkman again eased himself around the rear of the truck. He saw the speeding cab and stepped out to flag it. When he realized the cab was already in service, he began to hurriedly step back and out of the cab's way.

Birkman seemed momentarily perplexed by the resistance that he felt in the middle of his back, hindering his attempt to move back. The growing resistance was now propelling him directly into the path of the speeding cab.

The cabby was running late and driving faster than weather conditions permitted. His eyes widened as he saw the figure suddenly appear in his path. The cab hit the pedestrian with a solid blow, throwing the body against the rear of the truck from where it had emerged so unexpectedly.

As the cabby kept driving, he thought to himself that things like this ended up causing him too much paperwork to complete.

Forms for this, forms for that. No need for me to stop and get involved the cabby thought.

The force of being struck first by the cab and then by hitting the rear of the truck took its toll on the 74-year-old man. His limp body took its final breath as it lay twisted halfway on the street and the sidewalk. A few passersby stopped in the driving rain and gathered around the crumpled body.

A weary policeman emerged from the crowd and checked the body for vitals. "Looks like he didn't make it folks. Any of you a witness to what happened here? Come on now, who's going to help me out as a witness?"

Amidst mutterings of "I didn't see a thing!" the crowd dispersed. They had their own business to mind and didn't want to get involved.

Thirty minutes later the door to Alex Birkman's office opened. Max Ratek spun around in Alex Birkman's chair to look nervously at who had entered the office unannounced.

The figure's eyes swept the office and noticed that Ratek's nameplate was displayed prominently on Birkman's desk.

"A bit premature, aren't we?" the figure asked as he shook rainwater from the coat that he was now discarding.

Relaxing, Ratek grinned slyly, "I've always been able to count on you. How did it go?"

"He's dead. Poor codger didn't even see me sneak up behind him. Last thing he knew was that someone pushed him in front of a cab."

"How do you know he's dead?" Ratek probed.

"Cop checked him over and pronounced him dead."

"Did anyone see you leave or return?"

"Nope. Used the rear staircase and rear exit door. Good thing he walks slowly. I caught up to him at Pearl and followed him from there. What's next?" Grimes asked.

Ratek slid a sealed envelope across the desk.

"This is as agreed. Now my friend, we are going to paint a masterpiece of investment success! Wall Street will be my canvas. I'm going to become the Michelangelo of Wall Street."

The Put-in-Bay Resort Town
South Bass Island, Ohio
Fifteen Years Later

～

The 450 horsepower radial engine roared, as the red 1943 Stearman biplane spun down toward the blue-green Lake Erie water. As Emerson Moore fought desperately to regain control, his goggles pressed tighter to his face and his white silk scarf fluttered violently behind the leather helmet on his head.

His sunset flight had begun quite normally, in a plane he had borrowed from a friend. He took off in the exquisite machine from the island's airport, and made a low pass over the downtown area, before heading toward Rattlesnake Island. He circled Rattlesnake twice before climbing to the southeast and back toward Put-in-Bay.

Halfway to Gibraltar Island, Emerson decided to try some aerobatics; he started a shallow dive north of Gibraltar Island. He pulled up into a loop. As he reached the top of the loop, Emerson heard a loud TWANG as the plane snap-rolled to the left and nosed down into a spin. Its wings were sheared off as the plane impacted the water off Gibraltar Island.

Emerson died upon impact.

Two days later, Emerson's body, dressed in a dark blue suit, white shirt and blue and white striped tie, lay in the coffin in St. Paul's Episcopal Church on Catawba Avenue. A steady stream of mourners paid their respects and gave condolences to Emerson's Aunt Anne, a longtime Put-in-Bay resident, with whom he resided.

Aunt Anne had been dabbing her red eyes and paused as she saw a familiar-looking person with red hair enter the rear of the church and make her way toward the coffin. It was Martine Tobin, the beautiful married woman who had stolen Emerson's heart a year ago when she and Emerson had met for the first time on the island.

Martine placed her hand on Emerson's folded hands and looked carefully at the tanned, handsome 42-year-old face displaying a peaceful smile. This was a jolting end to her vivid dreams and wishes of the man she cared about so much. Tears welled up in her eyes.

Martine felt an arm on hers and turned to see that Aunt Anne was standing next to her. Tears streaked Aunt Anne's face.

"Martine, how kind of you to come!" Aunt Anne said sincerely.

"I had to come," Martine said sadly. "One of the Ohio State University workers on Gibraltar Island has kept in touch with me since last summer and e-mailed me about his death. It's the least that I could do."

"He was such a good man," Aunt Anne reminisced.

"Yes, he was. And I cared for him very much!"

"I know. I always knew."

"I just wish that things could have worked out differently for the two of us. I don't know how they could have. How can you care so much about two men—one, your husband and the other, Emerson?" Martine questioned sadly.

Martine and Aunt Anne stood alone in silence for a few minutes. Then Martine leaned over the coffin and slowly lowered her head closer to Emerson's face. She kissed Emerson on the cheek.

Emerson smelled her *Giorgio* perfume and opened his eyes. His body was wet from sweat despite the bedroom's air conditioning. He shivered—and not just because of the room's coolness.

He looked around his room at his Aunt's house and realized he had been dreaming. The only place that he saw the mysterious Martine since last summer had been in his dreams. And that was both a good thing—since she was married, and a bad thing—since he still yearned for her.

At the urging of his Aunt Anne, Emerson had returned to the resort town of Put-in-Bay on South Bass Island. It had been approximately a year since he had visited and encountered confrontations with Great Lakes shipping magnate Jacques L'Hoste and his son, Francois.

His aunt had persuaded him to sell his Arlington, Virginia home and move into her home on East Point. She had argued that he was her only relative and with her aging, she could use his help around the house. She was 66-years-old now. Besides, when she died, she told him that the house would be his—so he'd better start taking care of it.

Since Emerson's job as an investigative reporter for *The Washington Post* required him to travel and he worked out of his home most of the time, it was a fairly easy sell to his boss, John Sedler. Sedler also thought it would be good for Emerson to move to South Bass Island and away from the haunting reminders of the tragic death of his wife and three-year-old son in Washington. Emerson had won his battle with the bottle and seemed more emotionally stable now that a year and a half had passed since their deaths.

Emerson enjoyed the island life and quickly made many friends on the island. He especially enjoyed his relationship with Barry and Sybil Hayen—the owners of *The Put-in-Bay Gazette*. Many evenings found Emerson and Barry sitting together on Barry's front porch, which overlooked the harbor, and discussing story ideas and island events.

Emerson's circle of friends on the island quickly grew as a result of his aunt's introductions and his natural likeability with people. He enjoyed the relationships that he had with the owners of the Islander Inn, Ashley Island House Bed and Breakfast and The Vineyard Bed and Breakfast.

The restaurant owners and bar owners also became fast friends with him. He forged friendships with many of the island's entertainers including the one and only Pat Dailey—the island's legendary troubadour, Alex Bevan, Bob Gatewood and the wildman himself—Westside Steve.

Often, Emerson would stop by and visit with the DeRivera Park staff including Tom, Chuck and Jack. He donated time and his writing skills to the Lake Erie Islands Historical Society and to the Chamber of Commerce.

Then there were the water excursions, like fishing for Lake Erie's famous walleye and perch with the owner of Miller Ferry or Mr. Cassidy, the island's self-appointed historian and retired dock master—as well as Aunt Anne's sweetheart. He enjoyed sailing and boating in the surrounding water.

At times, there were the airplane rides with that rascally Dennis Watson, the owner of the island's only airline service, Dairy Air. The sides of the fuselage were painted in black and white to resemble the patterns of a Holstein cow. Emerson would accompany Watson on flights to Fremont or Detroit to pick up passengers and Denny would fill Emerson's ear with the history of the island and stories about island life and tourists.

Island life agreed with Emerson.

LaGuardia Airport
New York City

~

The flight attendant looked down the aisle as the 737 touched down at LaGuardia on schedule at 8:10 A.M. The well-groomed, 6 foot 5 and impeccably attired passenger in first class aisle seat 2B caught her eye and winked at her.

She smiled back courteously. A bit much for me, she thought. Tall, good looking and the way he dressed reeked of money and success—or all show. She had seen all kinds of men on her flights and enjoyed guessing about their careers and success levels.

The plane neared the jetway, and the flight attendant began distributing the suit jackets to the first class passengers as it was announced that passengers could use their cell phones.

The apparently affluent passenger in 2B took the jacket as she handed it to him, saying, "Thank you, Honey."

She smiled and continued distributing jackets to the other passengers.

The passenger slipped on his suit jacket. The charcoal pinstripe suit had been tailored in Italy from exquisite Italian wool and cashmere. He tugged at the cuffs of his blue shirt with its white pencil stripes and white collar and checked his French blue brick cufflinks. He gave a quick pull on his gold silk and cotton tie, which had been specially woven in England.

He reached inside his suit jacket pocket to retrieve his cell phone and speed dialed a number in lower Manhattan.

A voice answered the call. "You were able to catch a flight back this morning?"

Before speaking, the passenger glanced at the passenger seated next to him—the one who had initially tried to engage him in conversation for which he had little time. He had been irritated since his private jet had an engine problem and could not take off that morning to return him to New York. There had been no other jets readily available for charter. He berated himself for spending the night in Cleveland and not flying back to New York last night after the dinner meeting had concluded.

Seeing his seatmate busily finishing a crossword puzzle in the newspaper, the passenger replied to the voice on the other end.

"Yes," he said in a disgusted tone. "Is my driver here?"

"Yes, he's waiting in baggage claim."

"I should be in the office within 35 minutes. Set up a meeting in the conference room with the team. My dinner meeting went well last night. Chocolate doughnut is in play." He chuckled softly as he said the code words.

He didn't want to say more over the cell phone. There were investors who used scanners in hopes of picking up cell phone conversations and inside information so that they could front-run deals by buying stock in companies targeted for a takeover.

"Okay, we'll be ready when you arrive."

The passenger ended the call and returned the cell phone to his inside breast pocket. He stood with the other passengers and retrieved his leather overnight case from the overhead compartment. As he prepared to walk down the aisle, he took one last condescending look at his seatmate working furiously to complete the crossword puzzle. He turned and exited the plane.

The seatmate put down his copy of the *Cleveland Plain Dealer* and looked at what he had written in row fourteen across. There was space for a ten-letter word for an ice cream flavor.

The passenger had crammed seventeen letters into the small space. He knew that the answer was not what he had written. He had written "chocolate doughnut."

Emerson Moore folded the paper and placed it in his briefcase. He had expected the flight from Cleveland to be relatively quiet and had been pleased when his frequent flier mileage had enabled him to upgrade into first class. You could meet very interesting people in first class and pick up story ideas.

He stood and exited the plane. He needed to call John Sedler at the *Post* on a pay phone and tell him that he might be onto a corporate takeover attempt. It could make for an interesting cradle-to-grave story if he could piece it together.

"Chocolate doughnut? And you heard him say it's in play?" Sedler asked incredulously on the other end of the phone.

"I wrote it down as he was talking. What do you think about a story?" Emerson queried.

"I like it. Any idea who the guy was?"

"No. Wall Street type. Well heeled. Arrogant," Emerson responded. "And I wonder if there isn't a link to the Cleveland area since he was on the Cleveland to LaGuardia flight this morning. It must have been a short trip to Cleveland as he just had a small overnight bag. I'd guess that he met with someone there and decided to pull the trigger."

"Let's go for it then. See what you can dig up in New York. You've built up enough contacts there. And with you in Put-in-Bay, you're close enough to any breaking events in Northeast Ohio, if that is indeed where the target company is."

"Great. I'll get started. Coincidentally, I'm here to see Carl Chrisman."

"The reporter who used to work for us a few years back?"

"One and the same."

"Is he still with that public relations firm?" Sedler inquired.

"Yep. He's still working with them—and he's involved with their crisis management group. He may have some ideas."

"Be careful. Don't give away your inside track on this," Sedler cautioned.

"Carl and I have a pretty good relationship. I'll be careful, but I don't think I have too much concern about him."

"Okay then. Keep me in the loop. Good luck, Emerson."

"Thanks." Emerson ended the call and caught a cab to Chrisman's midtown office at Highsmith Partners.

Thirty minutes later the cab deposited Emerson at the Lexington Avenue entrance to Highsmith Partners. It was still early morning on a sunny, June day.

Birkman Investments
New York City

~

Max Ratek tugged on the cuffs of his blue shirt with the white pencil stripes and white collar as he strode into the office suite of Birkman Investments on the 20th floor where he had relocated the firm several years ago. He curtly greeted a number of his employees as he entered his private corner office with its inviting skylight.

Since taking control of Birkman Investments, he had grown the firm's wealth by his savvy investing and willingness to cross over into the dark side with some of his more unscrupulous dealings. A little inside information here and there helped boost his wealth accumulation. He had been careful in his dealings so that the SEC's Enforcement Division couldn't nail him.

He had grown the firm's reputation for taking significant stock ownership in underperforming companies and forcing management to give him board seats and heed his directions. The other pension fund managers would follow his lead and support him as they knew that he could drive the stock price up, make a good profit and exit the company.

Ratek was a passionate man, driven by unbridled greed and a passion to amass wealth. His warrior instincts had him on edge like a caged tiger ready to leap into a takeover battle anytime that he sensed he could make a huge return.

He never thought twice about the impact he had on the company's employees, customers or the communities in which they operated. His focus was on the short-term return, not people. Once he raped and pillaged, many of the companies did not recover. They folded or were acquired by competitors, resulting in loss of employee jobs and plant shutdowns.

He had worked hard to become the Michelangelo of Wall Street and relished the media's attention. He was a lightning rod for stories about investment houses with very high returns.

Ratek checked his messages, made one quick international phone call and walked to the conference room. He glanced at the clock as he entered. The stock market would open in the next few minutes.

Grimes was waiting for Ratek. With Grimes were Michael Searle, Birkman's top analyst; Jerry Olsen, Birkman's financial strategist; and Judith Beckwith, a financial analyst who was a statuesque blonde with a patrician attitude about her.

Ratek noted as he sat at his usual seat at the head of the long conference table that a copy of the financial analyses and the strategic takeover plan were awaiting him. He expertly clipped the end of the cigar he was holding and lit it.

"Jerry, I've confirmed our financing. Usual approach on the buy side?" Ratek asked.

"Right. We'll begin buying shares today through a couple of brokers who will help mask our interest. We'll balance the activity so as not to cause any unnecessary increase in the stock price due to buying pressure."

"We've got to keep the lid on this. Limit knowledge on a need to know basis! I don't want any of these other deal junkies to front-run this!" Ratek asserted as his adrenaline began to surge. Completing deals satisfied Ratek's inner need for gratification and added to his successful Wall Street reputation.

"Yes, sir. As we have always done. We will be preparing daily reports to show our share accumulation."

"Be sure to let me know when we get close to the 5 percent threshold on ownership. As we have done in the past, we'll hold off until the last moment before we complete the required filing with the SEC. Once we get to the 5 percent, go ahead and acquire more shares to take us up to the 10 percent ownership level quickly."

"Right. But then again, we'll be careful about running up the price needlessly," Jerry commented.

"Simon, I trust you've had your usual conversations about keeping this quiet with our two brokers who will be buying shares." Ratek waited for the response as he studied his cigar smoke curling upward.

"I met with the two of them separately last night and told them we'd be making the play and to keep their mouths shut. They understand the consequences." Grimes paused as he smiled evilly at the consequences comment. "Besides, they've their eyes on the commissions for the purchases."

"You're comfortable enough with these two brokers? I know we've used them before, but I want to mask our purchases as much as possible on this one." Ratek wanted more reassurance.

Grimes smiled slyly. "I met with them at their homes to underscore that I knew where they lived. And I told them as I was leaving that I hoped that their families continued to enjoy good health. I don't expect any problems with these two."

"Good." Turning to Michael Searle, Ratek asked, "You're still comfortable with the numbers and pro formas?"

Searle peered over the edge of his glasses. "Yes, I am. We've got a real opportunity to mine the hidden wealth there. The break-up valuation is holding."

Judith added coolly, "The over funded pension assets are deal sweeteners." Judith saw that Grimes had been staring at her as she commented. It wasn't the first time she had caught the pompous little rat giving her admiring glances.

Ratek saw the time on the clock on the conference room's wall. The stock market had opened. "Okay, let's get this juggernaut rolling. Jerry, make the call to the brokers."

Highsmith Partners
New York City

~

"Emerson! Good to see you!" Carl Chrisman greeted Emerson warmly in the lobby of Highsmith Partners. He had his briefcase in one hand. "I've got an emergency with a breaking crisis, but I can take a few minutes with you. I apologize. This just broke!"

"No problem with me. I understand. I get caught up in last minute demands on time."

"Let's grab a cup in the café on street level," Chrisman suggested.

"Fine with me."

"Hey, did I hear right that you sold your place in Virginia and moved out to an island in Lake Erie?" Chrisman asked his friend as they stepped into the elevator.

"Yes. It's about an hour west of Cleveland. Real idyllic. Moved in with my aunt who is having some trouble in keeping up the place. Beautiful sunsets, great rainbows, good fishing and boating," Emerson offered. "I'm using it as my base and travel from there when I'm working on stories."

"Sounds like a great place!"

"Still enjoying the public relations side of things?" Emerson questioned.

"Big time. It's the rush you get from working on these crisis management issues. Can you manage the situation? Can you make the client come across in the best positive light and take into consideration all the constituencies that you need to be concerned about? That's what it's about!"

"Can you tell me what crisis is breaking now?"

"Emerson, you know I can't tell you. It's confidential. If I told you, it'd be in the *Post* tomorrow."

"Carl, we go way back. You can tell me off the record."

"And since when does off the record mean anything?" Chrisman agitated.

"You know my integrity. I keep my word."

The elevator reached street level and they walked over to the café.

"Okay, Okay. It appears that one of the brokerage houses had one of its brokers falsifying statements for clients. The clients thought that their dollars were earning strong returns for them, but they were never invested. When a client wanted to withdraw from his account, the broker would rob Peter to pay Paul. He siphoned a lot of the money for his personal gain."

"And you want me to keep that quiet?"

"It seems to me that someone said it'd be off the record and that someone is supposed to be of high integrity!" Chrisman teased. He knew that Emerson would not break his word.

"Oh, you're killing me!"

"Not a word! You promised!"

They sat down at a table near the front window which overlooked the street.

Emerson sipped his coffee and picked up the chocolate doughnut that he had ordered. "Carl, when you look at this doughnut, does it trigger any thoughts about any company?"

"Just a doughnut company. Why?"

Emerson wanted to be careful as to how he worded his next comment.

"Just something that I overheard this morning on the plane. Guy was talking about a company that reminded him of a chocolate doughnut."

"Got me." Chrisman began devouring his bagel with cream cheese.

Emerson let his mind wander. What company headquartered in northeast Ohio had anything to do with chocolate doughnuts?

He thought about the principal industries in northeast Ohio. Steel? No. Healthcare? No. Nothing came to mind. Jewelry? Uh-uh. Polymers? Maybe, but what was the connection? Vacuum cleaners and sweepers? Don't think so. Tires? Hmm...tires? Could it be that obvious? Doubtful, but worth following up on. He had to start somewhere.

Emerson's eyes followed a policeman who had purchased a bag of doughnuts and was munching on a glazed doughnut as he left the café. The policeman walked over to a waiting police car and Emerson's eyes focused on the tires. Black and round like doughnuts.

Maybe the takeover target was a tire company in Ohio! Emerson recalled that Akron, Ohio had been the world's tire capital at one time.

Chrisman interrupted his thoughts as the police car pulled into traffic. "I apologize, but I need to run to this meeting. Maybe you can call me the next time you're in town and we can spend more time together."

"Sure, I'll look forward to it."

"It's not every day that you get to spend time with someone who has won a Pulitzer Prize for their investigative reporting!"

Emerson grinned modestly, "It's no big thing. Thanks for seeing me today."

They shook hands and Chrisman ran to catch a cab. Emerson caught the next cab for a meeting he had at Columbia University later that morning. He was anxious for some free time so that he could go on line and research his ideas about a tire company being the takeover target.

Fallsview Tire & Rubber Company
Cuyahoga Falls, Ohio
A Week Later

~

Fallsview Tire's corporate headquarters was located at the intersection of Front Street and Broad Boulevard where it overlooked the Cuyahoga River. It was just a short 30-mile drive southeast of downtown Cleveland and eight miles from downtown Akron.

Jay Oakes, vice president—investor & public relations, had been looking at a traffic accident from his third story office window which overlooked the river and the expressway on the other side of the river. He reached to answer his ringing phone.

"Oakes, here. How may I assist you?" he queried.

"Jay, it's Jimmy Malloy," the excited voice on the other end responded.

Malloy was the senior vice president of Flanagan & Son, the proxy solicitation and stock surveillance firm that Oakes had retained when he joined Fallsview Tire six weeks ago. They had worked together on numerous projects over the years and had a deep mutual respect for each other.

"Hello, Jimmy. What's up?" Oakes responded.

"I've got you on the speaker phone. Ed and Ann are with me."

It sounded serious. Ann Wright headed the proxy fight team and Ed Madigan headed the stock surveillance team.

"You've got my attention."

"It looks like you've got a player in your stock. By our estimates, we think someone has accumulated about six percent of your shares," Malloy explained.

"Six percent! Are you sure?" Oakes was fully focused on the discussion. This was not what he had expected when he joined Fallsview Tire. His employment had been full of surprises.

"Jay, it looks like two brokers are buying your shares. They've been buying in small blocks," Ed Madigan offered.

"How did you spot them?"

"They changed their strategy and began buying bigger blocks. We figured that they had hit the five percent level so whoever is behind this will have to file with the SEC within 10 days. Then the whole world will know who's interested in your company," Madigan explained.

"Jay, we're going to turn over every stone we can to find the beneficial owner of the shares," Malloy said confidently. "We're running ownership reports and Ann is going to look at voting tendencies of your institutional holders—whether they will support a dissident or not, just in case it's a dissident."

"Thanks, Jimmy. I need you guys to pierce the veil as quickly as possible and find out who's behind all of this. I'll inform management here. We may want to visit with you there and discuss strategy."

"No problem. Well, here we go again, Jay," Malloy stated.

"Yeah, here we go again. Talk to you later—and a big time thank you for everything you guys are doing on this one." Oakes ended the call. He and Malloy had been joking in a prior phone conversation that Oakes had a cloud following him—each company he had joined in the past few years ran into takeover problems, SEC investigations or some sort of crisis management situation. Oakes was becoming more concerned about the reality of the comments.

Oakes looked at his trading monitor and saw that the stock price was relatively stable. Trading volume seemed to be growing. They probably still had time to put together a strategy. Whoever the dissident was, he probably did not know that Fallsview Tire had an early warning system in place.

Oakes pushed back from his desk and thought for a few moments about the last six weeks on the job. He had joined the $6 billion company in June and on the first day of employment was directed by his boss, the chief financial officer, to prepare a press release. The release would announce that earnings for the quarter would be significantly below expectations. Wall Street expected to see 36 cents per share and they were going to deliver 4 cents per share.

This earnings shortfall was due primarily to integration issues and unanticipated costs with Millington Trucking Company, a company Fallsview Tire acquired six months ago. On paper the acquisition had made sense. It had huge win-win potential. Fallsview Tire would incur lower shipping expense by operating its own trucking company and the trucking subsidiary would be supplied with Fallsview Tire's tires which would help reduce their costs.

Employee turnover issues and problems with two different computer systems not communicating effectively had hidden the full impact of the problem until recently. The problem was much larger than anyone had anticipated.

The impact of the press release sent the stock dropping over the last six weeks from $36.00 on the day that Oakes began his employment to $16.00.

A week after the initial press release was issued, Oakes had been summoned into the office of company chairman and CEO,

Greg Owens. Owens had pulled another surprise. He told Oakes to write a second press release to announce the resignation of the company's chief financial officer. Oakes had been stunned despite knowing that rumors had been circulating that Owens was looking for a scapegoat, and might be targeting popular CFO Cliff Bronson. Oakes returned to his office to write the release as directed and wondered what the next surprise would be.

Once the release about the CFO's departure hit the press, Oakes was busy responding to Wall Street investors, stock analysts and the media, as well as trying to direct internal employee communications for a company that he had just joined and knew little about. It was a good thing that Oakes liked challenges.

Oakes left his office and went to the office of the company's chief legal officer, Joe Weimar. Oakes had developed a cordial and respectful friendship with the wiry and street-smart Weimar since the first day that Oakes joined the company.

Oakes entered Weimar's paneled office, an office much nicer than Oakes' office. Oakes used to jokingly complain that his office was the size of a broom closet when compared to Weimar's. Stacks of files and papers lined three walls of Weimar's office. Oakes had often teased Weimar about knocking over the stacks and causing more of a mess.

"Joe?" Oakes saw that he was interrupting Weimar's concentration on a brief.

"And what is it now? You get yourself in a jam that you need me to bail you out of or what?" Weimar asked good-naturedly with his deep voice.

"We've got a problem," Oakes started seriously. "Our stock watch firm just called and thinks someone has bought six percent of our stock."

"Do they know who?" Joe laid the file on his desk top and fully focused on the matter at hand.

"No. They are trying to pierce the veil and identify the actual owner, as well as what type of position this owner takes with companies. It could be an unfriendly dissident."

"Have you told Greg yet?"

"No. You're the first."

"Okay, let's go see him now. And don't run me down with that SUV of yours."

Oakes was relieved by Joe's reaction to the news and was careful not to hit Joe with his powered scooter.

Oakes had been relatively confined to the scooter or his high tech wheel chair for the last two years as he continued his battle with multiple sclerosis.

Oakes had a habit of looking at the bright side of life. He would banter others about his disease or the use of his scooter or wheel chair. The scooter he was using now had a wet black look and the new quiet running high torque motor which gave it a top speed of five miles an hour.

"Race you!" Oakes teased as he passed Weimar on their way to Owens' office.

"You're going to get a ticket one of these days," Weimar joked as Oakes narrowly missed striking the mail boy.

It took less than two minutes for them to reach the small office next to Owens' office. It was occupied by Owens' executive assistant, Lita Sterling.

"Is Greg available?" Weimar asked. "Lita, we need to see him right away."

Lita looked over the two visitors and sensed their urgency. She was a pro. In her loyal 32-year career at the company, especially the last two as Greg's assistant and the prior ten as the former CEO's assistant, she had seen many visitors vie for the CEO's time. She was at the point where she could quickly determine which visitors came with very serious matters, and which visitors were potential interruptions.

She could tell that this was urgent by the looks of concern on Weimar and Oakes.

"One moment and I'll check."

She ran a hand through her graying hair as she rose from her desk, knocked on Owens's door and stepped inside. She returned quickly.

"He'll see both of you now," she said as she held the door open for them. Lita stood about 5 feet 8 inches tall.

"Thanks, Lita," Weimar stated as he walked past the attractive assistant.

Lita closed the door behind them as the two entered Owens' large cherry-paneled office which reflected Owens' love of the outdoors. It was decorated with mallard duck decoys, trout nets and fishing rods, as well as mounted ducks, pheasants and a large buffalo head. Below the buffalo head was displayed an elk horn obsidian skinner which Owens had allegedly found in Montana and used to skin a buffalo which he had killed.

The fifty-six year old, balding Owens was quite a sportsman and enjoyed the fun of the hunt. He had been with Fallsview Tire for 24 years and had had a successful career in its marketing and operations group. He had been responsible for the extremely successful marketing campaign about putting the go in Fallsview Tire. It was no coincidence that his initials were G.O.

Owens had replaced the popular Steve Walent two years sooner than planned. Walent had elected to step down to spend more time with his wife, who was dying of cancer. He was sorely missed by employees who were still trying to adjust to Owens' more direct style. Walent's skill with employees and Wall Street had resulted in a very profitable company and high stock price. His shoes were big shoes for the inexperienced Owens to fill.

Owens' goal was to continue the growth and develop his own legacy at whatever the cost. His public facade was very appealing, but in private he could turn on you and shred subordinates. His style was to manage by fear when necessary.

"And what brings you two gentlemen to my humble abode this morning?" Owens asked as Weimar settled into a chair and Oakes positioned himself next to Weimar.

"Greg, it looks like we may have a problem with trading in our stock. Jay will explain what happened this morning," Weimar stated.

"We received a call from Jimmy Malloy who runs our stock watch service. They indicate that someone has accumulated about six percent of our shares through two brokers. We don't know who yet. They're trying to find out who's behind this. We call it piercing the veil of secrecy," Oakes explained.

Owens did not understand all of the intricacies of Wall Street and relied heavily on Weimar and Oakes to help him.

"I know we've had this discussion before, but tell me again

how the stock watch firm works," Owens said to Oakes.

"They have monitors that they are constantly watching and which are tied directly to the trading activities. They track settlement reports, talk with floor traders, our stock specialist..."

Owens interrupted, "Stock specialist. What do they do?"

"Every company is assigned a specialist on the floor of the exchange. His job is to coordinate the buying and selling of the shares like an auctioneer. The brokers contact him to make their purchases or sales. Sometimes the specialist will buy shares to a certain extent to support the stock price."

"Who do you think is buying our stock? Does the specialist know?" Owens asked hurriedly.

Weimar commented, "Greg, it's too early to tell. The specialist knows which brokers are buying but not who is telling the brokers to buy. It could be as simple as a major value player taking a position in our shares because they think we're a good buy right now. Or it could be a dissident who believes he can drive up the stock price by forcing us to give him a board seat or stirring up the other major investors. With our stock depressed right now, it could be wide open. There are filings that have to take place as mandated by the SEC and we can watch for the filing so we know who it is."

Oakes added, "And the stock watch guys will use their ears on the street to see what they can pick up. Many times they can beat the filing and that edge will give us extra time to plot our strategy."

"How long until they are required to file?" Owens asked.

"Within 10 days of securing five percent ownership," Oakes responded.

"So, you think this depressed stock price makes us attractive?" Owens quizzed.

"It could to a new investor," Weimar commented.

"Maybe we shouldn't have gone after that trucking company. I shouldn't have listened to Cliff about the synergy we would experience by buying Millington Trucking, nor about how well the integration was going. On schedule and below cost projections! He didn't know what he was talking about. Should have fired him sooner."

Weimar and Oakes listened as Owens talked about the recently departed chief financial officer. They both knew that the CFO had tried to discourage the purchase, but Owens would not listen to him.

"Joe, you've got a lot of contacts in New York. Who should we get to assist us on the legal side? I want us to start preparing."

"P. Dayton Ford is one of the top takeover lawyers in New York. I can call him to make sure his firm has no conflicts and can represent us."

"Conflicts?" Owens questioned.

"If they are working for the buyer, they can't represent us," Weimar explained.

Oakes cautioned, "We might want to hold off until we know who it is. If Ford is representing a dissident, we would tip our hand to them that we know about the stock accumulation. Can you give Malloy 24 hours to identify who it is? They're one of the best on the street. If it's a dissident, they typically use the same lawyers every time so we'll know who not to approach about representing us."

"Good idea. Tell Malloy he has 24 hours. I want you to get Carli involved on this. She's on vacation somewhere in Canada, so you'll have to track her down. Lita can make the call for you. I want the three of you to keep this quiet and be prepared to draft a plan once we know who in the world this is. Jay, I'm counting on your help because you're the only guy in our company who has experience in this type of matter."

"More experienced than I'd like to be," Oakes said. "One more thing."

"Yes?" Owens looked puzzled.

"These Wall Street guys can be like sharks. If any of the other funds get wind of this, they could move quickly to take ownership positions in our stock. They'll smell the blood in the water."

"Even more reason for us to do everything we can to keep this close to the vest," Owens responded.

"Greg, we'll get in touch with Carli," Joe added as he rose to leave the office.

"Keep me advised of any breaking developments," Owens instructed with deep concern.

Weimar and Oakes left Owens' office and confirmed that Lita had Carli Dansen's number. They asked her to call Carli at the lodge where she and her husband were staying in Alberta. Carli was the company controller and acting chief financial officer.

Weimar and Oakes returned to Weimar's office to await the transfer of the call from Lita. They didn't have to wait long.

"Hi, Joe. Hi, Jay," the buoyant Carli greeted them. "You just caught us. We're on the deck having an early breakfast before we go hiking up to Great Bear Lake."

"Having fun?" Weimar asked.

"A great time!" Then she paused as she heard something disconcerting in the tone of Joe's voice. "Is everything okay back there? You sound a bit glum."

"How would you like to take a hike back here?"

"Oh, oh. Tell me what's going on," the strawberry blonde said seriously.

Weimar and Oakes quickly relayed to her what had transpired that morning.

"This is serious. I'll catch the next available flight back. I'd hope to be in the office late tomorrow or first thing the next day. I'll call you when I change planes in Minneapolis."

"Sorry to ruin your vacation Carli," Oakes offered sympathetically.

"The forecast calls for rain the rest of the week anyway. See you soon."

Carli hung up.

"I'd better get back to my office and see if there're any messages for me and what the stock's doing now. I've got to call Malloy, too, and let him know that he's got 24 hours in which to identify whoever this is," Oakes said as he wheeled out of Weimar's office.

Birkman Investments
New York City

～

"I told you not to call me here!" an angry Ratek stormed as he recognized the voice on the other end of the phone.

"But, it was important. I have a tip for you," the caller said eagerly.

"Meet me tonight at Delmonico's at 7 o'clock. And don't call this number again."

"Sure, sure. 7 o'clock at Delmonico's."

Ratek hung up the phone and thought about the caller. Carney worked for one of the major investment banking houses and usually provided Ratek with good tips on deals that were in the works. The last one had cost Ratek's firm dearly when he purchased stock based on the tip and the deal didn't develop as planned. Carney didn't return his fees. He couldn't. He spent the money on the mistress he kept.

Ratek picked up the phone and speed dialed a number. "Simon, could you step into my office? We now have a dinner meeting planned for this evening."

Promptly at 7 P.M., a nervous Carney entered the front door of Delmonico's on Beaver Street. He told the maitre'd that he was meeting someone and was about to enter the dining area to look for Ratek when a short, smarmy-faced man stopped him.

"Mr. Carney?"

"Yes."

"You're here for the 7 o'clock meeting?"

"Yes. Who are you?"

"I'm an associate of the gentleman with whom you are meeting. Could you follow me please and don't say anything."

Carney followed the tough looking gentleman down a narrow hallway to the men's restroom. As they entered, the gentleman pulled a hand-held device from his pocket and began to run the device, which turned out to be a scanner, over Carney.

"What do you think you're doing?" Carney challenged.

The dangerous looking gentleman put a finger to his lips to silence Carney. The gentleman's tough stare sent a chill through Carney.

Grimes completed scanning Carney for any electronic eavesdropping equipment. "Can't be too careful these days, you know."

Carney nodded his head nervously.

"You're clean. Follow me."

Carney followed Grimes down the hallway and back to the restaurant's dining area where Grimes stepped aside to allow Carney to pass. Grimes gave Ratek a nod to signify that Carney was clean as Carney walked to Ratek's table in a dark corner of the restaurant. Carney sat down and quickly began to drink the Manhattan that Ratek always had awaiting him.

"Mr. Carney, do not ever call me on that number. You've been told to use a drop to get messages to me."

"I know, but this was urgent. I just learned that we may be taking a large position in a company that may be in play and I wanted to get the information to you so that you could move into the stock first and at a lower price."

Ratek's eyebrows raised as his interest was piqued.

"And what company is this?"

"Fallsview Tire & Rubber Company," Carney said triumphantly.

"Hmmm. And does your firm know who put the company in play?" Ratek didn't want to appear too anxious, but he was eager to learn as to whether the word was out that he was behind the play.

"No. They monitor the trading volume of a number of companies and saw a trend in volume increases in Fallsview Tire's stock trades. It's coming from two brokers, but they're not sure who's behind the buying."

"Interesting. I appreciate the information and do keep me advised of any breaking developments on this one. You'll find a briefcase on this chair between us with your usual fee. You still owe us for the last bit of breaking news that didn't pan out. So, just keep me in the loop on this one and I'll forget about the last one."

"Sounds fair to me," Carney responded quickly as he peeked to see the briefcase on the chair. The rent payment on his mistress's apartment was late and this would help him.

"I'm afraid I won't be able to join you for dinner as I've other plans this evening."

"That's quite all right. I really shouldn't stay either. I've plans with my family tonight," Carney replied.

Liar, Ratek thought to himself. "Please wait a few minutes before leaving. I'll settle the bill as I leave."

Ratek looked casually around the room to make sure that no one had been paying too much attention to the two of them. He rose from his chair, settled the bill with the waiter and left the restaurant. His car and driver were awaiting him as he emerged from the restaurant.

As soon as Ratek left the restaurant, Carney eagerly grabbed the briefcase from the chair and slowly opened it. He looked inside at the $25,000 in cash and quickly closed the briefcase. After waiting five minutes, which seemed more like an eternity, Carney felt that it was safe to leave the restaurant.

He turned left from the restaurant and began walking down Beaver Street. He was thinking about how pleased Nikki would be when he showed up with her rent payment. Nikki always had a special way of showing him her gratitude. As he hurried along deep in thought and eager anticipation, he didn't notice that he was being followed.

Fallsview Tire & Rubber Company
The Next Day

∼

"Jay, it's Birkman Investments and that marquee name, Max Ratek. You've got your hands full," Malloy warned Oakes over the phone.

Oakes responded, "Crap! They're one of the ones that like to come in and squeeze company management just to inflate the stock price."

"You got it. They're one of the major dissident players out there. They're bottom feeders, looking for companies in distress. If you don't turn it around, they'll get the other pension fund managers to circle around like vultures to support their initiatives and may force a sale of the company or a breakup. Sometimes the value of the parts is greater than the whole. They don't care at all about employees, customers or the communities in which they operate. It's bottom line greed.

"My team is putting together an analysis of your current shareholder base and their voting tendencies if they have been in a stock that Birkman is in. We'll also e-mail you a profile of the Birkman team."

Oakes recalled seeing Ratek's picture on the cover of a recent business magazine. The headline had stuck with him. *Ratek— The Michelangelo of Wall Street.*

He could paint a deal like no other dealmaker on the street. His approach with companies was ruthless and his strategies were legendary.

Oakes asked, "How's our trading pattern today?"

"Good so far. We don't see any order imbalance on the buy or sell side. Stock trading volume is above average, but we haven't picked up on any rumors yet that the street knows you're in play. Jay, it would probably be a good idea for you and your associates to come in for a strategy session."

"We were planning on it. Do you know if P. Dayton Ford usually works for Birkman?"

Malloy laughed. "No way. Ford and Ratek clashed a number of years ago on a deal and Ford has never forgiven Ratek for his failure to honor a handshake agreement between them."

"We may want Ford to represent us. I need to update our team. Jimmy?"

"Yes?"

"Thanks!"

"It's what I'm here for! Talk to you soon."

Malloy had a deep admiration for Oakes's business acumen and the manner in which he fought his MS.

Ten minutes later, Oakes caught up with Owens, Weimar and Carli Dansen as they headed to the corporate cafeteria for lunch.

"I've got news! Let's step into this conference room," Oakes suggested. The four of them quickly moved into the nearby conference room.

"Where do we stand?" Owens inquired anxiously.

"It's our worst nightmare. Jimmy Malloy just called and said that it's Max Ratek and his Birkman Investments firm. Once they secure significant stock ownership, they begin to demand action to improve the stock price and may demand a board seat so they can influence corporate profitability."

"Didn't I read about this Ratek recently?" Owens thought aloud.

"You're probably thinking about a recent spread in *BusinessWeek* where they dubbed Ratek as *'The Michelangelo of Wall Street.'* This guy is a dangerous threat to us," Weimar cautioned.

"Yes, I do remember reading about him. I believe *The Wall Street Journal* had some articles about his actions with regards to a number of companies in which he took ownership positions," Oakes added.

The usually upbeat Carli seriously probed, "Is the word out yet, or is it still quiet?"

"As far as Malloy can tell, the other vultures don't yet know that Fallsview Tire is a target. There's been a major increase in trading volume. Malloy is checking on the voting patterns of our current holders in the event that some of them have been involved with other Ratek-owned companies," Oakes explained.

"I think that we need to move quickly and put together a strategy for dealing with him," Carli suggested.

"Carli has a good point, Greg. We need to put together a strategy to address our various constituencies—our employees, our other investors, customers, suppliers, community and local government. Jay, do we know if P. Dayton Ford does work for Ratek today?" Weimar asked.

"Good news. I asked Malloy about that. Apparently, Ford and Ratek are at odds. There should be no problem in using him," Oakes replied.

Owens outlined a plan. "Folks, here's what I'd like you to do. I want you in New York tomorrow meeting with Jimmy Malloy and Ford. Figure out a strategy to address the various constituencies that you just mentioned and how we should deal with Ratek when and if he calls. I expect he will be calling. We also need to be ready for the media to come knocking at our door. Let's make sure that we all are in agreement with what the company position should be," Owens instructed.

The three nodded their understanding of the instructions.

"Okay, let's go to lunch. Jay, care to join us? We're going to the mystery meat palace and seeing what kind of fresh road kill they have," Owens joked as he thought about getting caught up in the hunt. He might be able to add this battle to his trophy case.

"Thanks, but I'll pass today. I want to stay close to my phone and the stock monitor."

"Okay then, let's go. Joe and Carli, let's be upbeat for our employees."

Owens, Weimar and Carli left the conference room and went to the company's lower level cafeteria whose large windows overlooked a series of waterfalls on the Cuyahoga River.

Birkman Investments
New York City

~

The phone's incessant ringing interrupted Ratek's conversation with Grimes. "Yes?" he said as he answered.

"It's me!" a jittery Carney responded.

"Didn't I tell you not to call me on this number?" Ratek angrily questioned.

"It's important."

"What is it now?" Ratek asked.

"I was mugged and robbed last night about two blocks from the restaurant. They beat me up and took the briefcase! I had to be treated at the hospital last night, but I'm out now. I need the money!" Carney's stress level was increasing.

"And what do you expect me to do? I'm not in the lending business. I'd suggest that you take more care with your possessions. Now, I must really go."

"But, I need cash. I've got to pay Nikki's rent or she'll dump me," Carney pleaded.

"Not my problem. Good day." Ratek hung up the phone and looked at Grimes. "Did you have assistance last night? I heard him say 'they.'"

"No. But when I was finished with him, he probably felt like he had been mugged by several people," Grimes retorted proudly as he slid the cash-filled briefcase across the desk. "I wore a ski mask."

"It seems that his amorous escapade may draw to an end. Pity. Pity. Combined with the return of my cash and the beating you gave him, it's the icing on the cake. It'll help make up for the last so-called lead he gave us."

Ratek began taking the cash out of the briefcase and placing it into the opened wall safe.

Aunt Anne's House
Put-in-Bay

～

Emerson completed his internet search of tire companies located in northeast Ohio. There were only three and one was a subsidiary of a Japanese tire company. Fallsview Tire was the only publicly traded company that was having serious financial difficulty.

Emerson sat back in his chair and looked out the window at the boats docked in the harbor and moored to the buoys. He gazed longingly at Gibraltar Island across the harbor, and agonized over his memories of Martine—the one who got away.

Emerson noticed the breeze rippling through the leaves of the trees on Gibraltar Island and thought it'd be a good day for a sail. He planned to finish up early and take a sail that afternoon. He glanced down at his Aunt's dock and saw the small red-hulled sailboat pulling at its lines as if it was eager to be set free in the breeze. It would be a fun afternoon.

Emerson turned back to his laptop and began to search *Yahoo Finance* for data on Fallsview Tire. He saw a growing trend in trading volume increases and that the stock price appeared to be slowly rising based on the trading demand and a low of $16.00 a share. He next reviewed the company profile and insider trading reports which showed no unusual activity by the key officer group.

Turning next to the press releases, Emerson quickly scrolled through several of the releases and saw that Fallsview Tire's profitability and stock price had plummeted recently. As he read through the releases, he saw that it appeared the troubles stemmed from the acquisition of The Millington Trucking Company. The releases indicated that management felt there was a synergistic opportunity to lower tire shipping costs by having their own trucking company and to lower the operating costs of the trucking company by providing tires at cost. On paper, it seemed to make sense and Wall Street's initial reaction a few months ago had sent the stock price up 20 percent.

Emerson accessed the SEC website to review the financial reporting documents. He was, by no means, a financial analyst, but hoped to glean some pertinent information from the filings. After a half-hour, Emerson shut down his laptop. He had seen the revenue growth through the last quarter, the profitability drop and rising selling and administrative expenses, but couldn't identify why Fallsview Tire would be a target. Maybe Emerson was on the wrong track and the target wasn't Fallsview Tire.

Emerson reached for his cell phone and dialed his ex-Navy SEAL buddy, Sam Duncan. Sam had hinted that he was doing covert work for the CIA and, at times, for other government agencies. Sam's network of contacts rivaled Emerson's.

"Sam here," the cheery voice answered.

"Hello, stranger. It's Emerson."

"E, how're you doing? I haven't talked with you in ages."

"Things have been going fairly well."

"Heard that you moved in with your aunt in Put-in-Bay. How do you like the island life?"

"It's great. Plenty of sailing, good weather and good people on the island. I've started to get plugged into the community here. Plus living here allows me to help Aunt Anne around her place."

"You haven't been through a winter there yet, have you?"

"No. And I hear they can be brutal! Snow and ice, plus the cold lake winds. Maybe I can talk Aunt Anne into going to Florida for the worst of it."

"Give me the warm waters off Florida anytime! Over that Martine girl now?"

"Sam, I honestly don't think I'll ever be over Martine. I just wish something could have worked out. She was like a dream!" Emerson lamented.

"Yeah. She's a real hood ornament!"

Emerson ignored the reference to Martine's beauty.

"Once in a lifetime, you have a chance to meet a woman who can be the center of your universe. I've been fortunate in meeting two women," Emerson responded as he thought about his deceased wife, Julie, and Martine.

"Martine could rock any man's world," Sam replied with unrestrained admiration of the untouchable beauty. "She can be in my dreams anytime! That husband of hers was a real nightmare. What a wimp!"

"Let's not dwell on Martine." Emerson changed the topic. "Sam, you know everybody. Know anyone at the SEC or any Wall Street analysts? Although with the group you run with, I'd hardly expect you to have contacts in those sectors."

"Nah. I don't run with that crowd. Too analytical in a business sense for me. But let me check the folks I know, they may know someone you can talk to. What's up?"

"Keep this relatively quiet. I'm tracking down leads to a possible takeover battle. I overheard a Wall Street type talking on his cell when we landed at LaGuardia a little over a week ago and it sounds like he's putting a company in play for a takeover battle. I'm going to uncover this as quickly as I can and break the story."

"Interesting but out of my bailiwick. Let me see what I can find and I'll call you on your cell. How's the weather there?"

"Bright blue skies and a good breeze."

"I read 'sailing this afternoon' in that description."

"You got it. I'll be enjoying a sail this afternoon!"

"Take your cell, E, and I'll call you within a few hours."

"Thanks, Sam."

"No problema."

Emerson shut off his cell and went downstairs to see his aunt.

When he entered the kitchen, he remembered that she had a meeting at the Lake Erie Islands Historical Society. Today, he would make his own breakfast.

Teterboro Airport
Teterboro, New Jersey

~

The Gulfstream corporate jet touched down smoothly at Teterboro Airport. Many corporate jets landed at the Bergen County facility managed by the Port Authority of New York and New Jersey, just a 12-mile ride from midtown Manhattan.

The sleek aircraft taxied off the runway and up to its designated parking spot. The door opened shortly after to reveal highly animated chatter between its three passengers.

"Oh, for crying out loud, Jay, let me help you. You're going to fall down the stairs if you're not careful," Weimar pleaded.

"Jay, you need to let Joe help you," added Carli.

"No. No. I can manage quite well as long as I support myself on the rails," replied a determined Oakes as he maneuvered himself slowly out of the aircraft and down the stairway.

"If you're trying to set the company up for a worker's comp claim, this is a dumb way to do it!" Weimar stated tenaciously.

Nearing the bottom of the stairs, Oakes retorted, "Nag, nag. Carli, we should have left him bound and gagged in the plane. And if you're not careful, Joe, you may end up in that way!"

"Oh! Oh! Think you're up to trying to gag a lawyer?" Weimar

responded with glee.

Oakes began to walk slowly toward the waiting car as the co-pilot and pilot, carrying Oakes' scooter, began to descend the stairs. Oakes was halfway to the car when his MS-weakened legs gave out and he landed flat on his back. When he saw his traveling companions rushing to aid him, Oakes threw both arms straight up in the air and yelled, "Ta dah! For my next tumbling act I will..."

"Now's no time for a nap!" Weimar said as he went to Oakes' aid.

"Joe, cut it out!" Carli stormed as she also bent to help Oakes to his feet.

Joe and Carli helped Oakes to his feet and took his arms to help steady him as they walked the remaining distance to the car.

Carli cautioned, "Jay, you don't have to prove anything to us. We love you just as you are."

"Jeesh! Okay you guys. Let up. It was just a little accident. I usually can do a short walk like this if I'm careful and slow," Oakes said.

"Note that the operative word here is 'careful.' As far as slow, you've always been a bit slow!" Weimar added as he saw another chance to take a friendly shot at his colleague.

They settled into the car for the drive to Jimmy Malloy's office.

Jimmy Malloy's Office
Lower Manhattan

~

Jimmy Malloy warmly greeted Oakes and his companions as

they entered Jimmy's inviting, oak-paneled conference room. The gregarious Malloy introduced his associates, Ed and Anne, before everyone settled into chairs surrounding the large conference table.

"Jay, it looks like your company is in for a rough ride with these S.O.B.'s."

"Jimmy, have you had past experience with Ratek?" Carli asked before Oakes could comment.

"On more occasions than I care to remember," Malloy replied with a raised eyebrow.

"We've assisted them on some of their takeover attempts in the past," added Ed Madigan.

Weimar and Carli looked questioningly at Malloy.

"That's true. This business is somewhat incestuous. We're mercenaries. We work together and then against each other. However, a deal is a deal. Sometimes we all are driven by our love of doing a deal—and winning the battle. Anne, why don't you pass out the copies of our scorecard for takeover battles in which we've participated."

Oakes had always appreciated Malloy's profound instincts and ability to be an aggressive competitor. Malloy's convivial manner exuded a confidence built on a plethora of powerful social and business connections.

Anne distributed the copies. "You'll see," she commented, "that we have represented the aggressor and the target. Our scorecard shows our effectiveness in winning for the side we represented."

"With a track record like this, why didn't Ratek hire you first?" Weimar probed.

"We think he tried," Anne responded.

"You think he tried! You need to explain yourself," Weimar pushed.

"We had an inquiry from an outside source as to whether we would be conflicted since we represented you. All the firms get inquiries when deals are being formulated, but you don't know which ones will be taken seriously. So you just can't get overzealous about the inquiry," Anne explained.

"But what we did do since your stock began trading so low and you had some earnings difficulty was to have my stock surveillance team watch your trading activity a bit more closely. We think that helped us identify the accumulation trend and spot Ratek more quickly than normal," Madigan added.

"Ed, you've always been ahead of the pack," Oakes stated as he recalled Madigan's work for him in the past.

A knock at the conference room door interrupted their dialog. The door slowly opened to reveal the receptionist.

"Mr. Malloy, I have Mr. Ford in the lobby to meet with you."

"Tell him that I'll be right there." Turning to his visitors, Malloy announced, "As we discussed, I invited P. Dayton Ford to join us."

"I'm looking forward to meeting him. He's highly regarded with respect to the legal issues of takeover battles," Weimar responded.

"Carli, I'll warn you that he's an older, southern gentleman who can really sweet talk the ladies," Malloy cautioned.

"Sounds like my grandfather!" she cooed.

Malloy left the conference room and quickly returned, ushering in the 60ish, white-haired, portly attorney. If he'd worn a white suit, he would have reminded people of a Kentucky colonel.

Ford's friendly and non-threatening style would cause people to drop their guard around him, and this enabled him to effectively break down communication barriers. Ford always thought that you could learn more with a touch of honey than vinegar. He was cunning and resourceful and in demand to represent companies and takeover artists.

Ford and Malloy were used to mingling with the elite of Wall Street. They counted many of the lawyers, investment bankers, proxy fighters, money managers, financial analysts and arbitrageurs as friends.

Malloy made the introductions.

"Well, how are you all doing this grand and beautiful morning?" queried Ford with a touch of a southern drawl.

"We've had better days. We assume that Jimmy has brought you up to speed about Ratek and his bunch taking a position in our stock," Carli stated.

"Yes, he did. He's given me the background information on the stock buying, your depressed stock price and the state of your business, including the consolidation issues with your Millington Trucking Company acquisition. This is some pickle that you folks are in.

"Before we go too far, let me tell you youngsters a story about attorneys. A surgeon, an architect and a lawyer were arguing about which of their professions was the oldest. The surgeon thought his was older because God took a rib from Adam to create Eve and you can't go back further than that. Well the architect said his was older because God was the first architect when he created the world out of chaos in 7 days. Then, the attorney who had been listening intently as, we attorneys are known to do, spoke up and said that the legal profession was the oldest profession. He asked who do you think created the CHAOS?"

Ford chuckled with the others at his little story and continued, but in a more serious vein. "Ratek loves to create chaos, too, but there are ways in which we can manage this chaos. You know he's one of the toughest to deal with. He'll probably demand board seats, want to sell off assets—sometimes the pieces of a company are worth more than the entire company. We call that break-up value. He'll eliminate jobs, and impact suppliers, customers and communities all in the name of increasing the return for shareholders. He doesn't really care about anything more than fattening his wallet and building his reputation. I didn't get a chance to look at your financials, do you have an over funded pension reserve?"

"Well, yes we do. What made you focus on that?" Carli asked.

"He is known for raiding pension assets also. You folks are ripe for a takeover."

"What are your initial thoughts about the direction we should take?" queried Weimar.

"I took a look at your company structure and saw that you don't have a staggered board or a rights plan to use as a shark repellant."

"No, we couldn't sell our chairman on implementing them," Weimar commented.

"There are four courses of action you can take in these types of situations. First, you could offer to buy him out at a premium. Second, you can find a white knight."

Oakes interrupted at this point when he saw the quizzed look on Carli's face. "A white knight is a friendly buyer who may be willing to operate the company with some minor tweaks rather than breaking it up or taking it through a major reorganization."

Ford continued, "Third, you can let him gain control of the company and sell it."

"Don't think we want to do that. That wouldn't be right for our employees or us!" Oakes said firmly.

"Jay, you're so pragmatic!" Carli teased.

"Someone has to be."

"Fourth, you can fight," Ford stated. "We can put in a number of takeover defenses."

"You could raise cash to buy him out by selling the crown jewels of the company," Malloy added.

"If you're talking about the tire business, which is our most profitable business, there's no way that we would do that. Neither the CEO nor the board would consider it. It's just not in the best interests of our shareholders," Weimar stated sternly. "Dayton, is there any basis you see for an injunction to block further stock purchases by Ratek?"

"There's really no true grounds on which we could request it. I think where this is heading is that you may need to look at a pension reversion so that you can capture the excess funding of your pension plan and somewhat protect your employees. I'd suggest that you meet with your investment bankers and obtain their advice in the event you wish to buy out Ratek's shares and make him go away. You should be preparing for Ratek's call to notify you that he owns your stock. That's one thing that he and his team like to do. They enjoy making the call to the company and telling them that they are a 10 percent stock owner. It's the shock value. But that's where you have an edge. Your buddies here spotted their stock accumulation. You need to rock them back on their heels when they make that call and do your best to manage them."

"I agree with Dayton. You've got a few days to prepare before this breaks in the media. You'll want to be ready for employee and media questions," added Malloy.

"Once the arbs sniff this out, you'll see more action in your stock price and it may start to climb—which may be a good thing for you."

"Arbs?" Carli asked.

"They're investors who take a position in a stock that's in play, hold the stock for a short time and then sell out after making a quick profit," Madigan explained.

"And bottom line, Ratek is in this for the bucks!" Malloy offered.

The meeting broke up and the Fallsview Tire group left to meet with their investment bankers before flying home at the end of the day to report to the CEO.

West of Rattlesnake Island
Lake Erie

~

The breeze was from the west and was rapidly propelling the small sailboat toward Rattlesnake Island, which was northwest of South Bass Island. The cell phone's ringing brought Emerson out of his quiet reverie of the lake.

Emerson picked up the phone and noted that the caller ID displayed Sam's promised return call.

"Hello Sam."

"E, my main man. I did some checking with some folks and you actually have someone you know in the area. I heard that he's a real rainmaker," Sam said with pride in being able to have an upper hand on his good friend.

"And who would that be?" Emerson asked with his curiosity heightened.

"Bob Welch!"

Emerson remembered Bob, who ran an investment banking firm in New York. They had met on several occasions at parties in Washington and Emerson and he had hit it off although their busy schedules prohibited them from having a strong friendship. They had a mutual admiration for each other.

Emerson had heard that he took an early retirement and lost touch with him.

"Where is he?"

"He's heading up some kind of stock trading training program at Kent State University, which is southeast of Cleveland. You might want to follow up with him and see if he can give you any insight on the story you're chasing."

"I'll do that. It'll be good to see him again. Maybe I can invite him up here for some sailing, too. Hey, when are you going to come visit me here? As I recall you certainly seemed to enjoy yourself on the island. In the short time you were here last summer, I understand that you became a stumbling legend at the Beer

Barrel. Or was it at the Round House?" Emerson teased his wild and ornery friend.

"Yeah, that's me alright, a stumbling legend. Seriously, I'd like to visit, but I'm heading out of the country for a project. Before I go I need to spend some time with a blue-haired babe, though," Sam responded.

Emerson guessed that Sam was going on another CIA assignment and knew better than to ask questions about it. But the blue-haired babe comment was fair game to pursue.

"Dating a punk rocker now?"

"Nope. It's my 80-year-old mother. Her hair and all of her friends' hair turned blue. It's those permanents that they get, you know what I mean?" Sam kidded.

"I should have known. That's probably the only female attention you get, too!" Emerson teased back.

"Nah, you know I'm a chic magnet. They find me irresistible!" Sam retorted good-naturedly.

"Okay Mr. Chic Magnet, give me a call when you get back into town and we'll try to get you back up here for a visit," Emerson said as he began to end the call.

"Will do. Over and out," Sam replied.

Emerson pocketed his cell phone and focused on his sailing. As the wind began to pick up, he rounded Rattlesnake Island to head for his Put-in-Bay home.

~

Oakes, Weimar and Dansen had just finished briefing Owens on the results of their previous day's meetings.

"Doesn't bode well for us," Owens deplored.

"Well, Greg, we can put in place a number of the takeover defenses that they have suggested and we can do that rather quickly. The staggered board will take shareholder approval and it's too late to get that on the agenda for the annual meeting in two weeks," Weimar said.

"We're looking into the pension reversion to see if we can reduce the attractiveness of our over funded pension assets. Our investment bankers are helping with the particulars," Carli volunteered.

"Pension reversion?" Owens asked.

"It's when a company takes the amount that is over funded and reverts it back to the company. It's not really our pension that was over funded. It was the Millington Trucking Company's," Carli responded.

"What's the amount of the over funding?" Owens probed Carli for the critical piece of information.

"About $40 million. We can use it for operations or dividend it to our shareholders."

"So we did make out from the acquisition!" Owens stated proudly.

"That's about the only thing that went right for us from that mess!" Weimar retorted.

"I need to call the board and notify them. I'd been waiting for the results of your New York visits before letting them know about this threat," Owens stated.

"Good luck in your call to Phil," Weimar warned.

Weimar was referring to Phil Webster who had recently been appointed to the company's board of directors. He replaced another board member who had unexpectedly resigned. Webster had been a fraternity brother of Owens at Yale and had built a strong reputation for his Cleveland company's real estate wheeling and dealing.

Webster had been highly vocal of late due to the stock's dropping price. He had purchased 25,000 shares at $41.00 when he first joined the board and was furious about the stock price drop to $16.00.

"Yeah. I'm not looking forward to that discussion."

The three of them left Owens' office as he called out to Lita to get Webster on the phone. Lita raised her eyebrows inquisitively as the three walked by her desk, but didn't get a response from any of them as to what was transpiring. Owens kept a tight rein on who knew what in his organization.

Only a minute passed before Lita called in, "Mr. Webster is on line one."

"Hello, Phil."

"Hello, Greg. What's new?" Webster asked as he wondered why Owens would be calling. Probably more bad news about another earnings forecast being missed.

"Well, it appears that we are headed for a takeover battle," Owens started slowly.

"Oh, isn't that just great! Just more negative publicity about the ineptness of the Fallsview Tire's management team and your ability to manage your company effectively," Webster whined.

The comment about his company was not lost on Owens. It was evident that Webster wanted to distance himself from his involvement as a board member.

"Well, I at least hope that whatever they want to do will raise the stock price and I can recover my losses," Webster continued sardonically. "Who's trying to take you over?"

"Max Ratek with Birkman Investments."

Webster paused for a moment.

"Well, you'll certainly have your hands full. He's one of the toughest ones out there. What have you done so far?"

Owens quickly informed Webster about the events surrounding their discovery of Ratek's foray into their stock and some of their basic plans to thwart his takeover attempt.

"Amazing. Good thing you had that Oakes on board to spot him. I didn't know that you were using a stock surveillance team to watch your stock," Webster mused. "Keep me advised of your plans."

"I'll do that to the extent that I do for any of the other board members," Owens stated strongly.

They ended their conversation.

Oakes' Office
Two Days Later

~

Oakes lay on the cot in his office. He felt drained and fatigued from the events of the last few days and the impact of his MS. His multiple sclerosis caused him to tire easily. Some days he felt that the MS was beating him and he struggled to show how macho he was in the workplace. Once he had joined the company and they became aware of his disease and its symptoms, they were very supportive. It had been Joe Weimar's idea to install the cot in his office so he could rest when needed.

He thought back to the strategy meetings with his public relations department and how they developed the various approaches to the governor, the mayor, Congressmen, the union, employees, retirees, community, suppliers, customers, media and investors. He and his team had put in long hours, but he felt that they had made significant progress in developing an action plan that could be ready to go in a moment.

There had been telephone conferences in Owens' office with Weimar, Carli, the investment bankers, Jimmy Malloy's team and P. Dayton Ford. They had developed what ifs and laid out their strategy with several backup plans for dealing with Ratek and his people once the news broke.

Oakes pulled himself from his cot and used his remote control to position his battery-powered wheelchair next to the cot. He slowly eased himself into the wheelchair that he was using that day. He wheeled up to his desk and checked his monitor for the stock price movement and share trading volume for Fallsview Tire. Trading volume continued to increase and the price had moved up a point.

The phone rang. Oakes reached over and answered.

"Jay Oakes here. How can I help you?"

"Jay, this is Michael Searle from Birkman Investments calling."

It was the call they had been expecting and it was ahead of the date on which Birkman had to disclose their ownership to the world.

Oakes felt a surge of energy invigorate himself as he responded, "Hello, Michael. We were expecting your call. Welcome aboard as a new shareholder."

There was stunned silence on the other end of the phone. Searle and Birkman Investments relished catching companies off-guard and using the element of surprise when they placed the initial call to the target company. It helped create an aura of strength and hostility for the Birkman firm.

Searle did not like the way this was starting.

"You know that we own your stock? How do you know that?"

"It's our business to know who our shareholders are. We're professionals here," Oakes responded. Oakes' comments and approach had been carefully crafted to set the appropriate tone when the first call was placed by Birkman.

Ratek was not going to be pleased when Searle reported the results of the phone conversation.

"Very good for you, then. The purpose of my call is to set up an initial meeting with your company to discuss what your folks are going to do to increase the stock price for your shareholders. We'd like to invite you as the investor relations contact and your CFO, or acting CFO in your case, to attend a meeting at our offices in New York in two days to discuss your plans. Can you make it?"

Just as Oakes and his team had expected. "Sure. Carli Dansen is our acting CFO. I'll also bring along our general counsel, Joe Weimar."

"That's agreeable." Searle provided directions, meeting times and ended the call.

Oakes sat back in his chair and smiled. So far so good. Everything was going as planned. He wheeled out of his office and down to meet with Owens, Weimar and Dansen to report how well the call had gone.

Birkman Investments
The Same Day

∼

"What do you mean they knew?" Ratek exploded angrily at Searle. Ratek paced in his office.

"This guy, Oakes, didn't rattle. He must be an experienced investor relations guy."

"I'll bet they're using a stock surveillance firm to monitor who is buying and selling their shares!" Ratek groused as he began to pace.

"Could be. That would explain why they knew we owned their stock. It also means that they may have already contacted their advisors and have a strategy for dealing with us."

"I'm not worried about that. The key strategy that I hope they have is how in the world they are going to restore shareholder value! How did he react when you invited them in for a visit?"

"Calmly. I think he expected it."

"Let's just see how this goes when we meet. See if you can find out whom they might be using on stock watch. I'll bet it's Jimmy Malloy! We know he does their proxy solicitation."

Searle rose from his chair and started for the door. "I'll follow up on it."

As the door closed, Ratek reached for the phone.

The Steakhouse Restaurant
New York City
The Next Day

~

They had flown into New York in the late afternoon, checked into their rooms and were having a late dinner at a restaurant, a block from their hotel, which had been suggested by the hotel staff.

Oakes, Weimar and Dansen made their way through the restaurant's sidewalk café, and into the less noisy and paneled interior. The outdoor café had been appealing and was somewhat secluded from the street by a 4-foot high wall topped with flowers.

Despite his numerous trips into New York, Oakes had never dined there. Over the meal they discussed their plans for the next day.

Finished with his meal, Oakes motioned to the waiter.

"Can you point me in the direction of the men's room?"

"Yes sir. It's on the second floor."

"And the elevator is where?"

Looking at the scooter, the waiter said apologetically, "I am so sorry, sir, but our elevator is out of service today. We could try to carry you up the stairs."

"Not very handicapped accessible, are you!" Oakes challenged. It had been a very tough day.

"Jay, would you like us to carry you?" Weimar offered.

"No. No. Let me see how I can handle this," Oakes said. Oakes scootered away from the table and over to the foot of the stairs. He looked up the long, narrow and steep stairs to the second floor. There was no way that he would try to navigate his way up the stairs and down to a restroom on the second floor. Oakes scootered out the front door.

A few minutes later he rejoined his associates at the table.

"Jay, did everything come out alright? If not, I can give you my empty water glass." Joe grinned.

"Joe, you are so bad!" Carli said good-naturedly.

"Watch this! Waiter! Could you come here?" Oakes asked seriously.

The same waiter returned and stood nervously next to Oakes. "Sir?"

"You might mention to the management that you're out of toilet paper in the sidewalk patio area."

The waiter looked aghast and ran to the maitre'd. A moment later he could be seen carrying a small shovel and broom and moving hurriedly to the entrance and the nearby sidewalk patio.

"Jay, you didn't?" Carli asked wide-eyed.

"Nah. I just took a leak out there, but there's no harm in letting them think that it's more than that," Oakes laughed.

Carli and Weimar shook their heads as they grinned at their travel mate.

"The next time I come to New York, I'll need to bring my stair climbing chair to avoid something like this again."

Carli leaned forward and asked sympathetically, "Jay, can you tell me a bit about MS? I'm really not that familiar with it."

"Sure. Multiple sclerosis is a chronic, debilitating disease that affects a person's brain and spinal cord. With MS, a person's immune system thinks a part of your body is a foreign substance and directs antibodies and white blood cells against proteins in the myelin sheath surrounding nerves in your brain and spinal cord. This causes damage to the sheath and ultimately to your nerves. The damage slows or blocks muscle coordination, visual sensation and other nerve signals," Oakes explained.

Weimar and Carli listened intently to Oakes' explanation. It would help them be more supportive of their friend and co-worker.

"How serious can it become?" Carli asked.

"It varies in severity, ranging from a mild illness to one that results in permanent disability. There are treatments that help modify the course of the disease and relieve symptoms. But, to date, a cure has not been found. Hey, you two can help find a cure!" Oakes declared.

"How's that, Jay?" Weimar asked incredulously.

"By supporting the National MS Society in their research. You can join me in the annual Spring MS Walk fund-raiser in the Cuyahoga Valley. Of course, I ride the trail.

"I'm interested," Carli said supportively.

Oakes continued, "About 400,000 Americans have MS. It usually surfaces in people between the ages of 20 and 50 and is twice as common in women as in men. My variation causes me to have periods of fatigue and I have trouble keeping my balance and walking, as you know."

"I'm so sorry, Jay," Carli consoled.

"Oh, he just uses it to get a little extra sympathy from people," Weimar jested.

"I do get extra attention and it does provide me a different perspective on life," Oakes reflected. "In the early stages of my MS, I wall-walked, then walked like a drunk. I'd fall once in awhile and people sometimes wouldn't help me because they thought I was drunk. Then I'd tell the zebra story.

"The zebra story?" Weimar asked.

"If you're in the front of your house and hear hooves pounding through your backyard, you might assume horses are running through your backyard. If you look, they might be zebras. You just can't jump to conclusions about people. Once I started using a cane, people started helping me."

"You've got it made now. Trading in the cane for a sweet ride!" Weimar noted.

"But Joe, think about my view. At my level, I see belt buckles, butts and hip pockets. I'm constantly dodging swinging bags, briefcases, purses and baby carriages. I'm lucky my kneecaps haven't been broken."

"Dangerous," Weimar mused.

"Daily travel is not the worst of it. The most dangerous part is in a crowded elevator. Think about it. You're in a sea of people and my line of sight is limited to people's butts and some of them are in stretch pants that they should be ticketed for wearing. In fact, some of them should be required to beep when they're backing up so I'd have a chance to avoid a collision. Then again, some of the views aren't that bad."

"Jay, you're a rascal!" Carli chided.

"Just trying to tell it like it is. Sometimes I get requests from people in crowded elevators to sit on my lap."

"Oh boy, I bet you accommodate them," Joe teased.

"Nah. They're usually senior citizens who think I'm cute. They really don't want a seat, they're just trying to be kind."

"How do kids treat you?" Carli asked.

"They're open and want to know about it. They'll come up to me and ask why I'm on a scooter or in a wheelchair. I tell them that the signals from my brain don't make it all the way to my muscles and that causes some problems with walking. They usually want to know if they can catch it and I explain that it's not contagious. I do offer them a chance to jump on my lap and take them for a quick spin. Especially in airport waiting rooms. It breaks down barriers and allows them to see people in wheelchairs or other mechanized accessories in a different light. We may appear a bit different, but deep down inside, we're just regular people. I tell them that God just made some of us extra special in this way."

"You're a saint, Jay," Carli said warmly.

"Maybe Saint Jay can put in a good word for Fallsview with his boss. I have a feeling we're going to need it," Joe said kiddingly.

Corner of Wall Street and Broadway
The Next Morning
8:30 A.M.

~

The cab deposited Oakes, Weimar and Dansen at one of the busiest corners in the city, Wall Street and Broadway. It was a beautiful crisp morning. Masses of people were entering the financial district and bringing a strong sense of high energy to the area.

Oakes enjoyed this corner. It provided a perfect viewpoint from Trinity Church and its graveyard filled with the illustrious forebears of New York to the looming buildings of Wall Street which created a shadowy canyon into which the masses poured.

"What a beautiful church!" Carli exclaimed as she gazed at the church's Gothic Revival architecture.

"That's Trinity Church. The original church was chartered in 1697 and ministered to the poor and the waves of immigrants who poured into the city. The church and the graveyard are listed on the National Register of Historic Places. I find the graveyard intriguing," Oakes said.

"I've always thought you had a rather macabre sense about you. Now, I'm convinced," Weimar quipped.

"Seriously, the graveyard contains the graves of a number of historical figures like Alexander Hamilton, William Bradford and Robert Fulton."

"And how do you know so much about the history of New York?" Weimar asked.

"When I first started working in investor relations, my first boss was a native New Yorker. Trips into the city to visit with investors also were filled with history lessons on the city and the stock exchange. I wouldn't trade what Mark Blitstein taught me for anything!" Oakes responded with deep admiration for his former boss.

As they waited for the traffic light to change, the three of them noticed an attractive blonde wearing a cream suit with a relatively short skirt purchase coffee at a nearby kiosk.

As she turned holding her coffee, a gentleman accidentally brushed into her and caused her to spill some of her coffee on her cream suit. They could hear the gentleman apologizing profusely. The blonde looked down at her suit and at the gentleman. She let loose with a stream of profanity and dumped the rest of her coffee from her cup on the man's suit and stormed away. The man looked down in disbelief at what happened and then briefly stared at her as she disappeared in the crowded sidewalk.

"Welcome to New York and the sharks of Wall Street," Oakes offered to his dazed companions.

"Sort of reminds me of my wife," Weimar jested.

The light changed and they crossed the intersection toward the New York Stock Exchange.

"Do you know why they used to trade stock in eighth's?" Oakes quizzed his companions.

"No, why?" Carli asked.

"Back in early colonial times, the most common coin was the Spanish Reale which was made of silver. Reales were often called pieces of eight because they could be cut into halves, quarters and eighths to make change. You've heard that quarters are called two bits, right?"

"Yes," Carli admitted.

"Two bits or two eighths make a quarter," Oakes continued.

"Pieces of eight. Interesting that the pirates of Wall Street also would deal in pieces of eight just like their sea borne namesakes!" Weimar observed.

Weimar and Carli stared at the imposing façade of the New York Stock Exchange as they walked by.

Oakes pointed to a towering, columned building at Wall Street and Broad Street. "That's the site of George Washington's inauguration as first President of the United States. The statue in front is Washington. The building contains the Federal Hall National Museum." Pointing farther down Wall Street, Oakes continued, "Alexander Hamilton founded the Bank of New York in that building in 1791. I've done some stock transfer work with the Bank of New York over the years."

They turned the corner and headed down Broad to the offices of Birkman Investments.

~

The receptionist ushered the three visitors into Birkman's opulent, 20th floor conference room with windows providing a view of the New York Stock Exchange at the corner of Broad and Wall Street. She quickly offered coffee and then left to locate the hosts of the meeting. The tables of the conference room were set up in a u-shape and the walls were lined with plaques and framed magazine articles about the success of Birkman Investments in turning around company performance. At the far end of the room was a large cabinet where liquor and soft drinks were stored.

The message to visitors was clear and intimidating: Birkman Investments expected results—even at the cost of breaking up a company.

Ten minutes had passed before the first of the meeting hosts arrived. It was a part of Birkman's strategy during first visits to increase the tension in the room. The door opened and a blonde woman brusquely entered the room. There was a coffee stain on her suit jacket.

The three visitors eyed each other quickly. If she handled work relationships the way she handled the stranger on the street, it could be a difficult meeting.

The blonde set her files on the other side of the room and walked rapidly over to the group.

Extending her hand, she stonily introduced herself. "I'm Judith Beckwith. I'm assisting Michael Searle with the financial analysis."

"Hello Judy, I'm ...," Weimar began.

Judith cut him off and stared intensely into Weimar's eyes. "My name is not Judy. It's Judith. Don't be condescending toward me!"

Not one to be intimidated easily, Weimar continued, "Well then, Judith. As I was saying, I'm Joe Weimar, general counsel. This is Jay Oakes, our vice president of investor relations and public relations." Then, very warmly, Joe introduced Carli. "And this charming lady is Carli Dansen, our acting chief financial officer and company controller."

Carli and Oakes smiled to themselves at Joe's introduction of Carli. They knew that he wanted to show Judith Beckwith that Carli was a cut above Judith.

The door opened again and Michael Searle entered the room. After a brief round of introductions, everyone took their seats. The two from Birkman Investments were seated directly across from the three visitors.

The three visitors couldn't help but notice that Judith's skirt had risen mid-thigh as she crossed her legs. They would discuss later how Judith used that as part of her intimidating tactics.

Searle opened the discussion.

"Thank you again for coming in to visit with us on such short notice. It's apparent, Jay, from our earlier conversation that you were already aware that we have taken a significant ownership in your stock."

"Yes, as we discussed," Oakes replied.

"Just to go on the record, we anticipate owning 11 to 12 percent of your company. This will make us your largest single stockholder.

The SEC filing, as you know, will be made four days from now. I'm sure you've been watching for it."

"That would be a safe assumption," Weimar said stoically.

"Here's what we are looking for: we expect to see a return of shareholder value to the $40 range and we expect to see it within the next two quarters."

"That's rather aggressive," Carli responded, visibly shaken by the short deadline.

"We have a reputation for being aggressive. Either you take steps to turn around performance or we'll take the steps and turn it around for you. And you know that we can leave bodies lying in our wake."

"I'd like to see your data supporting your key performance ratios, flow charts, financial analysis reports and competitive analysis of your markets within the next week," Judith demanded.

"Judith, we are willing to provide you with data that we would normally disclose publicly," Carli responded to the ice queen.

Weimar added, "Judith, as you know, we are not in a position to, nor is any corporation going to, disclose to you proprietary information. It is just not done."

The conversation was interrupted by the sudden entrance of Max Ratek into the room.

"I trust the meeting is going well," Ratek said as he looked at his two associates.

"We were just discussing the information that we need to review," Searle replied.

Weimar started, "Mr. Ratek, I'm..."

Ratek cut him off. It was the second time that morning that Weimar had been rudely cut off by the Birkman people. Weimar would remember the lack of courtesy.

"I'm not going to waste my time in getting to know you. Here's what I want you to do. I'm coming to your corporate headquarters for a meeting with your CEO next Monday. Make sure he's available for a one-hour meeting at 10 A.M. I'll want to review his strategy for improving the stock price. Tell him to be ready and don't waste my time."

"We'll check with him to see if he'll be available and get back to you," Oakes said.

Ratek's countenance flared. He put both hands firmly on the tabletop and glared at Oakes on his scooter.

"I didn't ask you to check. I told you that I'll be in to see him and to make sure that he's available. End of discussion. Michael, can we conclude this meeting?"

Searle looked at his boss and knew that it was time to close the meeting. He looked at the visitors and said, "The meeting is over. You have your marching orders."

Ratek, Searle and Beckwith left the room.

"What was that all about?" Carli asked. "They certainly want to see a lot of information."

"It's like a runaway train," Weimar commented thoughtfully.

"Yeah, and it's headed for a collision with us," Oakes said.

As she arose from her chair, Carli stated, "I expected our meeting to be more productive and longer. It didn't seem that we accomplished much."

"I think it was a part of their strategy of intimidation. Keep us off guard," Oakes explained.

"I agree. They wanted to make demands and set a tone. It was a ruse to strike fear in us and show they're serious. We can call Lita from the car and have her make sure that Greg is in the office for the meeting with Ratek," Joe said.

"If he's planning to be out of town, we'll need to convince him to change his plans," Carli added.

"Did you see how short that Judith's skirt was when she sat down?" Oakes asked.

"Couldn't miss it, could you? Another mind game. Just daring us to stare! Judith, what a piece of work!" Joe groused.

"Nice move in the warm way you introduced me, Joe. Making our little friend, Judy feel a bit less warm," Carli observed.

"She's a barracuda. I couldn't believe it when she walked into the room and we saw that she was the woman who dumped the coffee all over that poor guy. This is going to be a very serious test for us," Weimar cautioned.

Oakes responded, "At this point in the game, we'll let Ratek win a few small victories, but we'll win the war."

The visitors left the room.

Ratek's Office
New York City

~

"But we'll win the war," Ratek echoed mockingly as he switched off the conference room's hidden microphone. "These local yokels have no idea what they're in for."

He turned in his chair and faced Judith, Searle and Grimes who had joined him in his office.

Searle cautioned, "These folks didn't intimidate as quickly as some of the others."

"They all fall at some point. We'll keep the pressure up. They may be a little better coached and prepared than other company teams. But in the end, they all capitulate to us." Turning to Judith, Ratek added, "Nice touch with the short skirt. As far as the jacket goes, send the cleaning bill to me or go buy a new suit on me."

She knew that Ratek liked her in short skirts. For that matter, Ratek liked any female regardless of what they were wearing. She used her toughness to maintain a barrier between Ratek and herself. She saw what happened to other females who tumbled to his power easily. She relished the cat-and-mouse game they played.

"I may take you up on that. Well, this barracuda needs to excuse herself. I need to check the markets," Judith rolled the rrr's in barracuda and left the room.

Grimes' eyes followed her every movement as she walked out. She was the type that would never give the likes of Grimes the time of day.

Jimmy's Café
Chestnut Street
Cuyahoga Falls

~

Emerson pulled into the parking lot next to Jimmy's Café. After taking Miller Ferry from Put-in-Bay to Catawba, it had been a two-hour drive to Cuyahoga Falls. The drive had given Emerson ample time to recall the fun times he had in working with Lynn Arruda at the *Post*. She had resigned for personal reasons and relocated to Cuyahoga Falls two years ago.

Emerson had been able to locate her phone number and arrange this appointment with her. It would be good to see her and catch up. Following their meeting, Emerson planned to do local research on Fallsview Tire.

Emerson ran his eyes over the café where Lynn had suggested they meet. The building's unique, green, artsy exterior seemed to be more of a fit for Greenwich Village, Haight Ashbury or New Orleans rather than a conservative community like Cuyahoga Falls. Emerson would later learn that the artistic owner of the café had spent a considerable amount of his life in New Orleans.

Several customers were seated at tables with large green umbrellas in the fenced patio area in front of the building with its cornucopia of colors. Emerson's eyes were drawn to the carefully detailed chairs and benches in front of the building. There was an ambience to the little café that Emerson found to be especially appealing.

The slamming of a car door caused Emerson's head to turn and revealed his 45-year-old friend walking toward the café. Emerson quickly exited his car and caught up to her just before she walked through the bright red front doors of the café.

"Sunshine," Emerson called warmly.

Lynn spun around to see her old friend. Her eyes sparkled and her mouth was engulfed by her welcoming smile. "You remembered. Only you and my father ever called me, Sunshine."

She hugged Emerson and he took in the freshness of her blonde hair.

Emerson sighed, "Did you think I'd ever forget?"

Emerson had given her the nickname years ago due to her consistent exuberance. It didn't matter what was pressuring Lynn, she exuded a contagious optimism that flooded the office and had a calming effect on others. It was a character trait that Emerson had admired.

One day, he had started calling her Sunshine and was pleasantly surprised when she told him that he was only the second person to call her by that name. It seemed to just bring the two of them closer in their friendship.

Emerson continued. "You look good."

"Oh, sure. I'm still fighting the pounds."

"Aren't we all?" Emerson quizzed. If she was putting on weight, it was all in the right places he thought.

They entered the cozy café where they received a chorus of friendly hellos from customers seated at the tables inside and from the café's staff. Lynn quickly introduced Emerson to Bridget, the blonde bombshell; Eileen, John and Tim, who were café regulars; and the effervescent Kim, Buffie and Carla, who took their coffee orders.

Bridget offered, "We've got room here at our table if you'd

like to squeeze in."

"Thanks, Bridget. But we're going to sit outside. I haven't seen Emerson in years and we have some catching up to do."

"If you change your mind, the offer's still open."

"Thanks, Bridge!" Lynn responded.

"I'll send Jimmy out when he's available so he can meet your friend, Lynn." Kim called from behind the counter.

"Thanks, Kim!"

As they settled at the patio table in the far corner, Emerson observed, "Quite a nice group of folks here."

"They're great, aren't they? It's like the local bar where everyone knows each other and tries to help each other. A bunch of them recently got together to help one older gentleman move into a new apartment. He didn't have anyone to help him, but they heard about it and banded together to help. It's a real caring environment once you take the time to sit and get to know people."

At that point, they were interrupted by the appearance of a beautiful redhead wearing a rather low cut top which was straining to contain her ample bosom.

"Bon soir. Bon soir. Could I sing for you?"

"Emerson, meet Natalie. She's our resident French entertainer."

"I am not really French, monsieur, but I have fun doing this shtick," Natalie beamed.

"Nice to meet you. Let's have a song then!" Emerson responded.

Natalie broke out into a ballad about two lost lovers. She sang it from the bottom of her heart, full of meaning. Emerson and Lynn applauded at its conclusion and Natalie scampered inside.

"That girl's lungs almost popped out of her top on that last note," Emerson noted teasingly to Lynn.

"Emerson!" Lynn scolded mockingly. "Now tell me what you've been up to for the last two years."

Emerson relayed his past assignments and the loss of his wife and child with which Lynn commiserated. Emerson described his visit to his aunt on Put-in-Bay, his adventures on the island, his attraction to the very married Martine and his subsequent Pulitzer Prize award. He didn't reveal to her his current takeover project.

It was then Lynn's turn to share. She told Emerson the real reason for resigning and relocating with her two sons to Cuyahoga Falls to live with her aunt.

"I never wanted to share this with anyone at the time, but it had been so difficult financially for me to continue to live in Washington and raise the boys. They're 12 and 10 now. I've always kept my financial affairs private." She paused, uncertain if she was going to proceed and tell Emerson her secret.

"I had to file for bankruptcy. We just couldn't afford Washington, so we moved back home where I've been able to get the boys in good schools here in the Falls and regroup myself financially."

"I had no idea. Is there anything I can do to help you?" Emerson was shocked that this friend of his, who never seemed to have any problems, had kept her personal need so quiet.

"No, actually, I'm doing quite well now. I have a job in community relations at the hospital. We've been working hard to place stories in the local papers," she beamed.

Emerson's admiration for her fortitude took a giant leap forward. "Still have that ink running in your veins?" he grinned.

"I love the excitement and the deadlines. We all rush to get the stories out."

Emerson noticed a tall man wearing black rectangular glasses and with a thick shock of white hair approaching their table. He was about 57-years-old and had movie star good looks.

"Jimmy," Lynn cried out when she saw him.

Jimmy gave her a big hug and introduced himself to Emerson. "Welcome to one of the best-kept secrets in northeast Ohio."

Shaking hands, Emerson remarked, "Great coffee and you've got an unbelievable ambiance here!"

"Thanks. I liken it to walking inside of a tattoo. We've got a lot of characters here, including me. I heard you met a few when you were inside!"

"You've got a lot of really nice people here," Emerson added.

"If you two don't have plans tonight, I'd like you to join me over at Sutliffe II for the senior hula show tonight."

"Senior hula show? Here in Cuyahoga Falls?" quizzed Emerson.

Jimmy continued. "My 91-year-old mother lived for a number of years in Hawaii where she learned how to do the hula. She's now living in one of the local senior citizen buildings where she conducts hula lessons with the seniors. They all wear muumuus and put on quite a show. Even the building manager, Mary, gets in the act—and she's no senior. When that Sun Bunny gets moving, she steals the whole show."

"Sounds like a hoot, but I've got plans tonight," Emerson responded.

"It sounds so sweet of them to do that," Lynn cooed. "I'll go and bring the boys too. I'll get the details from you before I leave."

Jimmy excused himself so that Lynn and Emerson could continue their conversation.

"Emerson, you still haven't told me what brought you to Cuyahoga Falls. I can't believe it was just to see me. I know you better than that," Lynn sighed.

"I'd rather not say, at least today. Give me a little time and I'll let you know. You may know some folks in town that I can contact."

Lynn probed. "Emerson, tell me. Pleeeease."

"Like I said, give me a couple of days when I have more of the facts. Then we'll talk, but confidentially, since you're working with the media. I wouldn't want you to steal my story!" he feigned concern.

"Would I do something like that to my old friend?" she quizzed innocently and with a seductive smile as she reached over and squeezed his arm.

"I would hope not. You were always such a tease."

"Maybe, but it never got me anywhere with you," she flirted back.

Emerson grinned back at his good friend. They both had known for years that their special relationship was just that—a special relationship between two friends. Even with his wife gone now, Emerson still looked at Lynn as a very dear friend and nothing more. She was like the girl next door that boys had a special relationship with when they were growing up.

"Well, I need to run. I'm spending a few hours at Cuyahoga Falls Library and doing some research."

They hugged and Lynn went inside the café to finalize her plans to attend the hula show. Emerson took one last look at the cozy café before getting into his car and heading to the library. He looked at his MapQuest directions and turned left on Chestnut followed by a quick right on State Road.

As he drove north, he spotted Leopold Tire, an independent tire dealership. Emerson decided to pull in.

An energetic Dennis Leopold greeted Emerson as he entered the busy tire store. "How can we help you today?"

"Are you the owner?" Emerson asked.

"Yep, why do you ask? Are you selling something?"

"No, I'm Emerson Moore. I'm a reporter with the *Washington Post*. I'm here researching a story about the financial difficulties with Fallsview Tire & Rubber Company and wondered if I could ask you some questions. Could you step outside with me where it's a little quieter and I'll explain?"

"Sure," Dennis replied.

"I see by the sign on your building that you carry their tires," Emerson started.

"Sure. I carry their brand when I can get them for customers."

"You're having trouble with delivery?" Emerson probed.

"Oh boy, are we. Ever since they shut down two of their radial plants in Mississippi and Alabama, we've had problems in getting the tires we need for our customers. It seems that the distribution warehouse is always out of stock. Some sort of mix up in their production planning. Of course, Detroit gets the tires they need because they're the number one customer."

"And probably at a better price than you."

"That's correct! It hurts their profit margin big time—and it's hurting mine," Dennis stated firmly.

"So what are you doing about it?"

"I see what other tire brands I can get. I can't lose my customers."

"I understand. Would you mind if I quote you?" Emerson inquired.

"Nah. I usually speak my mind. People around here expect that from me. How are you set for tires? Want me to check?" the consummate salesman asked.

Emerson grinned. "I think I'm set for now, but I'll probably stop back to visit with you."

"Do that. Nice talking with you." Dennis hurried inside to wait on another prospective customer.

Jimmy Malloy's Office
New York City

~

"So that pretty well sums up what happened during our visit with Birkman Investments," Oakes noted as he, Joe and Carli finished a debriefing meeting with Jimmy Malloy's team.

"Be careful of that Judith. She eats people alive," Anne cautioned. "We've encountered her several times during takeover battles and she is just as remorseless as the others."

"If not worse," Ed added.

Jimmy sat back in his chair and looked at his three visitors. "You need to follow through on Ratek's visit to your office. It'll probably be confrontational and you better warn your CEO that his modus operandi is to catch the CEO off guard during this initial session. Your best strategy is a preemptive first strike."

"Preemptive first strike?" Weimar asked.

"Yes. Keep Ratek off guard. You've already made one major move that had to upset them. You spotted them in your stock and were prepared for the call."

"Thanks to Jay and your team," Carli acknowledged.

"You have got to keep the momentum in your favor. Hit them when and where they don't expect it."

"Have any advice on the next step?" Oakes asked.

"Let me think about it and I'll get back to you tomorrow." Jimmy reached for the phone and asked the receptionist to send Rick to the conference room. Rick was one of Ed Madigan's teammates. Barely a minute had passed when Rick entered the room.

"Jimmy, you needed me?" Rick asked as he looked at the conference room's occupants. His eyes widened in recognition when he spotted Jay Oakes and he nodded his head in greeting to Jay. They had worked together before on stock surveillance issues when Oakes was with other companies.

Jimmy began slyly and with a mischievous twinkle in his eyes, "Rick, I'd like you to arrange for a car and driver to take our guests to the airport."

"Glad to. There'll be three of you?"

"No way. Now I know what you're up to, Jimmy, you rogue!" Oakes stated. He turned to Joe and Carli and explained, "The last time that Rick arranged a car for me was when I was at my former employer and the chairman of the board, the president and I visited Jimmy and his team. Rick was asked to arrange for a car and driver to take us back to our hotel. The car looked like it was from Rent-A-Wreck and the driver had just got off the boat that day. He could barely speak English. The car reeked from smoke and had candy wrappers and empty beer cans on the floor. There were stains on the seats. The driver got lost and didn't know where the Grand Hyatt was. It was a mess! Good thing that my chairman and president were good-natured, but they still gave me a lot of trash about it and Rick. Rick, you remember that I called and gave you a hard time."

"Yep, I remember," Rick acknowledged.

"We have had a lot of fun at this end ribbing old Rick about this ever since. Haven't we, Ricky boy?" Madigan chimed in.

"Thought you'd enjoy telling the story to your new associates," Jimmy regaled with his infectious grin. "Seriously, Rick, arrange a car to pick them up downstairs in about five minutes."

"Got it covered. And Jay, I guarantee it won't be Rent-A-Wreck!" Rick left the room and the meeting closed.

Fallsview Tire & Rubber Company
Two Days Later

$\sim$

Since returning from New York, the Fallsview Tire team had been busy reviewing their financials and putting together their defensive strategy in anticipation of the upcoming filing and Ratek's visit. The phone lines had burned over the last 48 hours between Fallsview Tire's New York-based advisors and the corporate headquarters office on the banks of the Cuyahoga River. Fallsview Tire, at Oakes' suggestion, had retained Gary Welson from Dunhill & Easton, one of the top investor relations/public relations firms in Cleveland, to assist with their posturing.

During one key meeting, Welson had suggested an innovative approach to dealing with the upcoming filing with the SEC and Ratek's visit. It had never been used before, but its brashness could catch Ratek off guard. Welson thought that it would dovetail nicely with the way the Fallsview team had proactively managed the situation to date.

A knock on Owens' office door interrupted the brief meeting Owens was conducting with Weimar, Oakes and Dansen.

"Yes?" Owens asked as the door was opened by his assistant, Lita.

"Mr. Ratek and Mr. Searle are here to see you. Should I have them escorted here?" she inquired nervously. She had been a part of the hustle and bustle over the last two days and knew that this would be an important meeting with this outsider.

"Please do." The door closed. "I'd like you three to stay for the meeting with Ratek. If there's something confidential to discuss, then I'll ask you to excuse yourselves. I trust that everything is in place as we planned?"

"Yes," echoed Dansen and Oakes.

"I rather doubt that Mr. Ratek has any idea what's in store for him when he meets with us. It will be a firestorm," Weimar clucked confidently.

The young relief receptionist had been asked to escort the visitors to Owens' third floor, corner office perched overlooking the river and the adjacent freeway. The receptionist was obviously impressed by the sharply dressed businessmen she was escorting.

"Hi, I'm Rachel, and if you'd follow me, I'll escort you to Mr. Owens' office."

"Rachel, we'd be more than happy to follow you," Ratek flirted with a raised eyebrow at the attractive escort. Searle was silent.

Rachel blushed for a moment and asked, "Did you have any problems finding our building?"

"None whatsoever, my dear. Your president was kind enough to have a limo waiting for us when my plane taxied in at Akron-Canton airport."

They entered the elevator and began the ride to the third floor.

"You came on your own plane?" she asked in astonishment.

She had just recently graduated from high school and was easily impressed by the trappings of the business world, let alone the lavish excess of Wall Street.

"Yes, it's a Lear jet."

"Oh, that sounds so exciting!" she squealed. "Where did you fly from?"

"New York City, honey!" Ratek grinned as he responded to the impressionable young lady.

"I've always wanted to go to New York City!" she said excitedly.

"Tell you what I'm going to do." Ratek pulled out his pen and quickly wrote his name and number on a $100 bill, which he had extracted from his pocket. "Honey, here's my business card. You just call me and I'll send the jet in and fly you into New York for a date with me." He handed her the bill.

"Oh my, you shouldn't have done this!" she exclaimed. Rachel looked at the bill in awe as she turned it over to look at both sides. How romantic, she thought to herself.

Silly girl, you've probably just violated your company's ethics policy by taking a cash gift in excess of $50.00 from an outside business associate Ratek thought to himself. But then again, she might just call him.

The elevator reached the third floor and opened to reveal Oakes.

"Gentlemen, let me officially welcome you to Fallsview Tire's headquarters."

"Thank you, Jay. We're looking forward to a productive

meeting," Ratek icily informed Oakes.

"Good. So are we. If you'll follow me to Greg's office." Jay wheeled his scooter to the right and rolled the short distance to Greg's office.

Ratek observed the office décor as they walked down the executive suite. Not too extravagant, he thought to himself.

"I'm Greg Owens. You must be Max Ratek and Michael Searle," Owens effused cordially. Owens had recognized Ratek from the pictures in the magazine articles that he had reviewed. "I believe you already know Joe and Carli from their visit with you in New York. And Jay, of course, escorted you from the elevator."

"Yes. Yes," Ratek agreed impatiently as he took in Owens' office décor. It had the trappings of an outdoorsman, a hunter. Well, Ratek planned to turn the tables on Mr. Greg Owens. This time Owens was the prey. Ratek was the hunter and he was loaded for big game.

Owens motioned for them to take a seat at his conference table. "Please. Please, gentlemen. Now what exactly can we do for you today. As you know, we already are aware that you're a new shareholder of our stock—and a significant holder."

"Michael, could you give him the precise holdings, please?" Ratek requested.

"Yes, sir. As of the close of business Friday, we owned 10.6 percent of your outstanding shares which makes us your largest holder," Searle replied.

"And tomorrow is the SEC filing deadline if I understand the rules correctly," Owens stated rather matter-of-factly.

Ratek didn't miss the way in which Owens made his statement. "That would be correct. We plan to file first thing in the morning. Now, let's get down to business. I want to know what you're going to do to restore shareholder value. This Millington Trucking acquisition and its ensuing integration into your business has been a debacle. You've screwed it up from day one."

The Millington acquisition had been a pet project of Owens. He was the driver in selling it to the board and he knew that he was going to take a lot of heat because it had not gone as well as planned.

"We're taking steps. You probably noticed that our chief financial officer is no longer with us. To be brutally honest, I wasn't satisfied with his performance on the Millington acquisition. He..."

Ratek's cell phone rang. Ratek looked at the caller ID and then shut off his phone. A moment later, Searle's cell phone rang. Searle looked at Ratek who shook his head negatively. Searle shut off his phone too.

"Second guessing your former CFO? Come, come, my dear Mr. Owens, since when did you become an astute financial analyst? Your background is in sales and marketing. If you want to be brutally honest, I'd say the firing of your CFO was a ploy. He was your scapegoat. The word is all over the Street," Ratek retorted firmly.

Owens was caught off guard. He wasn't used to being addressed in this fashion by outsiders. He decided to ignore the comments rather than validate them with a reply. "We admit, as we did in the last quarter's press release, that our integration plans have not proceeded as planned. We are making adjustments to correct the misalignments in our plans..."

"I don't want to hear double talk! Just tell us what are the steps that you're taking to raise profitability and the stock price. Give me the top three actions that you're planning and don't waste my time or insult my intelligence!" Ratek demanded. "If I'm not satisfied with your responses, I may request a seat on your Board of Directors—something which you may not want to see happen."

At this point, Joe Weimar spoke deliberately. "Mr. Ratek, I believe Greg was starting to convey to you our plan. Perhaps, if you'd give him the chance."

Ratek didn't respond. He looked at Owens and waited.

"To be very clear to you, our basic strategy is to make sure that we can deliver the best products at competitive prices for our customers. By doing this we will be able to enhance the stock price, maintain customer loyalty, protect employee jobs and support the communities in which we operate," Owens explained.

Ratek interrupted. "I asked for the top three actions..."

This time Owens interrupted as he looked at his watch. "I was just coming to that. Coincidentally, we have a press release that was released in the last five minutes which announced a major restructuring of our company to restore share value." Owens slid a copy of the press release across the desk to Ratek.

Weimar and Oakes exchanged secretive smiles.

Ratek couldn't completely hide his look of surprise. He realized now that the cell phone calls were probably from his office to alert him of the press release. This was going to be an interesting hunt with a smarter than usual prey. A prey that tried to fight back. That would make the hunt even more enjoyable, Ratek thought to himself.

Owens continued with an increasing confidence. "First, we

will move forward in a significant cost reduction program, which we think will add to the bottom line. Second, we are announcing a 5 percent price increase across the board, which we feel will stick since the market tends to follow our increases and all of the tire companies are faced with weak earnings. Third, we are bringing in an outside consultant to help us finalize the Millington Trucking acquisition."

Ratek sat back in his chair and applauded slowly in a mocking manner. "Very well done. Do you play chess, Mr. Owens?"

"Well, yes, I do. Why do you ask?"

"You've made a strategic move this morning with your announcements. Be sure that you keep thinking several moves ahead," Ratek warned. "Otherwise, you may find yourself checkmated sooner than you expect!"

Ratek was pleased. He saw that his initial ownership was already forcing the company to take action to raise the stock price.

Owens reached inside another file and slid another release across the table. "Here's another move that we made this morning. I call it our 'preemptive first strike.' It's an announcement to the public that we've identified a speculative buyer of a significant number of our shares, and that we've met with that buyer today who will be filing his ownership position tomorrow. The release continues to state they we expect to work as closely with this new shareholder as we do with our other shareholders in restoring the stock price for all shareholders, but especially for our employee and retiree shareholders."

Ratek was taken aback by this divulgence. He looked at the subdued grins on the faces of the Fallsview Tire team. He had been outfoxed. They had front-run him by announcing his ownership the day before he had planned.

Owens continued, "Over the last two days, I've had confidential meetings with our mayor and our governor and invited our local retiree association to a late breakfast meeting in our cafeteria. They have been told this morning that we have a new major stockholder who is known for slashing retiree benefits. I expect that they are anxious to meet you."

Owens' phone rang. He stood up and took the call. "Yes Lita. It did? Good. They are out there? Good. Thank you."

"One more thing, Mr. Ratek. You should also know that a letter went out to all employees a few minutes ago announcing the contents of both press releases and our intent to protect employee jobs and their families at all costs. I wouldn't be surprised if you see some of our employees, retirees and members of the community, including our mayor, holding signs supporting the company as you leave the building this morning." Owens paused for effect. "I also understand that there's large contingent of reporters in front of the building. It's such a shame that you'll have to walk through them all to reach your limo, which will be parked across the street for your drive back to the airport."

Owens paused again. "What were you saying about playing chess?"

"It's not checkmate yet, Mr. Owens," Ratek replied stonily as he seethed internally. He had been outmaneuvered this time. "Michael, I believe that we have completed our mission. It appears that the threat of what we could force you to do has prompted you to initiate restructuring plans today. I would say that we accomplished what we needed for this visit." Turning back to the Fallsview team, Ratek said coldly, "Thank you for your time."

"We will all walk you to the front entrance," Owens said. They were looking forward to seeing the crowd that had gathered outside in support of the company.

As they exited Owens' office, Carli gave Lita a coy grin signaling that things had gone well. The ride down the elevator and walk to the building lobby were in silence.

The two visitors signed out at the receptionist's desk and turned toward the front doors. Through the glass, they could see a crowd of about 75 people, many of whom were holding signs with sayings in support of the company and against takeover raiders. Along the street, they could see the trucks of the major Cleveland TV stations with their satellite transmission dishes. A group of TV reporters and newspaper reporters had just finished interviewing the mayor and were gathered near the stone steps leading up to the lobby. They had been told that the dissident shareholder would be exiting the building shortly.

Across the street was the waiting Fallsview Tire limo. Ratek asked angrily under his breath to Searle, "Ready to run the gauntlet?"

"A gauntlet it is!" Searle replied, dreading the walk. "Whenever you are."

They opened the door and stepped out into the bright sunny morning which was quickly filled with jeers and the bright lights of the TV station cameras. Microphones and questions were thrust in their faces by the phalanx of reporters who seemed well prepared. They knew who he was and his firm's takeover history based on the questions that were being thrown at him.

Ratek stopped for one moment. "I will make one brief statement." He had to speak loudly in order to be heard over the jeers from the crowd. "My investment in Fallsview Tire is just that—an investment. I expect to see a return on my investment, just like you expect to see earnings on the savings in your bank accounts. My meeting today with top management triggered the restructuring that you saw the company announce this morning.

As you can see, my ownership interest in the company is already producing results. That is all I have to say at this point."

The reporters continued to pepper him with questions as they followed Ratek. Ratek and Searle made their way through the hostile crowd to the waiting car and quickly escaped into its relative security.

Turning away from their elusive speaker, the reporters rushed back to the front of the building where Greg Owens was standing and appeared to be ready to address the crowd.

"Folks, first of all, let me extend to you my heartfelt appreciation for your support this morning. At the last minute, so many of you showed up to help us today. The only thing we needed today that we didn't have was some tar and feathers and a rail to run that carpetbagger out of here."

The crowd roared at his down home humor.

"Seriously, folks, we are going into a major battle to protect the very life of our company. We've made mistakes and several missteps, but we are going to address them and do our best to maintain the viability of the company. My desire is to protect employee jobs and the communities in which we operate. I see Mayor Trabor in the crowd. Why don't you come up here with me?" The mayor joined Owens. "Ron, I just want you to know how much I appreciate the city's support and I know that I can count on you and your administration."

Mayor Trabor affirmed, "We're behind you and all of the Fallsview Tire employees. Isn't that right folks?"

The crowd roared their approval and the reporters threw a barrage of questions at Owens. "Sorry, folks, I need to get back to business. Everything else I have to say is in the press release."

Owens invited the mayor inside for further discussions, and the two entered the building closely followed by Weimar and Dansen.

Oakes was about to join them when Gary Welson and another dark haired individual caught his attention. Oakes waited for the two to make their way through the crowd.

"Gary, great job on getting the press releases out there and getting to the mayor this morning. You really outdid yourself in getting the crowd, the signs and the reporters out. Thanks. We owe you!" Oakes shook Welson's hand in appreciation.

"That's my job. I've got someone here who you should meet. You may have read about him last year. This is Emerson Moore from the *Washington Post*."

In The Limo

~

Ratek pressed the control to raise the privacy window between the driver and the passenger compartment of the limo and turned to Searle.

"They were too well prepared!" Ratek fumed.

"Max, they've been that way from the beginning."

"I think it comes down to two people driving this. It's that skinny general counsel and his scooter buddy."

"Yeah. They seem a bit experienced. You have got to hand it to them. That preemptive first strike stuff was a brilliant move. No one has pulled that rabbit out of a hat before!"

"Clever, weren't they? But they've only won the initial salvo of this battle. They may have blindsided us today, but they also gave away a critical secret."

"What's that?"

Ratek grinned slyly before answering.

"We now know to expect the unexpected! They won't pull this on us again."

The limo deposited the two visitors at the hangar where Ratek's jet awaited. It slowly made its way through the hangar area and stopped before pulling into the stream of traffic departing the airport grounds. The limo driver ejected the cassette tape which had been recording the conversation in the passenger compartment. The limo driver drove north on Route 77 towards the Fallsview Tire headquarters where he would present the tape to Greg Owens. Greg Owens didn't always tell everyone his plans either.

The limo driver had been working directly for him for a number of years and had provided Owens with inside information on other passengers, including fellow executives. The inside information had helped Owens move up in the company ranks.

Fallsview Tire & Rubber Company Headquarters
Front Steps

∼

Gary Welson continued, "He won the Pulitzer Prize for the Put-in-Bay exposé last year. We had met a few times over the years and I saw him here in the crowd and thought you might be interested in meeting him. I told him that you head up the company's investor relations and public relations function."

"Hello, Emerson. I read your story about the L'Hoste affair. Quite impressive!" Oakes greeted cordially.

"Thanks. Coincidentally there's a link to your company," Moore responded seriously.

"A link to us?" Oakes was dumbfounded. He had read the series with interest but didn't see any link.

"Yeah. The L'Hostes were actually working on the acquisition of Millington Trucking when their business blew up, so to speak. Both the father and son were killed. So the company had problems and the deal didn't go forward to completion. Then, Fallsview Tire bought it."

"Small world, isn't it?"

"Yep. It just keeps getting smaller," Welson added.

Emerson began to probe, "So what are you folks going to do about your new shareholder?"

Oakes saw it coming. He expected Emerson to steer the conversation to the issue at hand. Oakes thought that Emerson was very likable and wanted to open up to him, but then again he had to be wary of divulging information to a reporter, especially one whose investigative prowess was becoming more acclaimed.

"You want the company line?"

"Oh, come on now. You really don't expect me to settle for that!" Emerson countered quickly.

Welson interrupted. "Jay, let me help on this." Turning to Emerson, Welson continued, "You don't want to compromise Jay, do you Emerson?"

"What I want is the story. I've actually been chasing this for some time. Why do you think I turned up in the area? I've been running down leads and preparing a cradle-to-grave story about takeover battles."

Oakes eyes widened. "From cradle-to-grave. How long have you been in the hunt?"

"I got wind of this early on." Emerson explained what had transpired on his flight to LaGuardia and the conversation which he overheard. "Once I determined that the target was Fallsview Tire, I started my local research here in Cuyahoga Falls."

"That airplane flight of yours! Talk about being in the right place at the right time!" Welson commented.

"Yeah. Once in a while you catch a break like that. So, what's the real story here?" Emerson asked.

"In one word—win. We'll pull out all stops to make sure that these bandits don't get control of the company," Oakes stated determinedly.

"But, why? Based on my research, you folks haven't done such a great job in delivering shareholder value. Look at what's happened to your stock price, the way it's plummeted. You certainly aren't getting your integration of Millington Trucking handled. The only real reason for you to win is to protect your jobs!" Emerson said.

"It's more than that. We've got customers, suppliers, communities, and employees that we are concerned about," Oakes said.

"Whoa! You're company lining me! I know that you haven't been here long enough to develop that type of loyalty!" Emerson retorted.

"Easy, Emerson. You're really going in for the kill on this," Welson cautioned.

"Gary, he's giving me the company line. I want more than that!" Emerson replied.

"Okay, it's true that I've been here a short time. But I did learn the company tradition. It's a company that cares about its employees. For the last four years, it's been recognized by Cleveland's Employers Resource Council as one of the 99 best companies to work for in northeast Ohio. And you're right, we haven't done such a good job about keeping our stock price up for our investors and our retirees. Granted, we haven't handled the Millington Trucking integration well."

Welson interrupted. "Emerson, I'd think that it would be safe to say that a lot of their troubles started with the unexpected resignation of their former CEO, a man of vision and ability to get things done."

"So, you are saying that the current CEO can't get things done?" Emerson quickly interjected.

"I didn't say that. The new CEO was thrust into his position ahead of schedule and is working diligently to address the issues. Don't forget, he no longer has his seasoned chief financial officer on board," Welson said.

"Gary, now you're company lining me!" Emerson stated with frustration.

"No, I'm trying to have you understand several of the issues that are complicating the organization's progress," Welson offered.

"Emerson, the bottom line is that we strongly feel that we can resolve the issues in a much more humane way than Ratek would.

He'd come in and destroy the company. There would be bodies scattered from here to Wall Street. We've seen him do that at other companies," Oakes said. "We're working to resolve the issues. I'm seeing Owens going through a phenomenal spurt in professional growth. We all are. We think we can address the issues effectively and cause the least amount of heartburn to our employees."

"You think so?" Emerson asked skeptically.

"Yes, we are confident. We're bringing in outside experts to help us restructure the organization. Ratek is doing two things for us that will drive positive consequences," Oakes stated.

"And they are?" Emerson asked inquisitively.

"He's pulling us together and forcing us to make some tough decisions," Oakes said honestly.

"Well, I'm going to be following this closely for my story. I'll be around a lot and asking a lot of questions."

"All within reason. We don't try to give any preferential treatment to one reporter over another. It could backfire on us," Oakes answered.

"I understand. Thank you for your time. Gary, thanks for the introduction. I'll be back in touch." Emerson excused himself and returned to his hotel.

Kent State University
Kent, Ohio

∽

The next morning, Emerson headed east from Cuyahoga Falls

for the 20-minute drive to Kent State University. He drove through the tree-shaded streets of the picturesque college town with the nickname of the "Tree City." He had an early lunch appointment to meet with the former head of a New York investment banking firm, who had taken early retirement and was directing the financial engineering program for Kent State's School of Business.

Bob Welch and Emerson had bumped into each other on several occasions at a number of parties in Washington's social-political scene where they had both enjoyed each other's company and conversations about Wall Street trends.

Emerson had learned that a series of strokes forced Welch to take an early retirement. When Kent State contacted Welch about the university's plan to start a Masters of Science Program in Financial Engineering and the construction of a mock trading floor in the School of Business, Welch couldn't resist the opportunity and had agreed to head the program. It would be less stressful than his Wall Street days and he would be helping students develop their professional careers.

Emerson parked his car and entered the towering school of business where a graduate assistant escorted him to Welch's office on the fourth floor.

Welch heard the footsteps in the hallway and greeted his friend at the doorway.

"Long time no see, my Pulitzer Prize-winning friend. This isn't quite Washington."

"Yes, way too long and you're right—this isn't Washington. And it's not Wall Street either! But it is less stressful for both of us."

The two grabbed a cup of coffee and returned to Welch's office where Emerson informed Welch about the death of his wife and son, his adventure with the L'Hostes on Put-in-Bay and his relocation to Put-in-Bay to live with his aunt. He left out any mention of the elusive Martine.

Welch, in turn, caught up Emerson on the recent events in his life and his subsequent move to the university. "This has been a dream for me to join the university and direct this financial engineering program. It's based on the use of mathematical methods, computer science, statistics and economic theory to solve financial problems. We can run a number of scenario simulations to develop and understand a wide range of potential financial solutions. Let me give you a tour of our trading room."

The two quickly walked down the hall and entered the newly constructed trading floor. Emerson was in awe as they entered the room, which reminded him of the New York Stock Exchange and the trading floors of the Chicago exchanges. He gazed at the 25 trading floor workstations with Hewlett-Packard equipment and the maze of state-of-the-art information displays on the walls of the room. It was technology at its best.

"Impressive. Kent has made quite an investment here," Emerson offered.

"Here, students can simulate real trading floor activities and even access the training programs at the exchanges. They have access to the same data feeds and trading software that the major investment houses use. When the students complete their program, they're ready for the real trading floor," Bob explained. "It's interesting to see the attention that the major investment firms and brokerage houses are paying to this program. They're very interested in the program's graduates."

Looking down at his watch, Bob pronounced, "It's time for lunch. We're going to the Schwebel Garden Room across campus. It's run by the students in the restaurant management program and is located in the student center, just a short walk from here."

As the two left the trading floor, a fast-walking professor bowled into them. He had been reviewing a document as he walked.

"Oh, excuse me. I'm trying to maximize my efficiency. You know what I mean?" the busy, but outgoing professor explained as he hurried down the hall.

Welch smiled.

"That's Storming Norman Marks, one of the accounting professors. He's a real genius and favorite with the students. He also provides financial counseling to businesses in northeast Ohio."

"Seems very likable," Emerson mused.

"He is and he's a catch for the university," Welch added.

The two friends continued their chatter as they walked past Bowman Hall to the student center. They made their way through the crowded student dining area and took the elevator to the Schwebel Garden Room on the third floor.

As they entered the restaurant, Welch noticed the university's president, Dr. Carol Cartwright, seated at a table with a number of professors. She saw him and smiled an acknowledgement which he returned as he and his guest were shown a table overlooking the courtyard. They quickly reviewed the menu and placed their orders when the waitress arrived.

"Quite a campus here," Emerson noted.

"Yes, the university has gone through a major growth spurt. We're recently recognized by *U.S. News and World Report's* story on the best undergraduate business programs. We're the only university recognized in northeast Ohio."

"Impressive!"

"Yes, it's just another step in the right direction that the leadership is taking. But, come now, Emerson, I feel that I know you well enough that you wouldn't track me down just to get a tour of the trading floor and learn about the university. What do you really want to chat about?"

Emerson paused a moment before responding.

"Bob, I need your help on a story that I'm tracking."

"Would it be the Fallsview Tire story?" Welch probed.

"Good guess. But then again, how could you miss it with all the press it's been getting in the last 24 hours?"

"They're a big supporter of the university through their Fallsview Foundation. They also sponsor a rotating chair for retired executives to help with our MBA program. We all are interested in how this conflict with Max Ratek is going to play out. He knows every trick in the book."

"You know him?"

Welch smiled before speaking.

"Only at arm's length. He had approached our firm on several occasions to provide him with additional financing on several deals over the years."

"So your firm worked with him?"

"No, we didn't close the financing with him because ..."

Welch paused, uncertain as to whether to continue.

"Go on Bob," Emerson urged.

"Our sources indicated that Ratek was even more scurrilous than how he was portrayed in the press. There were rumors of payoffs and physical violence to the people he was associated with. Not something that we wanted to get involved with. Between you and me—and completely off the record—I'd guess that his accounting practices are questionable. If an investigation of his firm was conducted, the other major corporate scandals flooding today's news would pale in comparison."

The waitress appeared, served them their food, and left.

"This guy is really bad news, then," Emerson stated.

"Yep. He likes to think of himself as the Michelangelo of Wall Street. You've seen that written up in the media. I'd compare him more with the Antichrist."

"Strong statement!" Emerson concluded.

"Be careful how close you get to them. They know all the dirty tricks," Welch cautioned. "There is one thing, though."

"Yes?"

"Track down whoever is financing him on this deal. Whoever he has used over the years prefers to maintain a very low profile. He puts up the financing, allows Max to be the bad guy and keep some of the profits, and then quietly takes the majority of the profits without anyone knowing that he is the background."

"Any idea who it might be?"

"Not really. There have been rumors over the years. Could be someone offshore."

"Hmmm."

"If you want to add an interesting twist to your story, find out who that person is and reveal him to the public. Whoever it is, I'd guess they don't like publicity. You'd better be careful, too. They could be dangerous."

Having finished his meal, Emerson pushed back from the table. "Thanks for the advice. And I'll be cautious. With your contacts on Wall Street, could you make some discreet inquiries about who is funding Ratek?"

"I can, although I don't expect to come up with much. I would have more likely heard about who it was while I was working there than I would now. However, I'll make some inquiries."

"Thanks, Bob. I'll add this to my to do list. I'd better head back to Put-in-Bay. You ever been up there?"

"No, but it sounds like a place I'd like to visit sometime."

"I'll invite you up. I'll stay in touch as I proceed with my story."

"Please do. I've got my eye on this one for a variety of reasons."

Welch walked Emerson to his car.

Aunt Anne's House
Put-in-Bay

~

"You about done yet?" came his aunt's cheery voice from the other side of the screen door.

"Just about," Emerson responded. He had been painting the trim of the screened front porch and the door frame for the last hour. Living on the island rejuvenated Emerson. He was sure it was the fresh breezes that breathed a new life in him.

"I should be done in another 10 minutes."

"Well, I'm going to take the golf cart and run to the store. You need anything?" his Aunt asked.

"Nope. I'm set." Emerson had been replaying his conversation with Bob Welch. Bob's suggestion about finding the source of the financing was good. It was real good. He just didn't know how he would track it down.

Owens' House
Hudson, Ohio

~

Located north of Cuyahoga Falls, Hudson is a bedroom community for many executives working in northeast Ohio. The downtown area is filled with old homes and buildings that give it its quaint New England ambiance. Complementing the charming downtown area, are the old brick clock tower and the gazebo, where Sunday evening music festivals take place. It's a postcard delivered from yesteryear.

The stately brick colonial home of Fallsview Tire's CEO overlooked one of the greens and a water hazard of Hudson Country Club on the north side of town. Inside the home's four-car garage were Owens' new Corvette, his Cadillac De Ville, and his wife's Mercedes. Parked in the fourth spot was Owens' 1962 Corvette convertible. His pride and joy was tuxedo black with a black interior and had a 327/340 horsepower engine with a four-speed transmission. The auxiliary hard top was stored nearby.

Owens had recently acquired the car from Don Sitts, the affable owner of Don Sitts Auto Sales on Front Street in Cuyahoga Falls. Owens and Sitts met at a Corvette car show and became fast friends due to their mutual interest in Corvettes and the proximity of their businesses to each other in Cuyahoga Falls. It wasn't unusual for Owens to pop in and spend some time with Don over lunch talking about Corvettes or seeing the latest car that Don was restoring.

A meeting was taking place in the house's library, which featured a custom designed marble fireplace with fluted moldings and marble surround. Three walls were hidden by hand-built Schrock cherry bookcases and cabinets. Richly designed boardroom panels with pocket doors, and a huge window overlooking the golf course completed the room.

A shroud of anxiety covered the room as Owens met with his key advisors, Joe Weimar, Carli Dansen and Jay Oakes. Owens had called this after-hours meeting to discuss the strategy and review the plans for the upcoming annual meeting.

"The ballroom at the Sheraton has been reserved and so have rooms for the board members," Oakes confirmed to Owens.

"Good. And what about the press?" Owens asked Oakes.

"We're hosting a post-meeting press conference with you in one of the smaller conference rooms and then a small buffet lunch for them."

"Any investors coming that we need to pay special attention to?" Owens probed.

"A few. And I believe that they are friendlies."

"And we are anticipating that the press conference will go well. Joe, Jay and I have reviewed the potential questions and written responses for you. Here's the Q&A book," Carli said as she handed the thick book to Owens.

"And what about Ratek? What's he going to do since he missed the filing deadline for a shareholder proposal?" Owens asked.

"That's one major misstep he's made. This year, he can't try to change our board make up via a shareholder vote unless he pushes for a special shareholders' meeting. He would have to have it in the next few months and push a number of shareholder proposals. That would take the support of major shareholders," Weimar noted.

"And what would prevent him from getting that support for a special meeting?" Owens questioned.

"In two words—our turnaround. We would have to show the Street that we are successfully restructuring the company and that there is no reason for them to side with Ratek in order to increase the stock price," Joe said seriously.

"Which of our advisors are going to be here for the meeting?" Owens asked.

"P. Dayton Ford will be here with Joe. Jimmy Malloy will be with Jay and our accounting firm will be with me in the event that Ratek tries to throw a surprise our way," Carli stated firmly.

"And we're planning a few surprises for him," Oakes added.

"And what would they be?" Owens queried with interest.

"Greg, it would be better if you don't know right now. I can assure you that they're perfectly legitimate and won't open the company to criticism. Some of them are subtle. Others are not. I'll tell you about them as soon as they're finalized," Weimar explained.

"Jimmy Malloy gave us several of the ideas," Oakes added.

"Greg, the most critical thing we must do to make this annual meeting a success is demonstrate that we're in control. When Ratek steps to the mike to begin asking you questions, you need to make sure you don't appear rattled. Especially if he blindsides you with a question. Take your time in responding to him. Defer questions to experts on your staff," Weimar advised.

"Speaking of control, I trust that you've established a procedure to limit access to the meeting to only our shareholders and invited guests?" Owens wanted to be sure that the opportunity for disruption would be minimal.

"Yes. Meeting attendees will need to present a ticket to get in. The tickets were sent to any shareholder who requested one. Of course, that doesn't prevent a shareholder from passing a ticket off to someone else. Are you concerned about something in particular?" It was now Weimar's turn to ask questions.

"I seem to recall a few years ago a few disgruntled employees, who were also shareholders, asked questions," Owens responded.

"You're always going to have that risk."

"Good meeting folks. I appreciate your help this evening. Jay, will you need my help getting into your van?" Owens asked.

"No thanks. I have a lift that helps me get in," Oakes replied as he wheeled towards the door.

"Greg, care to join us for a dinner? We're going to the Inn at Turner's Mill," Carli offered.

"No. No. I'll just grab something here and start wading through this material you brought me. Reminds me of *War and Peace!*" Owens responded good-naturedly.

He escorted his three key advisors to the door who then departed for a late dinner at the upscale Hudson eatery.

Spago's Restaurant
Beverly Hills, California

~

"Joe, it's Margie. Did I wake you?"

Weimar looked through his tired eyes at the clock on the nightstand. It read 12:30 A.M. He wondered why his wife was calling him at this late hour. She had been attending a medical conference in Beverly Hills with a number of other doctors for the week.

"Why are you calling so late? Just to tell me that you love me and miss your passionate husband?"

Weimar loved to tease his pretty wife.

"Joe!" She sounded exasperated, Weimar thought.

"I'm at Spago's with Jim Aronson." Aronson was another doctor from the Akron area who had made the trip with her.

"You didn't have to wake me to let me know that you having dinner at Spago's, dear."

"Joe, stop it. Stop it right now. I called to let you know what I overheard at the table next to us. There were two guys, sounded like big money people, talking about Fallsview Tire."

Weimar sat up. He was fully awake now and in a serious mood. He had been reviewing the list of the largest shareholders and recalled that a few of the major pension fund shareholders were in the Los Angeles area.

"What did you hear, dear?" Being an attorney, Weimar didn't share confidential business dealings with his wife, just as she did not disclose confidential patient information to him. He hadn't told his wife anything more about the Fallsview Tire issue than what was already in the press.

"I wrote a few notes on my napkin. They were talking about voting for Ratek. That's the guy who's been buying all of your company's stock, right?"

She sounded worried to Weimar.

"Yes, Margie. That's the guy."

"Well, apparently they're not sure that he's going to be in the stock for long. They said something about a crash and burn."

"That means that he crashes his way into companies and leaves a burning mess in his wake after he's left and sold all of the assets. It's the way he operates. Did you hear anything else?"

"Just that these guys seemed a little uneasy about supporting him. They're talking about taking a short ride in the stock and bailing out. Then they talked about financials which I didn't follow."

"Thanks, honey. This is good to know. Maybe there are other investment funds out there that are uncertain about Ratek. His alliance of support could be fragile. We might be able to sway them to our side if we can show that we can turn things around. You've done good! How's your conference?"

"It's going well. I'm looking forward to tomorrow morning's sessions which focus on cancer breakthroughs."

"Is Aronson behaving himself with my pretty wife?" Joe was now relaxing and beginning to tease her again. The Aronson and Weimar families were close and often vacationed together.

"Of course, he is, Joe! I swear one of these days, I'm going to perform a lobotomy on you!"

"It may be too late. But better a lobotomy than a vasectomy, doctor," he retorted as he grinned.

"I hope you have nightmares tonight about just that! Just dream of me with that scalpel in my hand!" she enjoyed the repartee with her quick-thinking husband.

"Thanks, but no!" Weimar saw that he was fighting a losing battle in this friendly war of words. "Margie, you and Jim can have dessert on me tonight! Now, I'm going to try to get some sleep."

"Good night, my little stud." Weimar groaned at the comment which his wife just made in front of Aronson. He knew that he'd take a ribbing from Aronson the next time he saw him.

"Good night, my dear." Weimar placed the phone's receiver in the cradle and lay in bed. He replayed the comments about Fallsview Tire and fell asleep with ideas filling his mind.

Put-in-Bay
Lake Erie

~

The afternoon's wind from the west was propelling the small sailboat between Middle Bass Island and Gibraltar Island and toward Put-in-Bay's harbor. Emerson had started his sail that morning by tacking about 15 miles west of the islands before turning and running with the wind.

It had given him time to think about the events of the last few days and what his next steps would be in developing his story. He had been searching the Internet and calling friends who might be able to give him additional insight, including two phone calls to Bob Welch at Kent State.

He had talked with Lynn Arruda and agreed to join her to attend the weekly Cuyahoga Falls Front Street Car Show. She had explained that Jimmy, from Jimmy's Café, would be showing his car. Emerson enjoyed the older cars and driving his aunt's cream-colored 1929 Model A Ford truck with deep green fenders in the weekly Sunday afternoon island car parade.

Emerson had dropped the sail and carefully guided the small sailboat, now powered by its outboard, into its docking area in front of his aunt's house. Securing the boat, he ran up to the house's screened porch and entered.

"Good sail, Emerson?" his vivacious, 67-year-old aunt asked as he entered.

"Yes. Days like this make me thankful for moving here," Emerson responded.

"Oh, and I thought that it was days with your aunt that made you thankful for moving here. Now, my feelings are hurt," Aunt Anne feigned.

Emerson moved next to his aunt and put his arms around her to give her a bear hug. "Aw, you know you're the real reason I moved here. Someone's got to take care of you and make sure that that boyfriend of yours doesn't get out of line," Emerson teased.

He was referring to Mr. Cassidy, the white-haired, bearded, 73-year-old retired harbormaster who had been friends with Aunt Anne and Uncle Frank. Once Uncle Frank had died, their relationship began to develop. Mr. Cassidy, who had a habit of sticking his tongue out and licking his lips, also was the self-appointed island historian.

"He's quite the gentleman. He's going to be stopping by shortly to take me to dinner at the Boardwalk. We're having their famous bisque tonight. Would you like to join us?"

"Can't tonight. I'm having dinner with Barry and Sybil from the *Gazette* at the Crew's Nest. But, you could drop me off if you'd like."

"Okay, but you need to be ready in about 15 minutes."

"I'll run up and take a quick shower." Emerson scampered up the stairs being careful not to knock over any of her precious antique vases which were near the stairway.

Fifteen minutes later, the freshly scrubbed Emerson was helping his aunt into Mr. Cassidy's truck.

"Good to see you, boy," Mr. Cassidy beamed as Aunt Anne scooted next to him in the truck so that Emerson had room. "You should ride with us more often, so that Annie can sit next to me," he said with a twinkle in his eye as his tongue extended itself and licked his lips. "You can scoot a little closer if you'd like, Annie."

"Any closer and I'll be driving," she teased warmly.

Emerson grinned and thought how nice it was to see the relationship developing between the two of them. It had been about two years since Uncle Frank had died.

"What you been up to, boy? You haven't been around too much," Mr. Cassidy asked as he drove the truck past Perry's Monument and toward town.

"Working on a story about the takeover of Fallsview Tire. I've been doing some research and I'm going back to Cuyahoga Falls tomorrow for more research and to attend their annual meeting."

"Excuse me for interrupting, but we need to make a quick stop at the Silly Goose so I can drop off a small thank-you present to Jill for her donation to OWLS," Aunt Anne stated.

"Okay Annie, we can do that," Mr. Cassidy said as he turned left onto Toledo.

"OWLS?" Emerson questioned.

"Yeah, boy. It stands for the Old Woman's Literary Society on the island," he chortled.

"We came up with the name ourselves. We thought it was unique," his aunt explained. "We meet every two weeks and review books."

"And gab," Mr. Cassidy teased.

"Well, we do have to share information," she retorted.

The truck had turned right onto Delaware past the Puddle Duck Gift Shop and was approaching the Crescent Tavern. Mr. Cassidy stopped the truck in front of the outside patio area where the shaggy, red-haired Westside Steve was singing and entertaining a late afternoon crowd of revelers. He was wearing one of his trademark Hawaiian shirts and just ending a raucous song.

When he spied Mr. Cassidy in his truck, he shouted to the crowd, "Everyone turn around and look at the guy driving that old truck. On three, yell 'Hi Mr. Cassidy'. Ready now. One. Two. Three. Hi Mr. Cassidy!"

Westside Steve and Mr. Cassidy had been friends for years. Mr. Cassidy tooted his horn, waved back and drove on.

"I just love that kid. He's so full of energy," Mr. Cassidy said as they drove by the bright red Roundhouse Bar, Park Hotel, the Country House Gift Shop, Pasquale's Cafe and Frosty's.

"So, you come across anything real interesting in your story? Anything like what you found in that L'Hoste story you did a year ago?" Mr. Cassidy asked.

"Nothing yet. I'm working on a number of leads. I'm going to kick around a number of ideas with Barry and Sybil at dinner tonight."

"They're good people and have a lot of contacts. Wouldn't surprise me if they gave you some tidbit that would be very helpful," Mr. Cassidy mused.

The truck stopped in front of the Silly Goose on Catawba Avenue and Aunt Anne ran inside. She was back in no time and they headed to drop Emerson at Barry and Sybil's home on Bayview, overlooking the harbor.

"Need us to pick you up later?" Aunt Anne asked as the truck backed out of the driveway.

"Looks like it's going to be another nice evening. I'll just walk back."

The truck drove away to the Boardwalk as Barry appeared on their porch.

"Hungry?" the lanky Barry asked as he descended the stairs and greeted Emerson with a firm handshake.

"Sure. Where's Sybil?" Emerson inquired as he noticed that Barry's pretty blonde wife was not accompanying them as they walked toward the Crew's Nest.

"She's covering a special council meeting. She wanted us to go on and she'll try to catch up with us if it's not too late," Barry responded. "So what have you been up to?"

Emerson explained the events of the last few days as they reached the yellow and white complex housing the Crew's Nest and were seated at a table overlooking Bayview and the harbor. The private club offered members docking privileges across the street at its private docks and a host of amenities including swimming and exercise facilities. The club was also known for its fine, high quality meals and its wine cellar.

"You sure fell into this one with what you overheard on the plane," Barry commented as they watched a cruiser easing into one of the docks.

"Yes, that was the big break. It's going to be a cradle-to-grave story."

Their conversation then turned to island life and events as they enjoyed their meal together. As the sun began to set, they heard the bagpiper piping the sunset from Peach Point. The breeze carried the bagpipe's haunting music across the harbor.

"Shall we call it a night?" Emerson asked as he noted that the time was nearing 10:00 P.M.

"Sure. Sorry that Sybil didn't make it. She may have just got caught up in the council meeting and any follow-up interviews." Barry paused and then offered, "Let me think about your story. I may know someone who can give you additional insight into Fallsview Tire's financial distress. I'll check and get back to you."

"I appreciate any help you can give me," Emerson replied thankfully.

As they began to leave the Crew's Nest, a few boaters called for Barry to join them at their table and Barry excused himself. Emerson began his walk back to his aunt's house on East Point. He thought about the conversation with Barry and Barry's comment about knowing someone who might be able to give him additional insight as he walked. He hoped that someone with valuable information could be found.

Barry had lived on the island for years and knew so many people—islanders, summer residents and boaters. Emerson surmised that Barry's contact was a wealthy boater and investor from Cleveland who would have the inside track on what was happening behind the scenes.

Birkman Investments
New York City

~

Ratek was the last to enter his conference room. He glanced at his Rolex watch and surveyed the attendees, which included his team and his proxy solicitor and advisor, Peter Barkley from Wilton Partners. Over the years, Barkley had played a critical role in identifying voting tendencies of the major institutional investors. His advice helped Ratek in understanding which investors should be contacted and convinced they needed to side with Ratek and his team.

While Ratek didn't have a shareholder proposal for this meeting, he wanted to make sure the major shareholders would side with him as he began to make his demands on the company. At this point, Barkley felt comfortable the support was there, especially with the new shareholders who had taken ownership positions in the stock since Ratek's announcement of his ownership stake.

In anticipation of the need to call a special shareholders' meeting in the near future, Ratek had wanted Barkley involved from the start. Ratek would propose shareholder resolutions for the special meeting and would need Barkley's help in soliciting the votes and their subsequent tabulation. He might propose a new slate of directors of his choosing so he could obtain complete control of the company.

Barkley looked up from the computer screen that he had been intently studying. "All appears to be in order. We've got a couple of fund managers on the West Coast that I'm mildly concerned about, but overall, it appears that we have the support that we need."

"Good. Good," Ratek commented as he sat. Looking at Judith, he asked, "Anything more on the financials? You've been able to confirm that the pension reserve is over funded?"

"Yes, and ripe for the plucking," she grinned wickedly.

Grimes was sitting at the far end of the conference table and allowed his eyes to feast on Judith as she responded. He took in her full red lips and evilly thought to himself, "And so are you!"

Ratek saw Grimes staring intently at Judith, but ignored it. He knew that there was a certain tension between the two of them. As long as it didn't hamper getting their jobs done, he didn't interfere. Besides, Judith was probably as tough as Grimes, Ratek thought slyly to himself.

"Good," Ratek said.

"I've been preparing my questions for their CEO. I'm looking forward to walking up to that microphone and catching him off guard with some of my tougher questions. That country bumpkin has no idea what he's in for. We're going to drill down to the core of their problems and expose it for the world to see. When I'm done, he'll have no credibility!" Ratek stated arrogantly. "Are we set for the reception with the media the night before the special shareholders' meeting?"

It was Searle's term to respond. "Yes. We've got the lounge reserved at the Sheraton. We invited the press and TV crews to attend and they'll have an opportunity to approach you for brief one-on-one interviews."

Searle knew that the one-on-one discussions with the media fed Ratek's ego. Ratek loved stories about himself in the media. He didn't care if they focused on how successful or ruthless he was.

Searle continued, "After the meeting, we expect that you will be surrounded by the media for additional comments following your skewering of Fallsview's CEO. They'll try to catch you before they run up to his press conference."

"Very good." Ratek's eye gleamed at the prospect of the attention. Everything appeared to be going in Ratek's favor. "Good job everyone. Let's just make sure that we don't leave any stones unturned on this one. Keep up the good work."

Ratek excused himself from the meeting.

The Night Before The Annual Meeting
Cuyahoga Falls, Ohio

~

Having parked in the deck off Second Street, Emerson and Lynn strolled along the Front Street Mall north of Portage Trail looking at the cars on display at the weekly car show. The engines were glistening, the chrome spotless and the cars had been waxed with care for the show.

"Hey, you two!" came a cheery shout from one of the car owners.

Emerson and Lynn turned to see the gregarious Jimmy from Jimmy's Cafe approaching and capturing them both in a giant bear hug. "It's good to see you two."

"Hi Jimmy! We were finally able to get this hermit off the island and make a visit to see us!" Lynn said eagerly.

"I've got business here tomorrow. So this worked out fine. Which car is yours?" Emerson queried.

"This one right here," Jimmy said proudly as he stepped aside to allow them to view his emerald green, 1930 Ford Cabriolet with Billet wheels.

"Oh, Jimmy, this is really sharp!" cooed Lynn.

"I love it!" exclaimed Emerson as he looked at the convertible.

"It's got a 305 cubic-inch Chevy V-8 engine with a 350 transmission, stainless hugger heads, Turbo Sonic mufflers and Vintage Air. The grill is a '32 and we put in a dropped stainless headlamp bar."

Emerson and Lynn peered into the car's interior as Jimmy began to describe it.

"It's got 'Wabbits' burlwood dash, classic gauges with gold bezels, 'IDIDIT' anodized tilt steering wheel column, a Le Carra steering wheel and sculptured cloth upholstery."

Emerson let out a low whistle. "This is some car, Jimmy. There's nothing like it on the islands. You need to bring it up for Put-in-Bay's annual classic car show. This is a winner!"

"I have fun with this. It's just a little something to tool around in," Jimmy responded with pride. "I've wanted something like this all my life and finally broke down and looked for one. Found this on the Internet outside of Cincinnati."

"I bet this moves out!" Emerson stated in admiration.

"Enough talk about my car. Let me take you around and show you some of the others and introduce you to some of my friends."

He placed his arms around his two friends as he gently guided them down the mall and made introductions to Shelby with his 1966 white Mercury Monterrey, Mike and his 1937 burgundy Chrysler, Tommy and his 1938 cream Chevy coupe, Dayton and his 1970 blue Chevy El Camino, Lou and his 1931 red Ford Phaeton with a bright white canvas top, Rod and his turquoise and white 1957 Chevy, and Dennis and his 1956 orange and white Chevy Nomad.

Birkman Investments' Press Party
Sheraton Suites Hotel—Cuyahoga Falls

~

Located conveniently across the street from Fallsview Tire's headquarters and also on the banks of the Cuyahoga River, the Sheraton Suites provided the ideal facility for overnight annual meeting attendees and a ballroom for the annual meeting.

Birkman Investments had rented the hotel's Reflections Lounge for the evening and invited members of the press to attend in order to build relationships and gain support for their position in their takeover attempt. Ratek had a reputation as the master of the spin game.

Ratek and his team mingled with the reporters as the piano played quietly in the background in the cherry-stained room with large windows overlooking the river's water rushing through the rapids.

Ratek had guessed that Fallsview Tire's board members would be staying at the hotel and had left invitations for them to attend his reception at the front desk when they checked in. Ratek would do his best to build support—even with the enemy.

Emerson entered the Reflections Lounge. When he checked in at the front desk, he had overheard two reporters talking about the press party and decided to see if he could attend, even though he didn't have a formal invitation.

"And you are?" the attractive, expensively dressed blonde manning the nametag table asked Emerson as he approached. Armani, Emerson guessed.

"Not invited," Emerson responded with a grin. His warm smile had helped open doors for him before and he was hoping it would this time.

"Let's see if we can take care of that," she replied. "Who are you with?"

"You, if things go right!" Emerson teased.

"I don't think so!" the blonde snapped, dropping any pretense of niceties. "What newspaper are you with?" she inquired coldly.

"*The Washington Post*. Look, let me apologize. I didn't mean to offend you," Emerson offered.

Regaining her composure quickly at hearing that he was with *The Washington Post*, she responded, "Apology accepted. Sometimes, you just get tired of men hitting on you, if you know what I mean. I'm Judith Beckwith."

"Judy, I'm Emerson Moore," Emerson replied as he realized from his research that she was an analyst with Birkman Investments.

"It's Judith," she said as she printed his name and the newspaper's name on a nametag which she handed to him with a cool smile.

Too bad for a good looking woman that she has such an attitude, Emerson thought to himself as he affixed the name tag to his chest.

"Let me walk you over to meet Mr. Ratek," she offered.

Grimes and Searle overheard the exchange between Judith and Emerson. Their eyes followed Judith's body as she walked Emerson over to Ratek.

Commenting on her attractiveness, Searle said, "She can make a grown man cry!"

Grimes smiled slyly, "Not this man. One day, I'll make that predator cry. She'll beg for my attention."

Searle glanced at Grimes' face and saw an evilness about it. He looked for an opportunity to leave and excused himself to greet two newcomers. At times, Searle felt uncomfortable around Grimes.

Ratek had just finished talking with the business reporters from the *Akron Beacon Journal* and *The Cleveland Plain Dealer* and the editor from the *Cuyahoga Falls News-Press*. He was refilling his drink when Judith approached with Emerson. Emerson remembered Ratek from the plane flight to LaGuardia from Cleveland which had put Emerson in the hunt for the story. He wondered whether Ratek would remember him.

"Excuse me, Mr. Ratek. This is Emerson Moore from *The Washington Post*. He's just joined us unexpectedly," she said as a signal to Ratek that Emerson was not on the official invitee list. Judith returned to the registration table.

Ratek eyed Emerson and thought that Emerson seemed vaguely familiar. "Pleasure to meet you. Have we met before?"

"Not really. I believe we were on a flight together in first class from Cleveland to LaGuardia. You had talked to someone about chocolate doughnut being in play." Emerson knew that he was pushing it from the start.

Ratek retained his composure, but swore under his breath. "So, you heard my comment. How long did it take you to figure out who was in play?"

"I deduced it was a tire company that afternoon, but it took me a few days to determine that it was Fallsview Tire."

"Buy any of the stock?"

"Nope. Ethically, I couldn't do that."

"Ethics have nothing to do with it. You had an opportunity to make a solid return on an investment and you passed it up. The stock has increased in value since it was announced that I became a major shareholder," Ratek beamed proudly.

"I've seen your scorched earth approach to managing companies. You may increase a company's stock price, but you leave the company and people's lives in ruin when you're done playing with it."

Ratek was taken aback by Emerson's forthright manner, but only momentarily.

"You're wrong. Companies exist to provide a profit for their owners. Employees exist to make those profits. If they don't produce, then they and the company deserve what they get!" Ratek firmly stated.

"At whatever the cost?"

"At whatever the cost!" Ratek responded.

"Again, I disagree. You've overlooked leadership. Leaders exist to set strategic direction, motivate employees to perform and deliver results."

"I didn't overlook leadership. If they don't perform, they're gone," Ratek retorted angrily.

"Gone, but with big, fat golden parachute payments! Is that fair to the little guy? Leaders get paid for failing, but the little guy gets a swift kick in the butt as plants close and compensation and benefits are reduced. And investors like you make a killing in the process. Tell me where is the fairness in all of this?" Emerson argued.

"Welcome to capitalism! Who said it would be fair? Life's not fair to anyone." Ratek was becoming perturbed with Emerson.

Grimes had been scanning the attendees and keeping his eyes open for any potential incidents. He had been watching the exchange between Emerson and Ratek and saw its intensity increasing. He also saw that the conversation was drawing the interest of other media members. Grimes decided to join them in case Ratek needed him.

"You should know that I'm working on a cradle-to-grave story about your attempted takeover of Fallsview Tire," Emerson said.

"You made an error."

"An error?" Emerson asked.

"The use of the word 'attempted.' It will be a takeover."

"Maybe not. It sounds to me that you've run into a more formidable team than you're accustomed to dealing with."

"How so?" Privately, Ratek knew that this team was better prepared than any of the other teams he had run across, but he wasn't going to admit it to Emerson.

"I've talked with members of Fallsview Tire's team and heard how well prepared they were for you. Heard that they rocked you back on your heels when you made the initial call to inform them of your ownership position. Something that you're not used to, right?" Emerson was pushing the edge again.

Ratek was tiring at the impertinence of this reporter. Seeing Grimes at his elbow, he said, "Simon, why don't you chat with our friend here while I mingle with our guests." Ratek made one final comment as he began to walk away. "You can chat with him as he leaves our party."

"But I wasn't leaving!" Emerson agitated as Ratek greeted

another reporter.

"You are now, because you have just been uninvited." Grimes took a firm grip on Emerson's arm and began escorting him to the door.

Emerson began to protest and then decided to acquiesce. As they passed Judith at the doorway she gave Emerson an icy stare. What a group of misfits, Emerson thought.

Grimes returned to the room and approached Judith. "How did he get in here? He didn't have one of the pre-printed name tags."

"When I learned he was from *The Washington Post*, I let him in," Judith responded acidly.

"That was a mistake. Max is not happy about what happened. I'm sure that you will hear about it." Grimes stated harshly. "You want me to go to bat for you?" he asked as he allowed his eyes to travel the curves of her body.

"No. I can manage for myself. And quit looking at me that way. You're offensive!" she replied firmly. Judith didn't want to encourage any relationships with this toad. She was repulsed by his obvious interest in her.

"Don't say that I didn't offer." Grimes walked away with thoughts of her playing in his mind.

Fallsview Tire & Rubber Company's Board Dinner
Sheraton Suites

~

None of the Board members attended Ratek's press party in

the hotel's lounge. They were meeting with Owens, Carli, Weimar and Oakes at a board dinner held in the hotel's private dining room, the Library. It was a throwback to the opulent executive offices which prevailed through most large corporations. Its walls were lined with massive bookcases and one large fireplace. Views of the river were afforded by a wall of windows overlooking a gorge.

The eight Board members couldn't wait for the pre-board meeting the next day at 8:00 A.M. at Fallsview Tire's offices. They wanted answers from Owens that evening.

Webster started it. "Greg, I'm not satisfied by your plan to return the company to profitability. I reviewed the pre-board material and it just doesn't get it done fast enough."

Webster had been typically the most vocal of the Board members which was ironic. Webster was the only one that Owens had brought on board since moving into the CEO role. Owens had expected him to be the most supportive of his efforts since they were old friends. The opposite was true.

"It's a step at a time. We've got to walk before we can run. We're moving forward cautiously to make sure that we turn over every stone as we restore profitability. How do the rest of you feel about our approach?"

A general discussion ensued with the other Board members, half of whom were from non-profit organizations or academia and the other half from the business world. The overwhelming feeling was that the company's approach was the right approach. They wanted to give Owens a chance to demonstrate his leadership and turn the business around. They also didn't want to support the newest Board member who hadn't yet earned his stripes with the others, even though he had quickly become the largest shareholder on the Board. They knew his reputation for being successful, but weren't ready to embrace his ideas.

Webster probed further. "What about this annual meeting? Ratek has a history for causing problems at annual meetings. What are you going to do to prevent it at ours?"

"I'll let my team respond. Jay, who joined us a few months ago, has a strong reputation for crisis management and has been involved in a number of adversarial annual meetings. Jay, could you give them a brief overview?"

All eyes turned and focused on Oakes who was seated on his scooter at the end of the table.

"Sure. We know Ratek's mode of operations. Although I haven't dealt directly with him in the past, I'm acutely aware of his style. I've also contacted several of my peers at other companies who have had run-ins with him, and we're using advisors from Flanagan & Son in New York to coach us. We have a few surprises in store for Max Ratek if he uses some of his old tricks and we believe we've anticipated what could be some new tricks."

"Let me add to what Jay has stated," Weimar interjected. "We've also met with P. Dayton Ford, whom I'm sure many of you are aware, is the leading takeover attorney in New York. There is no love lost between him and Ratek. He's been advising us throughout the process and we are very well prepared."

Webster stared coolly at Weimar and Oakes, then looked at Owens. "I'm going to warn you that this Board had not better be embarrassed by Ratek."

"I don't expect that it will," Owens responded firmly.

Fallsview Tire & Rubber Company's Annual Meeting
Cuyahoga Falls

～

Tensions had been running high for both teams—Fallsview Tire's management team and Birkman Investments' team— as they both prepared for the annual meeting at the Sheraton Suites Hotel. The Sheraton Suites also overlooked the Cuyahoga River as it raced through the rocky gorge and the rapids that took the river down into the Cuyahoga Valley. The water swirled just as the minds of the key attendees to the annual meeting swirled.

The Fallsview Tire team had set up marketing displays of their key products the previous day for the annual meeting which would be held in the hotel's grand ballroom. Details regarding security, seating of the Board members and the press, standby medical attendants and vote tabulation had been resolved.

Carli was having an impromptu meeting with the outside accountants who had reserved seats near the front of the room so that they could easily respond during the question-and-answer session if they were asked by Owens.

Jay Oakes scootered over to Gary Welson to review some last minute details regarding the post-meeting session with the media.

Joe Weimar and P. Dayton Ford were talking about potential approaches that Ratek might try to pull at the last minute. Weimar was aware that Ratek had tried to get Board members to attend his press party the previous night, and that Ratek was throwing a breakfast meeting with the press that morning in the Riverfront restaurant prior to the start of the annual meeting. Weimar would be seated with Owens on the raised dais at the front of the ballroom to conduct the meeting.

Weimar chuckled to himself about some of the subtle tricks that they had set up to embarrass Ratek. It was going to be an interesting annual meeting. Weimar looked at his watch and saw that it was 9:45 A.M. The meeting started at 10:00 A.M. and all was going as planned.

It was at this point that Owens and the rest of the Board walked into the room. Owens strode to the raised platform and was quickly joined by Weimar as the Board members took their reserved seats in the first row.

"All set, Joe?" Owens asked somewhat nervously as he surveyed the ballroom and saw a number of shareholders had already been seated.

"It's all under control. Did the pre-board meeting go well?"

"They're all still nervous about what Ratek will try to pull today. Other than that, the pre-board went as well as can be expected under our current financial situation. One nice thing about Ratek's movement into our stock is that the stock price has climbed a bit for all of our shareholders to benefit," Owens responded.

There was a commotion at the rear of the room which interrupted their conversation and caused them to look at the source of the disturbance.

Entering the room and flanked by a phalanx of reporters and his team was Max Ratek. His height allowed him to tower over the group like some pied piper. The media smelled a very exciting annual meeting, especially during the question-and-answer period which they sensed Ratek would use to crucify current management—and, in particular, Owens.

Ratek's long stride quickly took him to the seats that had been reserved for himself, Beckwith and Searle, near the front of the room and near one of the microphone stands, which had been placed in the aisle for the question-and-answer session.

Oakes and Welson quickly appeared and directed the media to their reserved seats, three rows directly behind the company's board members. Welson took a seat with the group and Oakes scootered to the rear of the room from where he could address any unforeseen issues. P. Dayton Ford joined him in order to provide legal guidance.

Security had stopped three TV crews at the door and prohibited them from entering with their equipment. The company did not want the added distraction caused by the cameras, but more importantly, did not want to afford Ratek an opportunity to showboat for the evening news across the country.

The clock at the rear of the room showed 10:00 as Owens approached the podium.

"Ladies and gentlemen, welcome to Fallsview Tire & Rubber Company's annual meeting of shareholders. I'm Greg Owens, Chairman of the Board and CEO. I'll be conducting today's meeting as we formally present to you our financial results for the last fiscal year, share with you our exciting plans for growing our business and profitability, and address any other business matters which need to be discussed at this forum. There will be a question-and-answer session at the end of this meeting."

Ratek unconsciously licked his lips as he thought about the tough questions that he was going to pose to this untested CEO.

The closed door at the rear of the ballroom opened and shut quickly to allow Emerson to enter the ballroom. He had been on a phone call which had taken longer than he expected. Looking around the room, he saw several vacant chairs near the rear and moved to take one, nodding a greeting to Oakes as he walked by.

"I would like to introduce the Board members who are up for re-election this year to our shareholders." Owens briefly introduced each Board member and provided a brief biography on each. Owens was a bit perturbed when Webster stood and waved at the gathered attendees longer than what was necessary.

"Seated on my right is our company general counsel and secretary, Joseph C. Weimar. Mr. Weimar would you kindly provide our shareholders with the preliminary report of our proxy tabulation results?" Owens asked as he followed his script. He noted that the thick volume of potential questions and answers had been placed on the podium shelf where he would have easy access to it if he needed it.

"Yes, Mr. Chairman," Weimar formally responded as he began to read, "the preliminary results of the proxy tabulation show that 70 percent of the votes from shareholders had been counted. The preliminary results indicate that each of the Board members has been re-elected for the coming year and that the outside accounting firm has been retained."

After commenting on the results of the vote and announcing that the voting poll would formally close in 15 minutes, Owens began his report to shareholders. Most of it was already reported in the previously mailed annual report documents to shareholders and Owens regurgitated the data. He didn't try to hide the fact that the company was having financial problems. He couldn't. He provided a number of excuses about the failed integration of the trucking company acquisition and made sure to blame others including the former chief financial officer.

Owens did his best not to spend too much time here as he wanted to focus on the future and not dwell on the past. He shifted gears and began to talk about the future and their plans to roll out a new, profitable tire line. Displays of the new tire and banners lined the room.

Gary Welson turned in his seat and caught the eye of Oakes. They nodded at each other with concern as they saw Owens disregard their advice. Owens wanted to hype moving the company forward and not spend time in selling shareholders as to why they needed to support him and the company in the face of the threat from Ratek. He wanted to focus on additional profits from new products and not discuss costs.

Owens took a nearby seat as a series of ads began to roll on the huge video screen for what he called the tire of tomorrow, the Jupiter. His tag line was that it was "out of this world." It had a tread design similar to an alligator's hide and Owens liked to say that the tire would bite the road harder than your wallet.

Weimar winced as he watched the video of the ads flash across the screen. He had warned Owens that there were some concerns with some of the test results regarding tread separation, but Owens had dismissed them as inconclusive since the majority of the tests results were positive. Weimar hoped that Owens was right as further tests were being run.

With the video ads finished and closing comments made by Owens to end the formal portion of the annual meeting, Owens moved to the question-and-answer session.

Usually the question-and-answer sessions for Fallsview Tire consisted of a couple of retirees complaining about benefits costs each year and a non-profit organization raising an issue about the company's investments in countries with civil rights issues.

"At this time, I'd like to open the floor to our shareholders to ask questions. I'd like to let you know that you'll be limited to two brief questions. You should identify yourself, the number of shares that you own and state your question." Owens grinned to himself.

Almost every head in the room turned to look at Ratek in

expectation of his questions.

Ratek's head snapped up when he heard Owens' comment about limiting questions. He had a list of questions prepared which were intended to build upon each other and drill down into some areas which would show how inept Owens was in managing the company for shareholders. Ratek was furious with himself that he didn't see this coming.

At the rear of the ballroom, Oakes smiled to himself as he imagined how their strategy undermined Ratek's plans to dominate the question-and-answer session with questions from the floor.

A gray-haired, overweight retiree approached the microphone in the aisle and spoke. "My name is Nick Unger. I retired from this company as a retail stores division manager six years ago."

"Nick, you need to state how many shares you own. Got to follow the rules," Owens said gently to Unger who had worked for Owens at one time in his career.

"Oh, sorry about that Greg," Unger grinned at his informality with his old boss. "I own 1,200 shares and I've been reading in the paper about this new shareholder who's sitting over here. I recognize him from his picture in the paper. I'd like to know what you're going to do to protect our pension and benefits from him."

Unger grimaced at Ratek and returned to his seat.

"Nick, let me assure you and every retiree that we intend to maintain control of our company." Owens looked directly at Ratek. "We may have a new shareholder rattling his saber, but your senior management team and Board of Directors are taking appropriate actions to address all of our operational issues—and without the need of any intervention from outside meddlers."

A round of applause broke out from the group of retirees who were seated together.

Ratek leaned over to Judith and whispered in her ear as he handed her his list of questions. Judith stood and approached the microphone. She leaned over to talk into the microphone.

"Mr. Chairman, I'm Judith Beckwith with Birkman Investments. We are the owners of 10.9 percent of the common shares of Fallsview Tire. I have two questions to direct to you. First, why would Fallsview Tire move away from its core business and enter the trucking industry where you have no expertise?"

Owens had expected this question and replied, "The synergy between the two of us is obvious. We produce tires and they use tires, albeit retreads. But we have a retreading operation that can supply them with tires at a discount. They are in the hauling business. They can provide us with a discount on shipping our tires. On paper, it just makes sense."

"And what about you not having expertise? You didn't answer that for me," she said sternly as she shook her blonde hair.

"Granted we don't have the expertise at Fallsview Tire, but we bought their expertise. We have kept their management team with their years of experience intact."

"My second question is...," Judith started before she was interrupted by Weimar.

"I'm sorry Ms. Beckwith, but you have used your two questions."

"But the second one was a part of the first!" she responded defiantly.

"Again, I am truly sorry Ms. Beckwith, but you have used your allotted quota," Weimar firmly stated. He was tempted to call her "Judy."

Judith turned to look at Ratek who motioned her to take her seat. Furious, Judith sat down.

Ratek decided he would go next and took the list of questions from Judith. He eased his tall frame out of his seat and walked to the microphone. A look of frustration crossed his face as he realized that the mike was set at its lowest level and he would have to arch his back and his stance to an awkward angle in order to speak into it. He tried to raise the microphone, but it was screwed tightly in position. It gave an appearance of weakness in comparison to Owens who towered over him on the raised platform with an appearance of strength.

P. Dayton Ford jabbed Oakes in the ribs from where they sat at the rear of the room. This was just one of the subtle tricks that they had used.

"Mr. Chairman," Ratek began as the photographers snapped photos of him standing awkwardly. "I am Max Ratek with Birkman Investments and the owner of 10.9 percent of the common shares of Fallsview Tire. My first question for you is..."

Ratek didn't get a chance to complete his question as Weimar interrupted him. "Mr. Ratek, the Chairman stated the rules of the question-and-answer session as being that each shareholder was limited to two questions. Your associate has asked two questions on behalf of Birkman Investments' share ownership. Birkman Investments has had its turn and its allotment of questions. Would you kindly take your seat?"

Ratek's blood pressure began to surge at being outmaneuvered. He glared at Weimar and then thought for a moment before turning to the audience. "Is there anyone here who would exercise their right as a shareholder and designate me to ask two questions on their behalf?"

A couple of hands were raised from across the aisle and Ratek began to move toward them to obtain their shareholder information so that he could pose the question.

Again Weimar spoke. "Mr. Ratek, this is highly inappropriate and disruptive to our meeting as far as permitting sidebar conversations with other attendees as you gather information. I am sorry sir, but we just cannot permit it."

Ratek glared at Weimar again and was about to comment when a voice shouted from the front of the room.

"Here, here. Aren't we being a bit difficult to one of our largest shareholders?"

Everyone in the room looked toward the first row to see who was talking. Board member Webster was standing and challenging Weimar. Perplexed by this question from someone who was supposed to be on their side, Weimar looked at Owens who stepped in and took control.

"We are making every effort to provide equal time to each shareholder in this venue and not permit one shareholder to dominate this session. Some of you may not realize that we have had one-on-one discussions with Mr. Ratek and his team already and expect them to continue. I see no reason why we should permit him to question us in a public forum beyond what we permit our other shareholders. I see that we have been conducting this overall meeting for about one hour and we need to adjourn so that the Board can reconvene with its meetings. I thank you all for attending this morning and encourage you to ride on Fallsview Tire's products. Meeting adjourned."

Weimar strode over to Owens. "What a surprise from Webster at the end. You handled him well."

Looking at Webster and the other Board members as they filed out of the room and were escorted by one of the security guards, Owens commented, "I don't know what Webster is playing at. That was entirely inappropriate!"

Ratek and his team were making their way from their seats to the rear of the ballroom with the other attendees who were leaving.

"Nice trick they played with the microphone stand," Judith commented bitterly.

"Bastards! Did I look decrepit at the stand?" Ratek asked angrily.

"Very," Judith said coolly.

"Have a nice day folks," Oakes offered as the Birkman Investment team walked by Oakes and P. Dayton Ford near the rear of the ballroom. Ratek didn't respond, but just glared at his old nemesis, Ford, who was smirking ear-to-ear. This was one in the lost column for Ratek.

Emerson had left the meeting room and hurried after Ratek and his entourage.

"Excuse me, Mr. Ratek."

Ratek motioned for Searle and Beckwith to continue to the waiting limo outside the hotel's canopied conference center entrance and for Grimes to remain at his side. Ratek turned to Emerson, "Yes, Mr. Moore?"

"Tough meeting."

"Yes, it was a tough meeting for them," Ratek attempted to spin.

"No, I meant for you. It didn't appear that you were ready for their twist. They limited your ability to ask potentially damaging questions in a public forum." Emerson wasn't holding back. He liked to drill in when he was in the hunt for a story. He continued, "They really embarrassed you."

Ratek was not used to being talked to in this manner.

"Listen, smart ass. I did expect today's stunt," Ratek lied. "I know their little game. I just played into it to give them a false sense of security. I'm sure that they're celebrating about what they feel was a coup for them. Just watch what happens."

Emerson sensed that Ratek was lying. "What's your next step?"

"You think I'm going to tell you?" Ratek asked incredulously as he looked at his watch. "I've got to catch a plane."

Ratek and Grimes began to walk away when Ratek paused suddenly and turned toward Emerson. "None of this is for publication, understand?"

"I didn't agree to that up front. I have a story to do," Emerson replied.

"Don't cross me, Mr. Big Time *Washington Post* reporter!" Ratek threatened.

Emerson saw the evil look in Grimes' eyes as he stared at Emerson. Emerson looked at Ratek and responded, "Like I said, I have a story to do." Emerson turned and hurried away to catch the start of the post-meeting press conference with Owens.

Ratek fumed as they moved towards the waiting limo.

The Vaughn Boardroom had been set up for the press conference to be conducted by Owens. The TV crews had set up their cameras and lights and everyone was being ushered into seats by Gary Welson.

Owens, accompanied by Weimar and Oakes, entered the room. Owens' stride reflected his satisfaction in conducting a potentially tough annual meeting successfully. He took his place at the podium and beamed as he opened up, "Ladies and gentlemen, I'll take any questions you'd like to ask. You should have been provided with meeting highlights as you entered for this press conference."

A reporter from a Cleveland TV station was the first to ask a question, "Mr. Owens, you were rather abrupt with Mr. Ratek during the Q&A. How will this affect the manner in which he deals with you going forward?"

"I'd expect that he'll be a bit testy, but that's no different than how he's been with us so far."

The reporter followed up quickly, "So then, you have had a strained relationship with him to date?"

"I wouldn't say strained. He is known for his aggressive style. Next question?" Owens saw a hand in the air on the opposite side of the room.

"Why did you pull that stunt to limit questions from shareholders? I've attended the company's annual meeting for years and have never seen that pulled before," the reporter stated.

"Obviously, it was meant to provide all shareholders with an opportunity to ask questions and make sure that one shareholder did not dominate the time that we allowed," Owens responded.

"So what you are saying is that you didn't want to give Mr. Ratek a chance to ask potentially damaging questions?" the reporter deducted.

"I didn't say that!" Owens thought this was going a bit worse than he had originally anticipated it would go. "Sir, in the back. Your question?"

Emerson lowered his hand and stood to propose his question. "It appears that you're lacking solidarity in the boardroom as evidenced by the comment made by Mr. Webster. Could you tell us about the Board's support for you in light of the company's poor financial performance this past year?" It was a tough question and Emerson knew it when he proposed it.

A bead of perspiration appeared on Owens' brow as he thought before answering. Webster's comment had caught him completely off guard and he wasn't really sure where it came from or what Webster's motive was. He was also irritated with the way that Webster made a big deal at waving to shareholders when he was introduced. He wasn't sure what Webster was up to, but he would find out when he went into the board meeting which would begin after the press conference.

"I believe that Mr. Webster was giving us all an example of how independent our Board members are and that they are also independent in their thinking and discussions during board meetings. What was the second part of your question again?"

Emerson asked it again. "Could you tell us about the Board's support for you in light of the company's poor financial performance this past year?"

"They are very supportive of the company's financial performance. They realize that companies run through a down year every once in a while. This year's performance has been challenged by the acquisition of Millington Trucking and we are working our way through turning things around so that we can deliver the appropriate results for our shareholders. Did that answer your question?"

"No," Emerson replied stoically. "You didn't comment about their support for you."

Privately, Owens was somewhat concerned about their support, especially with the grief that Webster had been giving him lately over the phone. Webster had been demanding that he drive down from his Cleveland office to get more personally involved in turning around the company. Just another notch in his personal belt of accomplishments was what Owens had perceived. To date, he had been successful in thwarting Webster's attempts.

"They challenge me as they should in their roles. But they are firmly supporting me. Otherwise, I wouldn't be here," he added smugly. "Next question."

Emerson thought that Owens sounded a bit hesitant as he responded. Perhaps he wasn't as secure as he tried to portray.

The press conference continued for another five minutes before Oakes scootered to the front of the room to announce that Owens needed to leave to attend the board meeting across the street at the corporate headquarters.

"Let me make one final comment to you in closing. There's a report of a thunderstorm moving into the area and bringing torrential rains. I am personally concerned about each of you getting home safely today. I hope you're riding home on a Fallsview Tire!"

The reporters chuckled at the self-serving advertisement as Owens left the front of the room to attend the board meeting.

Ratek's Limo
Cuyahoga Falls

~

Ratek and Grimes entered the rented limo which was awaiting them in front of the Sheraton Suites. The limo was whisking them to Akron-Canton Airport where Ratek's private jet would fly them back to New York.

The limo was pulling out of the Sheraton's parking lot when it happened. Ratek's anger exploded with a series of expletives. Once he had exhausted his vocabulary, he began to calm down, although not by much.

"That son-of-a-bitch Owens threw us a curve with that Q&A limitation. No one has pulled that stunt on us. It was probably the idea of that bastard P. Dayton Ford. He's still simmering from the whipping I gave his client in the steel deal." Ratek was referring to a takeover of a steel company two years ago in which he soundly beat Ford's client.

"This was embarrassing with so many members of the press present," Judith commented.

"Michael, why didn't you see this coming?" Ratek asked his other analyst.

"Can't see them all, boss. We do our best," Searle replied quietly.

"Your best was not enough today. Word is going to reach our financier on this deal—and it won't be pretty for me. That means, you guys are going to go under a lot of heat, too. Simon, I want you to rent a car at the airport and dig around. See what kind of dirt you can come up with on any of the key players at Fallsview Tire."

"Okay. I'll see what I can find."

"Focus on Owens." Ratek instructed. " And check out that reporter Moore. He's an arrogant twit!"

"I'll get right on it, Max," Grimes assured his boss.

They replayed the events of the meeting on the way to the airport. The limo dropped the team at their jet and Grimes entered the airport to rent a car to use for his investigation.

Fallsview Tire & Rubber Company Board Meeting
Cuyahoga Falls

~

Owens entered Fallsview Tire's boardroom where the Board members were seated around the large conference table and waiting for him to convene the meeting. Owens ignored the accolades from the Board members for setting Ratek back on his heels.

He looked directly at his old friend, Webster, and demanded, "What in the hell was that showboating about? Did you think for one minute that your grandstanding would convey that this Board is not in unity on how we should move forward?"

Webster began, "Public perception of our unity..."

Owens interrupted with his voice rising, "You didn't use that brain of yours one iota. I expect complete and total loyalty from this Board!"

Owens was talking tougher than normal, but felt that he had that liberty since he and Webster went back to their college days. They had been friends, and again Owens was responsible for adding him to the Board.

It was now Webster's turn to be outraged. "Don't you think for one moment that you can talk to me in that manner! Even though I have the shortest tenure on this Board, I'm the biggest shareholder of any of your Board members. I speak my mind when I see inequity and I felt that you were being unfair to Ratek with the silly game you played about limiting questions. He is our biggest, single shareholder now and we owe him respect."

"Respect be dammed!" Owens retorted.

"Why throw gasoline on the fire? You've got to listen to his ideas about turning things around. If they're good and we improve profitability and the stock price, we all win," Webster explained toughly.

"That's not his modus operandi. He usually sells off assets and fires company executives. I might also add that he typically rids companies of their current Board members." Owens paused for effect and looked around the room at each of the Board members. "And none of you would want to go through that embarrassment, now would you?"

Webster began to respond and then thought better of it.

Owens then focused the Board members on the agenda and began to conduct the meeting which would eventually conclude after several serious exchanges late in the afternoon.

Vaughn Boardroom
Sheraton Suites

~

Other than a few TV crews still loading up their equipment, the press conference attendees had left the room. Emerson, Weimar, and Welson were walking with Oakes as he wheeled his scooter through the conference center doorway and they exited the building into the fresh morning air.

They had been talking about the meeting and how well it had gone.

"There's just one thing," Emerson started.

"And that is?" Oakes asked.

"With Ratek, you've just unleashed the whirlwind! I think he'll come after you full force now."

"Let him do just that. We have more tricks up our sleeve," Weimar grinned smugly. "You see, Ratek has never run into a team like ours before! Oh, did I just say that?" Weimar kidded.

Welson added confidently, "Seriously, Emerson, the team at Fallsview Tire is better prepared than any that I've dealt with in the past. They've Malloy and Ford involved as counselors in New York, Oakes' experience in investor relations and they identified Birkman's ownership before Ratek expected it."

"You forgot to mention that Fallsview Tire has an ace general counsel, too!" Weimar chided at not being mentioned.

They smiled gratuitously at Weimar's comment.

"Okay, Joe, a great general counsel, too!" Welson added.

"I hear what you're saying but I think he's going to take it up a notch. When I did my research, I spent some time reviewing the steel company takeover two years ago. Weren't there a couple of unsolved murders or unexpected deaths involved?" Emerson inquired seriously.

Weimer became very serious. "Yes, I'm quite aware of them. No one could prove any direct links between Birkman Investments and the deaths. There were rumors and they were circulated by your counterparts in the media."

"You know that one of the deaths involved a company's general counsel?" Emerson probed.

"Of that I am very much aware! It was P. Dayton Ford's brother, but unfortunately no one could prove a thing!" Weimar said stonily.

Oakes had been relatively quiet during the exchange. It was now his turn. "Emerson, are you aware of something that we need to know?'

"Nope. Just concerned that your scheme today may backfire on you."

They had reached the intersection of Broad and Front Street. Looking across the street at Fallsview Tire's headquarters building, Oakes wrapped up the conversation with Emerson.

"Emerson, thank you for your concern. Joe, it might not be a bad idea to put the company security team on notice to be especially aware of anything unusual for the next week or so."

"I agree," Weimar said.

"We need to get back to the office, Emerson, in case they need us to answer any questions at the board meeting. Thanks again for your support," Oakes stated.

"This is one time that I'd like to see the big company win, but you need to do the right thing with your employees!" Emerson commented.

"We'll do our best!" Oakes responded as he scootered down the cutout in the sidewalk's concrete and began to cross the intersection. "Thanks again!"

The three continued across the intersection and Emerson returned to his car for the drive back to the South Bass Island.

Birkman Investments
Later That Day

~

Ratek was pacing back and forth in his office. He had fumed during the entire flight from Akron-Canton Airport. It wasn't so much about what had transpired as it was about the phone call that he needed to make. He knew that he had to call before the results of the annual meeting broke on the evening news, although he fretted that it was already on the news wires. He needed to be the one to break the news. He couldn't have done it on the plane as his team was on board and he didn't want them to see his nervousness.

Still standing, Ratek picked up the phone and dialed the private number.

The phone was answered on the third ring.

"Yes?" the voice answered.

"It's Max." Ratek waited to make sure that they could talk.

"One moment," the voice responded. Ratek overheard the next few comments. "I need to take this call now. Could you kindly excuse me for a few minutes and then we can reconvene? Thank you." Then a pause as people left the office on the other end. "I can talk now. It seems that you've had a rather disappointing day."

Ratek's heart sunk. The news must have reached him already.

"If you mean things didn't go quite as planned, then yes. But it's nothing that changes our overall strategy or stock ownership," Ratek explained nervously. At this stage, he didn't need to lose his financial support on this deal.

"I expect you to close the deal promptly so that I secure the terms of our agreement. The return ratio on my investment is non-negotiable. Is that clearly understood?" Sir Edward Hollingsworth said emphatically as he puffed on his cigar. His new, five-year-old face looked taut but intense. The face-lift had gone well since he had used the best plastic surgeons that his money could buy.

Sir Edward wished that the rest of his rotund, 61-year-old frame would do well with surgery. He had tried a number of diets and nutritional escapades under the close supervision of a multitude of doctors, but none had worked. Sir Edward could not control his number one passion, his love of food. He was the ultimate *bon vivant!* Stomach bypass surgery had been suggested, but that would mean that he would not be able to eat as much. Now why would he want to sacrifice his one great love, he had asked the doctors.

They had responded so that he could pursue his second great love. He had teased them when he answered money. Money was probably tied with his quest for food. But his second great love was in squiring beautiful models. It gave an appearance of his sexual vitality even though it was a somewhat false appearance. His unfortunate bout with prostate cancer had virtually destroyed his ability to consummate relationships. He had deferred doctor visits when he knew that there was a problem. How he wished he had taken better care of himself in that area!

"Sir Edward, has there ever been a problem with me in the past? I've always delivered the terms of our agreements," Ratek spoke firmly.

"May I remind you of the steel deal? It was very precarious at times," Sir Edward recalled stoically.

"But we got it done!" Ratek reassured him.

"Messy, very messy! I don't like to be involved when the matter gets out of control." Sir Edward was referring to the deaths that had taken place during that takeover battle. He knew that he was at arm's length, but didn't want any of the taint to spill over onto him. Sir Edward's style was to remain in the background as best he could. There were rumors in the major financial markets that he was the deep pockets for many company takeovers. He preferred to maintain a low profile and reap the return on his investment.

He had made his millions at a young age when he had married into a small British shipping business and became its managing director. He sold the business for a handsome profit to a conglomerate in which he invested his proceeds. Sir Edward saw himself rise swiftly through the organization due to his business prowess and eventually controlled 30 percent of the conglomerate's stock. He then took the conglomerate private and shrewdly made additional acquisitions which resulted in substantially increasing his personal wealth.

"As I stated, I'll deliver the return. There was no real damage done today," Ratek reassured Sir Edward.

"But, perception, my boy. You appeared weak. Never, never appear weak to anyone. As they say, don't let them see you sweat! I really must return to my meeting. I'll be watching your progress," Sir Edward warned.

"We'll get it done!" Ratek said confidently as they ended the phone conversation. Ratek placed the receiver in its cradle and plopped into his chair. He spun around to look out the window of his office and onto the late afternoon shadows that were creeping down Broad Street.

Sheraton Suites Hotel
Cuyahoga Falls, Ohio

~

The light green rental car was parked in the hotel lot. Grimes had found a park bench from where he could watch Fallsview Tire's headquarters.

He had spent a couple of hours two blocks away at Cuyahoga Falls Library researching local newspaper articles on the company and any stories about its executives. He found little value in his research as he didn't turn up any scandals or information of interest, other than the fact that Owens liked Corvettes and the previous CEO had been highly esteemed.

He learned one other point. The librarian mentioned that he was the second person doing detailed research on Fallsview Tire. When he asked who else had been in, she responded a reporter named Emerson Moore.

Nosy reporter Grimes thought to himself. He'd be watching out for him, too.

The sight of a glistening black Corvette convertible with the new Jupiter high-speed performance tires interrupted Grimes thoughts. The sleek car emerged from the underground parking lot at Fallsview Tire's headquarters. The black beauty moved quickly to the end of the drive where it paused momentarily before its 340 horsepower engine propelled it quickly into a left hand turn onto Broad Boulevard and across the bridge over the Cuyahoga River.

Its tires gripped the road as the car screamed through its first turn and the driver deftly steered the lunging speedster under the Route 8 overpass and turned another screaming left onto Route 8's entrance ramp and pointed the vehicle toward its Hudson home.

As the car turned onto Broad, Grimes caught a good look at the driver and recognized Owens at the wheel. A plan began to form in the back of Grimes' mind, one that would repay Owens for embarrassing Ratek at the morning's annual meeting.

Miller Ferry
Off South Bass Island

∽

The sky was bright blue and filled with the screams of sea gulls swooping and diving at the ferry's stern as passengers threw them scraps of food. The ferry's engines began to slow as it approached its dock on the south side of South Bass Island.

Its bow swung around 180 degrees as the pilot began to reverse the ferry into the dock so that the cars and trucks on board could be unloaded. The ferry's crewmembers carefully threw lines to the dockworkers to secure the huge ferry to its dock. Watching the entire operation was like watching poetry in motion. Emerson was impressed by the way the pilot and the crew maneuvered and secured the large craft with no apparent effort, even in the worst of conditions.

Emerson recalled one run to the island when they had tried to outrun a storm and the storm caught them a short distance off of South Bass. Emerson had been sitting in his car in the first row of the bow. When the storm hit, the water was filled with white caps and began to surge. The ferry dipped between the troughs and huge amounts of water had cascaded over the bow, drenching Emerson's car. He had been glad when the trip was over and the storm blew quickly toward Cleveland to the east.

Emerson began to climb down the stairs to the main deck. He had spent most of the trip catching up with Billy, the ferry's owner, in the pilothouse. Emerson was interested whether anyone had been apprehended in the ferry incident a few days earlier. During the night, someone had sneaked onto the docks and untied the lines of both ferries to cast them adrift. When the dockworkers and crew arrived at 6:30 the next morning, one ferry was found to the east and, fortunately, aground on the beach and not the rocks 100 yards farther east. A team was formed to retrieve the ferry from the beach and inspect it for damage.

Billy had called Denny Watson at Dairy Air to begin an aerial search for the other missing ferry as Billy and a team of crewmembers set off in Billy's boat to start their own search. Within a few minutes of searching Lake Erie's waters, Watson radioed down to Billy that the ferry was adrift about two miles southwest of the island. Billy and his crew raced to the site and, due to the relatively calm lake, were able to easily board the ferry and return it to its dock.

They had been very fortunate that no major damage had been inflicted on the million-dollar ferryboats. The Put-in-Bay Police were investigating, but the pirates had not been identified.

The huge ramp on the ferry's bow was lowered onto the dock and the vehicles on board drove off. Emerson joined the other passengers in disembarking and walking up the big hill to catch a ride into town on the bus.

Almost halfway to town, Emerson motioned for the bus to stop at the island airport. The old blue bus eased to a slow stop in front of the white building that served as the airport's overall lobby, ticketing and administrative office.

Emerson jumped off the bus and took a look to his left to see if Dairy Air's planes were in. They were, so it meant that Denny Watson was probably in also. The door slammed shut behind him as he entered.

"Denny needs to get that door fixed one of these days," said Jane, the blonde haired airport administrator, with her usual huge smile and cheery disposition. "You never see his planes go lacking for attention, though."

"And that would be a good thing," Emerson noted. "Is Denny around?"

"Upstairs sleeping. I'll get him for you." With that, she grabbed a broomstick and knocked hard on the ceiling above her three times. A grumbling voice could be faintly heard from above in response to her knocking.

"That's how you wake him?" Emerson inquired, stunned.

"Only thing that works with him. He just shuts off the alarm clock and rolls over, takes the phone off the hook and turns off the two-way radio. We just keep pounding on the ceiling until he comes down. Here, let me do it three more times."

She grabbed the broomstick again and pounded the ceiling

three more times as she smiled.

Another muffled shout could be heard. This time, they also heard two feet hitting the floor and footsteps crossing the small bedroom above. It was shortly after that they saw Denny emerge from the doorway to the second floor.

"What's all the commotion about?" he said as he ran his hand through his tousled gray hair. He then saw Emerson standing by the counter and asked, "So, are you the reason that she woke me from my beauty rest?"

"It'd take you more than an hour to catch up on your beauty rest, my dear," Jane interjected.

Emerson smiled. "I was just talking with Billy on the ferry coming over and he said that you helped him in spotting the ferry southwest of here. Any ideas of who did it?"

"Working on another story?" Denny quizzed Emerson cautiously before he answered. The last time that he helped Emerson on a story a little over a year ago, he had ended up with a hangar destroyed by fire, and a torched airplane, not to mention second degree burns on his hands.

"Not this time. I was just curious." Emerson liked the friendly, rascally Watson who owned Dairy Air. He spoke his mind and went out of his way to help the islanders.

"Nope. There were a bunch of college counselors on the island that weekend. Heard they got loaded and actually were kicked out of one of the downtown bars. Now that's an event in itself. From what I heard, they were still wound up. They could have been looking for some pranks to pull. No one can prove a thing though."

"That's a shame. Billy sure was lucky not to have either boat seriously damaged," Emerson commented sincerely.

"That he was. Haven't seen you in a few days. What have you been up to?"

Emerson quickly told Watson and Jane about the events of the last two days at Fallsview Tire's annual meeting.

"That kind of stuff is way beyond me. Just give me my planes and a bit of the wild blue yonder. That's all I'm interested in!" Watson said.

"Especially if he has a pretty, single passenger," Jane added as she smiled.

"And just what is wrong with that? I'm single," Watson retorted. Turning to Emerson, he continued," It's been awhile since you've flown with me. I'll be making a run to Detroit on Friday, want to come along?"

"I'd love to. Let's see how my schedule goes with this story and I'll get back to you."

Emerson said his goodbyes and walked out front to catch the next bus into town.

Aunt Anne's House
Put-in-Bay, Ohio

∽

After writing a story for the *Post* and e-mailing it, Emerson took a quick shower and changed into fresh clothes. He bounded down the stairs and into his aunt's kitchen. The kitchen was filled with the warm aroma of an apple pie baking in the oven.

"I swear that I don't see much of you anymore," Aunt Anne teased. "Still working on that takeover story?"

"Yep, it's coming together in pieces, like a puzzle. It'll be interesting to see what the ending picture looks like," Emerson mused as he watched his aunt digging through some clutter on the shelves of her refrigerator.

"I wonder if this ham salad is still good. I made it a few days ago."

"I'll test it for you," Emerson volunteered.

"I don't want to risk it," she said as she set it on the counter. "Why don't you throw it away?"

Emerson picked up the ham salad and headed through the house toward the big-screened porch with its panoramic view of Put-in-Bay's harbor. As he entered the porch, he was surprised to see the door opening to reveal Mr. Cassidy.

"Hey, boy, what kind of trouble are you up to?" the crotchety Mr. Cassidy asked as he ran his tongue across his lips.

"Not much. I'm meeting Barry and Sybil for dinner at the Top of the Bay." Emerson was referring to the newest restaurant on the island which was perched on the roof of the Gran Islander Inn on Catawba Ave. It offered unparalleled views of the sunset and the island.

"That's quite a restaurant they've there. Meeting with Barry and Sybil, huh? About that tire company story?" Mr. Cassidy asked curiously.

"Yes. They're putting me in touch with a guy up here who used to work there. He may be able to give me some additional insight," Emerson replied.

"Yep, we've got people here from all over. It's just amazing how this little island attracts people from everywhere. Did you ever hear the story about Barry and Sybil's dog?" Mr. Cassidy asked as he settled into a chair.

Emerson set the ham salad on the end table and sat in a nearby chair. "No, I haven't."

"Well, it's one of the funniest things that ever happened here on the island. Barry and Sybil moved here about 20 years ago from Cincinnati. They both were involved with a small time newspaper there and summered here on the island. Every year, they found it more difficult to return to Cincinnati. Well, when the opportunity came to buy the *Put-in-Bay Gazette*, they pounced on it. Barry, being the thrifty guy that he is, found the cheapest movers that he could to pack up a truck with their household goods.

"Barry actually drove the truck to Sandusky where he hired two boys who were dumber than dirt to unload the truck the next day. Well, sir, these two boys went fishing and didn't get around to bringing the truck over to the island for three days. It didn't matter since Barry and Sybil weren't arriving for a few more days. The boys finally brought the truck over and began unloading it. That's when it happened."

"What happened?" Emerson was on the edge of his seat.

"The boys saw that Barry's dog was dead. It had been loaded in the truck and the boys didn't know that it was in there. It was all curled up, but dead."

"What did they do? I bet Barry was upset," Emerson guessed.

"Them boys beat feet back to Sandusky, buried the dog, found themselves a look-alike dog and brought it back to Put-in-Bay. They tied it up in the front yard to that big old oak tree. Made arrangements with one of the neighbors to feed it and went back to Sandusky."

"I'll bet Barry was surprised when the dog didn't answer to its name," Emerson offered as he thought about the situation.

"Oh, Hell's bells, boy. Barry called them boys when he saw the dog. Before he could say anything, the one boy asked how his dog was doing? Barry replied that it was kind of funny to arrive and see that dog running around. When it had been loaded, it was stuffed. It seems that it was his grandfather's dog and grandfather had it stuffed because he couldn't stand the thought of it being buried. It was just sort of passed down from generation to generation," Mr. Cassidy chuckled as he saw the look of surprise on Emerson's face.

"What did Barry do with the dog?"

"Oh, he had those boys come back over and take it back to its real owner. That's one of the funniest things that's happened here. I wish I could have seen Barry's face when he saw that dog tied to the tree in front of the house," Mr. Cassidy smiled.

"Emerson?" came his aunt's voice from the kitchen.

"I'll be right back," Emerson said to Mr. Cassidy as he rose from his chair and entered the house to see what his aunt needed.

A few minutes later, Mr. Cassidy joined the two of them in the kitchen. He was carrying an empty container, the container which had held the supposed spoiled ham salad.

Aunt Anne stared at the empty container in Mr. Cassidy's hand.

"James Cassidy, did you eat that ham salad?" she asked with concern.

"Sure did. It was really good," he chortled.

"It was spoiled. You've just poisoned yourself!" she exaggerated.

"Oh, I'll be fine. I've got JC above watching over me. I could be a poison tester and handle poisonous snakes if I wanted to," he exaggerated back to her.

"Here, you just set yourself down right now and take some Pepto-Bismol or you'll be sicker than a dog in two shakes," she instructed.

The dog comment made Mr. Cassidy and Emerson exchange grins. Better him than me, Emerson thought to himself.

"Well, I need to meet Barry and Sybil. I'm going to take the golf cart unless you need it, Aunt Anne," Emerson stated as he looked at his watch.

"I won't be needing it. I think I'll be nursing a sick patient here. You shouldn't have eaten that ham salad!" she admonished Mr. Cassidy.

Mr. Cassidy winked at Emerson as he realized that he would be on the receiving end of some TLC. Emerson left the two of them to their patter and drove to the restaurant.

After finding a parking space at the side of the hotel, Emerson raced up the first flight of stairs to the Blue Iguana restaurant where he stuck his head in to say hello to Sully the bartender. The Blue Iguana was one of Emerson's favorite restaurants on the island—not only for the food, but also the ambiance.

Stepping into the Blue Iguana was akin to stepping into the Florida Keys and breathing in the Caribbean atmosphere. From the bamboo matting on the walls, to the colorful painted parrots hanging from the ceiling to the gaily painted tabletops in blues, greens, oranges and yellows, the restaurant conveyed a sense of the tropics.

The good-looking, genial Sully was effortlessly exchanging barbs with two scantily-attired females seated at the bar and paused for a second to nod a greeting to Emerson. Seeing that he was preoccupied, Emerson waved and continued down the hall to the stairway to the third floor's Top of the Bay.

Emerson climbed the stairs and stepped out into the open-air restaurant with its panoramic views of the island and Lake Erie's waters. It was one of the highest points on the island and usually packed with early diners and then with the bar crowd and a DJ for dancing. The Top of the Bay offered afternoon drinking, dancing and a rooftop pool to cool off from the heat.

At one end was a covered canopy for those seeking refuge from the sun, while umbrella tables offered some protection to the other diners. A small raised swimming pool sat in the middle of the restaurant with the bar located overlooking Catawba Avenue. The Caribbean theme from the Blue Iguana carried over to the Top of the Bay.

Emerson heard his name shouted and saw Barry and Sybil seated at a table near the northeast corner of the restaurant. He promptly made his way through the crowd to join them.

"Another beautiful evening," Emerson greeted his two friends.

"Every evening on Put-in-Bay is a beautiful evening," Sybil said thoughtfully. She and Barry loved living on the island year-round.

"Heard an interesting story about you two moving up here," Emerson teased. "Something to do with a dog that was reborn!"

Barry chuckled, "You can just imagine our surprise when we drove up to the front of our new home and saw that dog tied to that old oak tree. Sybil and I just looked at each other when we saw him. We just cracked up!"

"Getting rid of that stuffed dog was one of the best things that happened to us here," Sybil mused.

"And you deserve the best. That's why you have me!" Barry kidded Sybil lovingly.

"This is getting rather heavy. Maybe I should go," Emerson said as he began to stand.

"Sit down, Emerson. Barry is just being his ornery self," Sybil grinned.

The waitress arrived and took their orders. She wore her hair in a big hairstyle that soared for the heavens.

Emerson couldn't resist as he took in the amount of hair and hair spray that the waitress had to use to make that head of hair so flamboyant. "I bet your hair doesn't move one centimeter in a nor'easter."

She had been used to comments about her hair and had a supply of comebacks. "Big hair makes my butt look smaller," she said as she pirouetted for the table. "I can't do anything about my short legs, but I can add height on top."

"Yeah, and I'm losing height on top," Barry added as he thought about his thinning hair.

Still chuckling, they placed their orders with the good-natured waitress.

"Anything new on your takeover battle story?" Barry asked with interest.

Emerson relayed the happenings at the company's annual meeting and that he had e-mailed a story to the *Post* for publication in the morning's paper.

"I never did get back to you with that contact I had. I brought it with me," Barry said as he handed Emerson a name and phone number on a piece of paper. "This is the guy who used to work at Fallsview and may be able to give you insight into their operations and problems. He's a pretty good guy."

Emerson took the note. "I'll give him a call tomorrow and see if he has anything that I can use."

"He'd probably love to hear about the shenanigans at the annual meeting. That deal with Ratek standing at the lowered microphone is priceless as is the limit on the number of questions a shareholder can ask," Barry noted. "Do you have any concerns that you may have pushed Ratek too far with some of your questions?"

"Nope. What are they going to do? Kill me?" Emerson questioned somewhat fearlessly.

"From what we know about you..." Barry started.

"And read about you," Sybil added.

"You have a tendency to cross boundaries, at times, during your interviews. One of these days, it could catch up with you," Barry cautioned.

"Okay, guys! It's not like I'm in one of the most dangerous professions in the world today," Emerson countered.

"Just be careful," Barry said as their dinners were served.

They small-talked about island events for another 45 minutes and then went to their respective homes.

Don Sitts Auto Sales
Cuyahoga Falls, Ohio
The Next Day

~

Owens eased the black Corvette off of Front Street and down the sloping drive to the service department entrance where he parked his car. He hadn't noticed that a car had been following him since he left his home that morning. The car drove past the dealership one block and parked in front of Falls Taxi's office.

Owens entered the service department, shouting greetings to Ted and Becky as he made his way to Don Sitts' office. Don had left a voice mail for him to stop by and see the 1966 Chevelle that he was restoring.

The affable Don looked up as Owens entered his office.

"Greg, you got my message!" Don said as he stood and greeted Owens.

"Yep, I need a little stress break after what we've been going through the last few weeks," Owens responded as they walked through the service department and entered a building at the rear of the property.

"Things have been tough, haven't they?" Don asked with concern.

"Yes, they have. I'm just hoping that we can pull this out of the fire," Owens said openly. He felt comfortable with Don, someone that Owens admired. He had a strong work ethic and had been able to move up from the ranks from a mechanic to the successful owner of this family-run business. At times, Owens was envious of Don's success.

"There she is," Don said as he pointed to the light blue Super Sport which was up on blocks.

"Nice car!" Owens said as he admired the great condition of the body and interior.

"We're working on the engine, adding a lot of chrome. Changing the wheels and putting on new tires. We should be done in about 10 days," Don explained.

"Just beautiful," Owens added as his eye took in the car's detail. "What kind of tires are you putting on this one?"

Don expected the question and answered quickly, "Your new Jupiter tire. How could I put on anything else?"

After five minutes talking about the car, Owens glanced at his watch. "I better be going back to the sweatshop. Let me know when it's ready, I'd like to go for a ride in it!"

"You've got it. I'll call you," Don responded.

Owens returned to his car and eased onto Front Street, cut over to Second Street and sped to the headquarters building. He didn't see the car that pulled out of a parking space in front of the Falls Taxi office to follow him.

Birkman Investments
New York City

~

Ratek was pacing furiously in his office as he replayed the phone conversation with Sir Edward Hollingsworth that he had just completed. Hollingsworth was enraged with the play in the press that Ratek had received that morning as a result of his poor showing at the annual meeting.

In a dramatic change from his past practice, Hollingsworth had demanded that Ratek set up a meeting between Owens and Hollingsworth at Hollingsworth's brownstone. And Hollingsworth did not want Ratek to attend, which caused Ratek angst.

Ratek looked up Owens' number and dialed. He had formulated a plan on his approach to Owens. Owens' assistant, Lita, answered the phone and connected Ratek through to Owens.

"Now, if you're calling to complain again about yesterday..." Owens started.

"Actually, I'm not. Rather, I'm calling you to let you know how impressed I was with the way your people foiled my plans," Ratek stated.

Owens was suspicious. What could make this tiger change his stripes like this? He would listen.

"It appears that I've underestimated you," Ratek continued as he played to Owens' ego. It was a strategy designed to lower Owens' guard and pull him into the lion's den.

Owens bit on that comment. "You're not the first, nor will you be the last. That's why I've been so successful."

"I can see that. The reason for my call is to invite you to a private, confidential meeting with my financier. He usually maintains a low profile in these types of situations, but he is so impressed by your abilities and the reports in today's newspapers that he'd like to meet you personally."

Owens beamed, "Well, of course. I can understand why he'd want to meet me. When would he like to meet?"

"Tomorrow evening at 7 o'clock at his place on the Upper East Side. It's a quaint little place. Are you available?"

"Yes, I am," Owens responded with utmost confidence.

Ratek provided him with the address and hung up as Owens made arrangements for his flight into the city. Owens advised Weimar and Oakes of his plans to go into the lion's den.

"Why would you want to visit this financier?" Weimar asked Owens incredulously.

"I may be able to convince him to pull his financial support for Ratek," Owens beamed with a sense of false confidence.

"What do you think, Jay?" Weimar asked his cohort.

"I think it'll be tough to convince someone, who apparently is the quiet money man and has probably made a lot of money backing Ratek, to back out of the deal. He or they know Ratek's reputation for increasing the stock price of companies that they target. I just don't know if it will be effective," Oakes said with concern.

"I'm going in. Whoever this mystery financier is, I'm sure that he's never met anyone as astute as me! This is going to be a full-dress power meeting," Owens said with a display of bravado. Owens rose from his chair and returned to his office.

"This will be interesting to watch," Weimar said uneasily.

Sir Edward Hollingsworth's Residence
Upper East Side
New York City

~

Ratek's hired limo pulled up in front of the Hollingsworth residence which was on Park Avenue, just north of 70th. A doorman stepped out from underneath the foyer to open the limo's door for Owens.

Impressive, Owens thought to himself as he exited the vehicle.

Owens entered the building and took the elevator to the 14th floor where a uniformed butler greeted him as he exited. Owens was shown into the residence which spanned three levels and 8,500 square-feet of living space. The elegant entry gallery had a 13-foot ceiling, a limestone floor and a huge Louis XV carved marble fireplace. To the right, was a curved staircase in marble and wrought iron.

Owens was shown through two mahogany doors into a reception area outside of the library. The butler knocked at the library's door and then ushered Owens into the stunning, chestnut paneled library which was double height and had parquet floors with antique rugs and fine tapestries on the walls.

An impeccably attired Sir Edward was standing next to a ceiling-to-floor length arched window with flowered swags overlooking Park Avenue. Sir Edward's hand rested on the corner of a mahogany serving cart filled with an array of beverages.

"Mr. Owens, it is indeed a pleasure to meet you. Could I offer you a drink?" the cherub-faced Sir Edward asked.

"Scotch and water would be fine. You can call me Greg," Owens offered.

Pouring the scotch carefully, Sir Edward said pretentiously, "And please feel free to call me Sir Edward."

I'd rather call you your royal high ass, Owens thought to himself as Sir Edward handed the glass to him. "Why, thank you."

"Come, why don't we sit over here?" Sir Edward motioned to a chair directly opposite the massive wood-burning fireplace. Sir Edward sat in a chair with his back to the fireplace.

Out of the corner of his eye, Owens realized that a larger than life size painting of a voluptuous nude was above the fireplace's mantel. He averted his eyes so as not to stare at it as he felt Sir Edward's eyes on him with a hint of glee. Owens realized that the painting was an appropriate fit with the decadent lifestyle that Sir Edward pursued. Owens sipped his drink nervously.

Sir Edward enjoyed the uneasiness that Owens seemed to be experiencing from where he was sitting. Sir Edward looked over the rim of his drink glass at Owens. There was an uncomfortable silence in the room. Sir Edward spoke first.

"I have a question to ask you, and it may be the wrong question."

"Go ahead and ask," Owens was anxious to move forward with the discussion and learn why Sir Edward had wanted to meet.

"You saw this takeover attempt coming, of course?" Sir Edward asked cunningly.

"No, not really."

"You appear to be confused. How could you not anticipate a run at your company when your stock value is so depressed?" Sir Edward asked incredulously.

"We were working diligently to restore shareholder value," Owens replied.

"To me, it appeared only in a very trivial way. Don't you recognize who is your real adversary in your feeble attempts to turn around the company?"

"Sure, it's Ratek and his gang at Birkman Investments," Owens responded defiantly.

"No, it's not. You're the real adversary to your company. Your lack of leadership in turning around the company demands that you turn the company over to people who know what they are doing, people who are driven to obtain results!" Sir Edward said firmly.

Owens' head snapped up at the comment and he felt himself staring unconsciously at the painting over the fireplace. He dropped his eyes. Owens was stunned by the comment and its audacity.

Sir Edward continued. "The fact of the matter is that you should step down from your position as Chairman of the Board and CEO, and turn your company over to one of your Board members so that the appropriate actions can be taken."

Owens paused and thought for a moment before answering. He needed to get his blood pressure under control and not have a knee-jerk reaction to this pompous bastard.

"Totally out of the question," Owens retorted.

"I can lay it out for you in poetic language. You have an opportunity to overcome a growing prejudice against you in the financial world. The *crème de la crème* feel that you're not doing the job. Why do you want to continue to put up with the bruises when a golden parachute awaits you?"

Owens had been a fighter all of his life. From high school sports to climbing the corporate ladder, Owens was a fighter. Maybe all of his approaches weren't as ethical as they should have been, but Owens knew that he was not going to quit. "I've no plans on leaving the company. If you're going to try to beat me, bring it on!"

"There is only one reality, my dear Greg. You will end up losing in the end. Why don't you think it over for 24 hours and then call me?" Sir Edward asked as he handed a white business card with his phone number to Owens.

Owens took the card and looked at it, then he crumbled it and threw it on the rug under his chair. "Not interested. Unless there is something more important to talk about, I think our meeting is concluded."

Owens stood from his chair, making sure to keep his eyes averted from the painting.

Sir Edward stood also. "Your brilliance is misdirected. I'll show you to the door."

Sir Edward escorted Owens through the reception area and the massive foyer to the residence's front entrance.

Owens had to wait a few minutes for the limo to return and take him back to the waiting corporate jet at Teterboro for the flight home. He replayed the evening's conversation over and over.

Tomorrow he planned to meet with Weimar, Dansen and Oakes to rework their strategy.

Ratek set his glass of scotch on the desk and reached for his ringing phone.

"Hello?" Ratek said.

"He refused to step down," Sir Edward said emotionlessly.

"I understand," Ratek said.

"Good."

Sir Edward's message was clear and to the point. Ratek dialed Grimes' cell phone number. Grimes was parked near Fallsview Tire's hangar at Akron-Canton Airport and answered on the second ring.

"Hello, Max. How did the meeting go?" he asked curiously.

"Not well. Not well at all. It's a no-go from his position," Ratek replied exasperated.

"I gotcha!" Grimes said to convey his understanding of what the next steps would be.

"Good night and good luck!" Ratek meant it as he hung up the phone. This whole takeover attempt was an enigma.

Grimes reached for the small satchel on the passenger's seat.

Fallsview Tire & Rubber Company Headquarters
The Next Day

~

"He actually asked me to step down, the son-of-a-bitch!" Owens said as he was wrapping up his meeting with Weimar, Dansen and Oakes in his office the next morning.

"And your answer, of course, was a definite no?" Weimar asked.

"You can count on it. I think that we have these guys on the run. They know we're fighters. That's why he had me fly in for the meeting with him," Owens stated. "One thing funny about this guy."

"Yes?" Carli asked.

"He tried to play a mind game with me. He had me sit where I would have to view this huge painting of a naked woman above his fireplace. Sorry, Carli," Owens said in deference to her. "Well, I didn't bite. I didn't look at that painting although it was obvious that he wanted to catch me looking at it. I first saw it when he seated me and quickly turned my head away."

"Sounds like something more like Ratek would do. I'll have to check out this Hollingsworth with Jimmy Malloy," Oakes stated.

"Think they'll back off now?" Owens asked, knowing what the answer would be.

"No. If anything, I'd bet that they will accelerate their efforts to take control," Weimar responded.

"Okay then. Jay, I want you to call Malloy and have him fly in here for a strategy meeting with us tomorrow morning."

"I'll call him," Jay responded.

The meeting continued for another 30 minutes before it adjourned.

At the end of the day, Owens eased the black Corvette convertible from the underground parking garage at Fallsview Tire's headquarters and up the ramp to Broad Boulevard where he paused to wait for an opening in the traffic. Seeing his chance, he accelerated quickly, perhaps a little harder than normal, likely due to the pressure he was under.

The car flew out of the ramp and flashed through a left turn to head east on Broad Boulevard toward the Route 8 expressway. As the car began to cross the Broad Boulevard bridge over the Cuyahoga River, two explosions came from the driver's side of the car, one was behind the front tire and the second was in front of the rear tire.

Nearby cars were damaged by the shrapnel. In the confusion of the explosion and smoke, other cars swerved to avoid crashing into one another, but to no avail.

A look of bewilderment and then fear flashed across Owens' face as the force of the blast catapulted the Corvette's left side high in the air and rolled the Corvette over the bridge's rail. Owens' briefcase was thrown from the car, but Owens' seatbelt trapped him securely. The car's forward momentum carried the burning, spiraling car head-on into the riverbank on the opposite side of the river where it crushed itself and killed the fast-driving Owens.

The twisted remains then dropped upside down to the rocky river bottom as the river's rushing water treated it as another rapid. Owens' battered body was still strapped into his seat.

Fallsview Tire would be looking for a new CEO.

A crowd began to gather to view the wreckage as sirens could be heard from the rescue vehicles conveniently located a block away at Cuyahoga Falls Fire Station Number 1. But there would be no need for urgency for Owens' sake.

Several cars pulled over on the expressway bridge and the southbound entrance ramp from Broad Boulevard to the expressway. People left their parked cars and looked down from the high vantage point upon the still-smoking Corvette.

A lone figure clutching something in each of his hands walked away from the edge of the southbound ramp which overlooked the Broad Boulevard bridge and the river. The figure had seen everything from the moment that Owens had pulled out of the garage. In fact, he had been the trigger for the events.

The figure walked over to his parked car and threw the two remote detonators in a satchel on the back seat. He then drove the car south on Route 8 to Akron-Canton airport where a corporate jet was waiting to return him to New York.

Grimes smiled evilly and with pleasure at his accomplishment. After talking with Ratek the previous night, he had planted the Semtex underneath the Corvette while it had been parked outside the Fallsview Tire hangar at Akron-Canton Airport, awaiting Owens' return from his meeting with Sir Edward.

Grimes' car picked up speed and easily moved into the southbound traffic heading through Akron and on to the airport.

Owens' Office
Fallsview Tire & Rubber Company

～

Weimar, Oakes and Dansen were seated around the conference table in shock after returning from viewing the wreckage from the bridge deck. Fallsview Tire & Rubber Company's security personnel were the first to learn about the crash due to a number of phone calls placed to the company by bystanders who witnessed the Corvette as it pulled onto Broad Boulevard. By racing to the crash site and working with rescue personnel, two members of the security team confirmed that it was Owens' car.

Weimar looked at the blank stares on the faces of Oakes and Dansen. "This is certainly an unexpected event. We'll need to move quickly as the wire services will be picking this up. Jay, why don't you start drafting a press release and I'll call Greg's wife. Although with all the press already here, I'd expect she's already aware. I'll have Lita set up a conference call with the Board members so that we can talk about an interim chairman and CEO."

"Do we have a formal succession plan for Owens' position?" Carli asked.

"Funny thing about that is that we don't for Owens. We have a plan for virtually every key position in the company, but Owens was reluctant to name a potential successor or start grooming one. I think that he was concerned that the Board could replace him quickly if he faltered and that was the reason for his reluctance," Weimar explained.

"Joe, who would have ever thought that something like this would happen?" Oakes asked.

"Just remember what I said before about some of the

takeover attempts that Ratek's been involved with in the past. This isn't the first mysterious death. There were several suspicious deaths that were never solved. I'm expecting a call from the police chief momentarily. Mayor Trabor has already called and offered his condolences, as well as a commitment to have a full investigation. He's pretty upset about this happening here. Cuyahoga Falls has a strong reputation as a safe and quiet community," Weimar added.

"Do we still want Malloy in here tomorrow for a meeting?" Oakes asked.

"Yes, and I'll call Dayton Ford. We'll probably want to have a conference call with him and discuss strategies for dealing with Ratek," Weimar stated.

"Owens' death weakens our position, doesn't it?" Carli asked.

"Ratek, if he was behind this accident, just cut off our head. We've got to figure out how to grow a new head—and the right head. Lita?" Weimar called as the other two began to leave the room, "I'm going to need you to help me set up some calls."

Lita, carrying a pen and a pad, entered the office to help Weimar with the necessary calls. Her eyes were red from crying.

Birkman Investments' Corporate Jet
Akron-Canton Airport

~

The jet gathered speed as it roared down the runway to lift clear on its way back to New York. Grimes had waited till the plane cleared the ground before he made the call to Ratek.

"Any breaking news?" Grimes asked his boss as he looked at his watch. It had been 40 minutes since he had left the site of the explosion.

"Yeah, it's all over the TV and news wires. It appears that Fallsview Tire's CEO was killed today when his car exploded and catapulted over a bridge into the river. Our phones have been ringing off the hook. Reporters are asking what impact this will have on our plans to go ahead with wrestling control of the company," Ratek responded.

"What did you say?" Grimes asked eagerly.

"First, I offered my condolences to the family and the employees of Fallsview Tire. Then, I explained that with his death, there was even more reason for us to move forward with our plans," Ratek replied smugly.

"Did they announce an interim CEO?"

"They're planning a press conference tomorrow morning at 10:00. It will be interesting to see if they pick the right person. I expect trading in their shares will be halted until after the conference."

"I'll see you in the morning then," Grimes said.

"Okay, Simon. And, Simon...?"

"Yes?"

"Nice job."

"Thanks. I'll tell you more when I see you."

Aunt Anne's House
Put-in-Bay

~

"Emerson, come down here quick," his aunt yelled up to Emerson who was in his bedroom on the second floor.

"Yes? Is everything okay?" Emerson asked as he bounded down the stairs and into the living room where his aunt was glued to the 6 o'clock TV news.

"Aren't you doing a story on Fallsview Tire?" she asked hurriedly.

"Yes, why?" Emerson was curious about her anxiousness. He glanced at the TV and saw film of a wrecked black Corvette being lifted from a river.

"Their head guy was just killed in a car wreck."

Emerson sat down. "Turn it up a bit."

Aunt Anne increased the TV's volume and sat down.

The on-site news reporter continued. *"...was pronounced dead at the scene at 5:35 P.M. Witnesses to the accident stated that two explosions were heard before the driver lost control of the black Corvette and the burning car plummeted 60 feet to the Cuyahoga River bed. Several cars in the area were damaged and two occupants of other cars were hospitalized. Joining us now is Fallsview Tire's spokesman, Jay Oakes. Mr. Oakes, how is the company handling this loss?"*

The camera panned back to show Oakes seated in his scooter. Jay replied, *"This evening, Fallsview Tire is a company in mourning.*

We lost our company's leader, but we also lost a good friend, husband and father. Our prayers are with his wife and family."

"Can you tell us what impact this will have on the current takeover battle that you are immersed in?"

"We expect that we will continue to do our best for our shareholders, employees and customers. This company has a long history of being a good corporate citizen and we'd expect that to continue. I really must excuse myself as we're preparing for tomorrow's news conference when, I'm sure, we will have more details to share with you and your viewers."

Emerson and his aunt watched the rest of the news story about the accident and then she turned the TV off.

"What do you think?" his aunt asked.

"It smells. I don't like it. There have been other deaths of a suspicious nature during takeovers involving Ratek," Emerson commented.

"Now, don't you get yourself mixed up in something that could harm you," his aunt admonished.

Emerson grinned. "Aunt Anne, I'm always careful. I'm going upstairs to get on my laptop and check out some of the news wires. Looks like I'll be attending a news conference tomorrow morning." Looking at his watch, Emerson continued, "I'm supposed to meet some friends at the Boathouse tonight. Alex Bevan is playing and I don't want to miss it. I'll probably make it an early night so that I can catch the first ferry out tomorrow."

"You just be careful," his aunt warned warmly.

"I will!" Emerson emphasized.

Owens' Office
Fallsview Tire & Rubber Company

～

The clock on the wall read 7:15 P.M. Weimar, Dansen, Oakes and Lita had been working diligently to cover as many bases as possible and prepare for the morning press conference. Weimar had urgently summoned Oakes and Dansen to his office.

"You better take a seat, Carli." Looking at Oakes, Weimar said, "It's a good thing that you're already sitting down."

"What's up, Joe?" Carli asked nervously. She didn't like the serious look on Weimar's face.

"You're not going to believe what the Board has decided to do." Without giving them a chance to comment, Weimar continued, "They're naming Webster as interim chairman and CEO!"

Almost in unison, Oakes and Carli uttered in disbelief, "No way!"

"Yes, it's unbelievable! Most of them are too busy or don't want to get directly involved here. Webster actually wanted it. In fact, he demanded it as the Board member with the most shares. So they gave it to him. It made it easy for the Board since they won't need to conduct a search for a new CEO," Weimar lamented.

"Will there be a search for a permanent CEO?" Carli asked.

"Don't know yet. Webster wants to meet with us at 7 o'clock tomorrow morning to go over the press conference and what he expects from us. Jay, you need to know that he's bringing along his company public relations guy to write a speech for him to use tomorrow. We should each review it to make sure that we don't have any serious issues. But then again, he can override us since he's the boss now," Weimar noted.

"I'll do whatever is necessary," Oakes commented.

"I think we all will," Weimar added. "You guys better wrap up and head home. Tomorrow's going to be a long day."

"Any news how Owens' wife is taking it?" Carli asked concernedly.

"Pretty hard. I talked to her on the phone and I'm stopping by the house on the way home tonight to see her." Weimar responded.

"Heard anything from the police?" Oakes wondered.

"Yes. They stopped in and talked with me for about 15 minutes. They're still in the preliminary stages of the investigation. I had our security folks meet with them also and I told them to cooperate as much as possible," Weimar said.

Carli and Oakes left Weimar's office and headed for their respective offices.

Oakes was battling the fatigue from his MS as he rode to his office. The stress over the last few hours was draining his energy level. He knew that he needed to rest well this evening so that he'd be ready for another emotionally charged day.

Boathouse Bar and Grill
Put-in-Bay

~

The Boathouse was located on Hartford Avenue, across from DeRivera Park and a half block from the public docks and the Jet

Express' dock. The light blue/gray exterior was framed with white trim, and a white picket fence separated the pedestrians from the sometimes bawdy and inebriated customers seated on its outdoor patio. The patio area was one of Emerson's favorite areas, especially when Alex Bevan was playing.

Alex was a Cleveland area and Lake Erie troubadour, songwriter and record producer who also was a Put-in-Bay regular. The friendship between the two of them dated back a few months to when Emerson interviewed Alex for a story for the *Gazette* and purchased his *South Shore Serenade* CD. Emerson loved his songs and his uncanny ability to sing the words to a song so rapidly. Emerson felt that Alex had a bit of rap in his background.

As he approached the bar, Emerson heard Alex's voice filling the air with his musical notes. Emerson saw the singer perched on a stool in the patio area and grinned at him as he was able to snag a table near Alex from a couple who were leaving.

Alex was a bit ornery, similar to Emerson's good friend, Sammy Duncan. In fact, Emerson thought that his other three singer-friends, Pat Dailey, Westside Steve and Bob Gatewood, were in the same category. Ornery but fun, and in some ways, all four of them reminded Emerson of pirates. Their swashbuckling appearance contributed to that perception.

A cute waitress appeared at Emerson's side. Seeing that Alex was completing his set, Emerson ordered a drink for Alex and a glass of wine for himself. Emerson was still careful about his drinking as a result of his previous drinking problem a year and a half ago. The waitress returned quickly and set the drinks on the table.

Alex set down his guitar and joined Emerson who slid Alex's drink across the table to him. He took a long drink. "Thanks, Emerson."

"Glad to support one of my favorite people," Emerson stated in a friendly manner. Observing the crowd, Emerson commented, "Full house tonight."

"Yep, another good night. Lots of good-looking chippies here tonight," Alex observed with a smile as his eyes took in some of the female scenery packed into the Boathouse.

Emerson grinned. He knew that he had to introduce Sam to Alex. They were alike in many ways.

An attractive redhead walked past the two and Alex's eyes took in every move of her svelte body. "Whoa. That one just sucked the breath right out of me," he groaned.

"Down, boy," Emerson teased.

"How's the newspaper business?" Alex asked inquisitively.

"I'm working on an interesting story about a takeover attempt." Emerson gave Alex a summary of what had transpired since he first stumbled onto the story.

"And it started with you overhearing this guy on the airplane! Wow!" Alex said in amazement.

"You just don't know what you can pick up when you listen," Emerson commented.

"Like I've always said, loose lips sink ships!" Alex noted with a grin. "Time for my next set to start."

"I won't be staying long. Got to head in to Cuyahoga Falls for that press conference. Love your singing!"

"Thanks, Emerson, and thanks again for the drink."

Alex pushed away from the table and returned to his stool where he began playing and singing again. Emerson stayed for three more songs and reluctantly left for home.

Emerson walked down Hartford and turned east on Bayview as he headed towards his aunt's house on East Point. It was a peaceful evening with a fresh breeze coming across the bay from the west.

Emerson's eyes took in the towering Perry's Monument, which was brightly illuminated for all to admire.

Fallsview Tire & Rubber Company Press Conference
Cuyahoga Falls

~

The small auditorium off the Fallsview Tire's lobby was filled with reporters and TV crews awaiting the start of the press conference. Gary Welson was mingling with the reporters when he saw Emerson seated in an aisle chair about halfway back from the front of the room.

"Have any tough questions planned for today?" Welson kidded Emerson.

"Not yet. It depends on what is said during the conference. Should I direct any tough ones to you?" Emerson teased.

"Yeah, right!" Welson grinned.

There was movement at the front of the room as Jay Oakes scootered to the front of the stage and next to the podium.

"Good morning, ladies and gentlemen," he started as he looked over the conference attendees. "We'll be starting the conference momentarily. To make it easier on each of you, we will provide you with a copy of the speech and background information as you leave the auditorium this morning. It'll also be loaded on our website."

Emerson's eyes focused closely on Oakes. Something was amiss. Oakes didn't seem to be himself this morning and Emerson didn't think it was related to his MS.

Oakes scootered back from the front of the stage to a position where he could observe the attendees. A minute later, the door opened and a man wearing glasses with dark frames and with a mustache strode to the podium at the front of the room. Emerson recognized him as the Board member who had stood at the annual meeting in defense of Ratek. Emerson's heart sunk at the thought of the potential of this jerk taking a leadership role in the company.

"Good morning. I'm Phil Webster. Until yesterday evening, I was just a Board member of Fallsview Tire, albeit the Board member with the largest number of shares. Due to the tragic event yesterday, the Board has appointed me as Fallsview Tire's interim chairman and CEO. I firmly believe that this was done in recognition of my business prowess and past successes!"

Emerson groaned inwardly. This guy's ego is going to be a problem he thought to himself. It's significantly bigger than Owens' ego ever was.

"Greg, wherever you are now," Webster paused momentarily to look upward with a look that came across as insincere, "I want you to know that you'll be missed."

How theatrical could you get, Emerson thought. This guy was a piece of work.

"I want to assure everyone that I will not let yesterday's tragedy cast a shadow upon the hard work that the Fallsview Tire & Rubber

Company team has done in restoring shareholder value. I expect to do my best as I restore the stock price and take firm control of this company."

Emerson groaned again at the constant use of the word "I." This foretold of a difficult time for the folks at Fallsview Tire who were used to being part of a team.

"That concludes my prepared comments this morning. I'll be announcing my plans to turn around the company value as soon as I can formulate them. As you can well imagine, with such short and unexpected notice, I did not have an opportunity to formulate them this morning. I'll take a few questions now."

Emerson noticed a short, ruddy-complected man with a portfolio step next to Webster. He must be Webster's personal press secretary, Emerson mused as he raised his hand.

"Yes?" Webster said as he looked at Emerson.

"In your opening remarks, you didn't say anything about starting a formal search for a permanent Chairman and CEO. Do you plan to transition from interim to permanent?"

Webster glared coldly at Emerson and then answered, "It would be premature for me to respond to your question." Webster turned his head to acknowledge a reporter on the other side of the room.

Before the reporter could pose his question, Emerson continued. "You're dodging my question. Let me restate my question. Do you want to be the next permanent Chairman of the Board for Fallsview Tire? Yes or no?"

Webster's head snapped around to Emerson. His stare bore a hole through Emerson.

"It would be inappropriate for me to comment."

"By not denying your interest, I'll interpret your answer as a yes." Emerson countered.

"I can't help you with your conjectures," Webster stormed.

The man at Webster's side ended the strained exchange. "I believe we have a question from this lady on the other side of the room."

All heads turned to the other side of the room with the exception of two—Emerson's and Webster's assistant. The assistant gave Emerson a smug smile at accomplishing the derailment of Emerson's probing questions.

Emerson looked at Oakes seated at the rear of the stage. He appeared to be pale and uncomfortable. Emerson reflected that the Fallsview Tire team was going to be in an awkward position when it came to working with this egomaniac.

Weimar had been watching the press conference from the rear of the auditorium. The day had gone from bad to worse—and it was only 10:15 in the morning. The 7 o'clock meeting called by Webster with Weimar, Dansen and Oakes had been a virtual disaster.

It was apparent that Webster had little respect for them. He planned to make his own decisions about the company's direction and he indicated that he would need very little input from them. He had already brought with him his own personal public relations parrot, Theodore Ploose, who was going to review every communication issued on behalf of the company before it went out, effectively cutting the legs right out from under Oakes. Not only was Webster going to be difficult to deal with, but so was Polly the Parrot, as Weimar nicknamed him.

Weimar focused on another reporter asking a question.

"Mr. Webster, do you feel that you'll be able to win this takeover battle that you have now inherited?"

Webster thought a moment before responding.

"It depends on what the definition of win is. The ultimate win is that shareholders win."

The reporter pressed, "Sir, what about your employees and customers?"

Polly the Parrot stepped forward at this moment and looked at his watch. "I am so sorry, but Mr. Webster has another meeting scheduled and must run so that he's not late. We must conclude our conference now. Thank you all for coming this morning," he said insipidly. He and Webster strode out of the auditorium followed by a defeated-looking Oakes.

There was a general moan from the group as they felt that they didn't get the information that they needed from the morning meeting. They began to file out of the auditorium.

As Welson walked past Weimar, he rolled his eyes in disbelief. "Good luck. Let me know what I can do to support you and Jay!" Welson said sincerely.

"Thanks, Gary. This is going to be a tough one!" Weimar responded as he began to return to his office.

Birkman Investments
New York City

~

The TV in Ratek's office clicked off as Ratek turned with a huge smile to face Grimes. "They picked the right one!" he smirked.

"That guy is a real idiot," Grimes said with glee.

"This plays right into our plan," Ratek said as he speed-dialed Hollingsworth's number to pass along the good news. This would take some of the pressure off of Ratek.

Owens' Office
Fallsview Tire & Rubber Company

~

Webster and Polly the Parrot walked briskly into Owens' office. Webster's eyes swept around the office at Owens' personal possessions—the mallard duck decoys, trout nets and fishing rods, the mounted pheasants and ducks, as well as the buffalo's head. He walked over to the buffalo head for a closer look and noticed the buffalo-skinning knife. He picked it up and looked at it closely, then threw it on the floor.

He yelled to Lita, "Get in here and get this junk cleared out of here. I'll be back in an hour and I expect this all to be gone. Do I make myself clear?"

Lita was aghast at the manner in which he was acting. She nodded her head to indicate her understanding and began to take down Owens' personal items.

"Get help if you need it!" Webster stormed as he walked, closely followed by his parrot, down the hall to Weimar's office.

Lita picked up the phone and arranged for several employees to assist her with boxes for packing the personal items. Working with this new boss was going to be very challenging, she thought, especially with his condescending demeanor.

Weimar looked up as the two stepped into his office. "I was just going to call you to tell you that Malloy is in the lobby for our meeting."

"Cancel it! Tell him to fly back to New York. I'll let him know if I need any advice from him. Go ahead now. Call the lobby. You're wasting my time!"

"But you said you wanted to meet with him when we talked yesterday," Weimar said.

"I did not. You apparently misunderstood me," Webster lied.

Weimar picked up the phone and called the lobby receptionist. "Rose, could you tell Jimmy Malloy that we regrettably have run into a complication and will not be able to meet with him at all today. Please apologize on my behalf for the unnecessary trip he made here to see us. Thanks, Rose."

Weimar hung up the phone and looked at Webster. Weimar was very adept at concealing his anger as he thought how he'd like to castrate Webster. It seemed like the tone that Webster set during that 7 o'clock meeting was continuing.

"Get Oakes down here!" Webster demanded.

Weimar called Oakes and within minutes Oakes scootered into the Weimar's office. The look on his face showed that he wasn't happy to see Webster and the parrot sitting there.

"I want your feedback on how well I did this morning at my press conference," Webster ordered.

"I thought you were absolutely splendid...," the parrot started.

"Not from you, imbecile!" Webster interrupted. "Oakes, you go first!"

Oakes took a deep breath before starting. He sensed that Webster had a strong adversarial style and dealing with him would be like walking through a minefield.

"Your opening comments were direct and to the point. However, I think the Q&A with the reporters was strained." Oakes switched from a direct style to an indirect by using the pronoun "we." "We seemed to take an antagonistic approach in responding to the reporters' questions."

Seeing that Webster was on the verge of erupting in anger, Weimar stepped in and commented, "I'd agree with that, Phil. It seemed to me that the company would have been better served had we taken a softer approach with the press. It was an opportune time to make a positive first impression."

"You guys don't know what you're talking about. What I showed them today was that I'm a take-charge person. I showed them leadership, don't you agree, Ted?" Webster asked as he turned to the parrot.

"Yes, sir! My exact thoughts. You showed decisive leadership, Phil," the parrot responded hurriedly.

"We really need to talk about where we are in this takeover battle, our strategies for defending it and other potential issues," Oakes suggested.

"Right, Jay. We do need to discuss them, Phil. And Carli should join us to talk about the financial implications," Weimar added.

"I agree," Webster said reluctantly. "Call her to join us and bring me up to speed on everything that you've been working on.

I want to know more about this Malloy and what his firm does and whoever the attorney is you are using in New York."

Weimar called Carli to join them and they worked late into the day reviewing strategies and everything that had transpired. They had paused to move to Webster's now barren office to eat sandwiches which they ordered and had delivered in the late morning from the company cafeteria.

The overall tone of the meeting was adversarial with Webster constantly challenging and demeaning Weimar, Dansen and Oakes. Webster also threw several condescending remarks at Lita when she was called into the meeting from time to time. It was a very long day for Weimar, Dansen and Oakes.

At the end of the day, Webster ended the meeting and he and the parrot returned to Cleveland. Weimar, Dansen and Oakes were sitting in Oakes' office. They were absolutely drained.

"Some meeting!" Oakes stated slowly. It was apparent to Dansen and Weimar that of the three of them, Oakes was the worse for wear. He was beat—and it was due to the combination of the stressful meeting and his MS.

"Yes, sir! My exact thoughts!" Weimar said as he mimicked the parrot.

"Joe, cut that out! It has been a long day!" Carli said. She was drained too and she didn't have MS.

"The guy is a flat-out jerk! We know it and, if the world doesn't know it by the evening news, they will soon. And somebody needs to declare open hunting season on that parrot. He should be stuffed!" Joe retorted. It was hard to keep the feisty Weimar down.

"What are we going to do?" Oakes asked.

"Our jobs may not be around long if he starts treating everyone here like that. We'll start seeing people bailing left and right is my guess," Weimar stated philosophically.

"What's your take on how serious he is in fighting this takeover?" Carli probed.

"I'm not sure. Jay, where did our stock close today?" Weimar inquired.

"Up one dollar," Oakes responded after looking at his computer screen. "Trading volume appears to be normal."

"Interesting. Glad that volume and the price didn't spike significantly upward. That's all that egomaniac would need. Carli, I'm not sure how motivated he is in fighting the battle. You guys will know this shortly for filing purposes, so I'm going to tell you what the Board did. The Board granted him 100,000 stock option shares. If he can drive the price up $10 a share and sell the company, the change-in-control feature on his stock options is triggered and they vest 100 percent. He walks away with a cool million for potentially a couple of month's work."

"But don't we have the same feature on our stock options?" Carli asked.

"Yes, we do. But our options are priced so high that we won't see any benefit from it. Just this carpetbagger benefits."

"Please tell me that the parrot didn't get any stock options," Oakes pleaded.

"Thank goodness, no. That would have been the last straw," Weimar responded.

"Good," Oakes sighed with relief.

"I'm ready to call it a night, guys," said Carli.

"Me too," Oakes quickly agreed.

Pufferbelly Restaurant
Kent, Ohio

~

Emerson found street parking near the front of the old Kent train depot which had been converted into the Pufferbelly Restaurant. After the press conference, Emerson had called Bob Welch at Kent State to set up an early dinner so that he could drive back to the island that night. He spent most of the afternoon conducting on-line research at the Cuyahoga Falls Library and had checked the on-line news reports regarding the press conference. He shook his head as he saw the bad press that Webster was getting as a result of his arrogance. Webster was playing in the Wall Street arena now with investors, and not in his privately held real estate company.

Emerson walked through the two sets of doors and found Bob waiting for him.

"I've been watching Fallsview Tire's stock on-and-off all day since the news broke," Bob said after greeting Emerson.

"How are the markets treating them?"

"I'd say they're taking a wait-and-see approach. They're trying to digest the full impact." The waitress showed them to a table near the railroad tracks which ran along the banks of the Cuyahoga River. "It could make Fallsview Tire more vulnerable to Ratek."

They placed their orders and continued talking.

"How so?" Emerson quizzed his savvy friend.

"Webster doesn't know anything about the tire business and even less about the trucking business, let alone how to integrate a trucking company into the tire company. He made all of his money from real estate investments in Cleveland."

"Hmmmm," Emerson said.

"There is one approach that Fallsview Tire could take, although I'd find it very unlikely that they'd pursue it."

"And that is?" Emerson asked.

"A white knight."

"You mean a friendly buyer?"

"Yes, but I'm not sure that Webster is in this for the long haul. Where's his motivation to see the company survive?"

"Little, unless he wants to be the permanent CEO. When I asked him today if he wanted to be the permanent rather than interim CEO, he did his best to dodge answering me," Emerson noted.

Their dinners were served and they continued their conversation.

"I think he's in it to get his money back from his investment. Why would he want to give up his lucrative position in his real estate business? It doesn't have anywhere near the problems that Fallsview Tire has," Welch offered.

"True."

"There's something else that could be driving him to sell

quickly," Welch hinted.

"And that is?" Emerson asked.

"Typically, in these types of situations, new CEO's are given huge stock options. If that happened here, he'd cash in big-time," Welch suggested. "You'll know if he did by reading the company's filings on the SEC's website."

They continued their hypothesizing for the balance of the meal and concluded with Welch agreeing to visit Emerson in Put-in-Bay.

Webster's Office
Fallsview Tire & Rubber Company

~

"Lita, get Max Ratek on the phone for me!" Webster called out from his office. He had arrived at the office early that morning with the hope of seriously addressing a number of the issues.

"I don't have his number. I'll have to get it from Jay," she called back in to his office. It seemed that she did little more than blink and Webster was looming over her at her desk.

"Let me make this clear to you: you are my assistant. What goes on in my office, who I call and talk with and what you type for me is confidential. If there is any breach of confidentiality I will fire you! Is that clear?" Webster fumed.

"Yes, Mr. Webster," Lita responded carefully, but professionally. Challenging would be an understatement in describing what it was going to be like working for Webster. Looking back over her career, she had worked for all kinds and she was able to successfully adjust to their unique styles. This would be a tough adjustment.

"Here's his number. Get him on the phone!" Webster stalked back into his office after pulling Ratek's business card out of his wallet and giving it to her.

Lita was surprised that Webster had Ratek's card. She wondered what he was doing with it as she dialed his number and made the connection.

"I have Mr. Ratek on the line for you, Mr. Webster," Lita said as she leaned in toward Webster's office and called in to him. She didn't see Jay Oakes in the doorway. Jay spun around quickly before she turned her head and scootered to Weimar's office.

Webster picked up the phone and turned his high back chair away from the doorway to his office. "Max, it's Phil. You've heard by now that I've been selected as interim chairman & CEO of Fallsview Tire."

"Couldn't miss it! It's all over the wire services and the TV news. You were magnificent in your press conference!" Ratek said as he played to Webster's ego.

"Thank you. It's easy when you know how to handle yourself," Webster droned inanely. "It's a shame about what happened to Owens. They're still trying to figure out what caused his car to explode."

"Yes, a shame," Ratek smirked to himself.

"But now the company has a leader that they can count on," Webster said in self-aggrandizement.

Weimar and Oakes entered the outer office area where Lita sat. They had quickly formed a plan when Oakes told Weimar whom Webster was calling.

"Lita," Weimar started.

Lita looked up and then nervously inside of Webster's office. When she saw his back to them, she relaxed a bit.

"I need to see Webster." Weimar looked into Webster's office. "Oh, I see he's on telephone. Any idea who he's talking to? I'd like to interrupt."

Lita worriedly looked in Webster's office again before answering. "It's an important call and I don't think you'd better interrupt."

That's all that Weimar had to hear. It sounded like Lita had been told by Webster not to divulge whom he was talking with. Lita seemed nervous and not herself. Weimar moved forward with the little plan that he and Oakes had quickly concocted.

"We can wait. Lita, I don't think that Jay knows some of the stories that you've told about your ex-husband."

Lita brightened up a bit as she enjoyed trashing her ex. She turned to Oakes and began some of her stories without noticing that Oakes had positioned himself where he could hear Webster talking on the phone.

"Yes, when I married Mr. Right, no one told me that he thought his first name was 'Always.'"

Oakes and Weimar made a show of chuckling.

Taking in Lita's 5-foot-8-inch height, Oakes asked if her husband had been tall also.

Lita responded with a grin, "Only when he stood on his wallet! But when I was finished with the divorce, he wasn't as tall."

They continued to chuckle as she told her stories and Oakes

kept one ear tuned to the one-sided conversation in Webster's office.

"I was curious as to how the company spotted me accumulating their stock so fast?" Ratek inquired.

"They told me that they used a stock surveillance firm run by Jimmy Malloy. You know him?"

"So that's how. I was suspicious that they got a jump on us by using him. I know Fallsview uses him for their proxy solicitation. Yes, I know Jimmy. All the players know one another and work to conceal themselves until the very last minute that they have to disclose anything. By the way, I didn't get a chance to thank you for attempting to support me at the annual meeting. I appreciated your effort," Ratek said as he continued to feed the ego.

"I thought it was the right thing to do. You know that Owens reamed me in the board meeting for my antics?"

"No, I didn't. I am so sorry about that," Ratek said in a tone dripping with false sincerity which was lost upon Webster.

"You know that the Board gave me 100,000 stock options to take this position?"

"No, I didn't. You deserved more," Ratek said. "Do I still have your support as we discussed over dinner in Cleveland a few weeks ago?"

"Yes, even more so. With me in charge, I can truly be instrumental in passing control to you," Webster beamed as he calculated what his stock options would be worth when Ratek took control of the Board of Directors and the company.

"Good. Now tell me how your team has planned to defeat my attempt."

Webster began repeating everything that he had learned from Weimar, Dansen and Oakes the previous day.

As Webster began reciting the details, Oakes had had enough. "Lita, on second thought, we can talk to Webster another time. The more that I think about it, it's not really important. Joe, let's go back to your office."

"I'll let him know you stopped by," Lita offered. She had enjoyed talking with the two of them.

"That's not necessary, Lita. I'd really prefer that you don't mention it," Weimar cautioned as he and Oakes headed to his office.

When Weimar asked in the hallway how things went, Oakes said, "When we get to your office, I'll tell you. You're not going to believe this!"

Weimar's Office
Fallsview Tire & Rubber Company

$\sim$

"That S.O.B. was spilling his guts to Ratek about everything that we told him yesterday!" Oakes said incredulously.

"He what?" Weimar asked not believing what he just heard.

"You heard me right. I didn't even know that the two guys knew each other. This explains why Webster stood up for Ratek at the annual meeting!" Oakes lamented.

"You think he's dealing with Ratek about letting him take control of the company?" Weimar asked with deep concern.

"Absolutely!" Oakes responded grimly.

Oakes thought for a moment and then, frustrated, stated, "There's not much that we can do."

"Not much at all," Weimar confirmed. "He's the Chairman of the Board now. He'll still need the Board's support and, then there'll be a special meeting of the shareholders to approve the change in control, or put Ratek's slate of Board members in place. He's our boss and we'll need to support him as much as we may not like it."

"Joe, what if someone leaked to the press that Webster and Ratek are in cahoots?" Oakes thought for a moment.

Weimar looked at Oakes and said, "Now, Jay, I could never counsel you as the company's legal head to do something like that. If I were to ever become aware of someone planning to leak confidential information, I'd have to take action on behalf on the company." Weimar looked hard at Oakes.

Oakes read the look and said, "Of course, you would. I was just brainstorming. Well, I need to go and see what kind of trouble I can get into."

Oakes grinned as he scootered out of Weimar's office.

"Jay, seriously remember my words of warning. I wouldn't want to be compromised," Weimar yelled after Oakes.

"I'll remember," Oakes said as he sped down the hallway.

Aunt Anne's House
Put-in-Bay

~

Emerson was on the cool cement floor of his aunt's garage

changing the oil on her 1929 Ford Model A pick up truck. It was primarily used for the island's Sunday afternoon parade of antique cars and street rods. The cream colored truck with the dark green fat boy fenders had been his uncle's pride and joy before he passed away. Now it was his responsibility to care for the truck, wax it and, especially, to drive it in the Sunday afternoon parades when he was on the island. The truck held a special meaning for him and his aunt.

The ringing of his cell phone caused him to ease himself out from under the truck and take the call. He stood near the garage doorway and breathed in the freshness that the morning drizzle was bringing to the island air as he looked towards the isthmus connecting East Point with the main part of the island and Perry's Monument towering in the sky.

"Hello?"

"Emerson, it's Lynn Arruda," the voice responded.

"Hey, Sunshine! I've missed you on my last couple of trips to Cuyahoga Falls. Still drinking that good coffee at Jimmy's Café?"

"Yes, I am. Emerson, can you drive down here? I've got something important to tell you," Lynn said earnestly.

"Someone asked the sweetheart of Cuyahoga Falls to marry him? I knew you wouldn't stay single long," Emerson guessed.

"Emerson, stop it. This is very serious. I need to talk to you in person."

"I've been making so many trips down there someone should be giving me frequent driver mileage. Is a trip really necessary?" Emerson dreaded another drive down there if it really wasn't important. "Can it wait for my next trip down there?"

"It's about Fallsview Tire."

"And you can't tell me over the phone?" Emerson pleaded.

"No, I've got some inside information that I need to deliver personally to you," she said with an air of mystery. "It's critical. Trust me!"

"Got my attention." Emerson looked at his watch and thought how long it would take to finish the oil change. "Can we meet at Jimmy's Café at, say, 4 o'clock?"

"Yes. I'll see you then. We both need to make sure that we aren't followed. See you at four!" Lynn hung up.

Emerson set his phone down and returned to completing the oil change as fast he could with his mind spinning thoughts about Lynn's cryptic call. Her comment about potentially being followed concerned him.

Jimmy's Café
Cuyahoga Falls

~

The rain had followed Emerson most of the way on his drive to Cuyahoga Falls before blowing off to the northeast. The sun was just breaking through the clouds as Emerson pulled into the café's parking lot off of Chestnut.

No one was seated at the outdoor umbrella patio tables as Emerson entered the café and laughed when he saw the new sign announcing that the café was a no-gossiping zone. He glanced at his watch and saw that he was five minutes early.

"We haven't seen you in some time," Jimmy greeted Emerson enthusiastically as he approached the uniquely painted coffee bar.

"I've been swamped," Emerson responded as he smiled at the gregarious owner. Jimmy had an aura about him that permeated the atmosphere with friendliness and care. He was so likable that Emerson wished he lived closer to Jimmy so that a strong friendship could grow between them.

"Coffee?"

Emerson licked his lips. "Yes, as long as it's a Jimmy's Special. Just add a little extra chocolate syrup on this one. You can call it a Jimmy's Special with an Emerson twist!"

A tall, dark-haired, attractive female walked behind the coffee bar. "Honey, can you make a Jimmy's Special with a dash of extra chocolate syrup for Emerson. Emerson, have you met my wife, Carla?"

Carla turned to look at Emerson and he saw that same level of radiance glowing from Carla as Jimmy had. Two peas in a pod Emerson sensed.

"Hi, Emerson. Heard a lot about you, especially from Lynn. She sounds like she's knows you very well." Carla was frothing the milk for the special drink.

"Hi, Carla. Yeah, we go way back to working together at the *Post* in Washington. Have you seen her today? I'm supposed to meet her here."

Carla set the Jimmy's Special in front of Emerson. "No, not yet."

Emerson raised the hot drink topped with a mountain of whipped cream, chocolate syrup and cinnamon to his lips and tasted the thick whipped cream. "Hmmmmm," he moaned as the delight slithered down his throat. "I'll grab one of the tables outside and wait for her."

"I'll dry off the seats for you," Carla offered as she followed Emerson out the door with a towel in her hand and quickly dried a couple of the rain-drenched chairs at the far table.

Emerson took a seat. He didn't have to wait long before Lynn parked her car in the lot and looked back in the direction she had just driven, trying to notice if anyone had followed her. She waved at Emerson as she energetically ran inside the café. "Let me grab a coffee and I'll join you."

Two minutes later, she was seated at Emerson's side. Emerson leaned over to her and said, "Now tell me, Sunshine, what's so secretive and urgent that I needed to see you in person?"

Lynn took a couple of gulps of her coffee and looked up and down the street. Then she blurted it out. "Webster has an alliance with Ratek!"

Emerson set down his coffee. He was stunned. "How do you know?"

Lynn moved closer. "You've got to protect my source. I don't want him getting into trouble. He could be fired. Got your word on it?"

"Of course. Now, tell me what's going on," Emerson urged.

"This friend of mine works at Fallsview Tire and overheard Webster talking with Ratek. He's very suspicious that Webster is going to let Ratek take over the company."

"When did he overhear the conversation?"

"This morning."

"What else did he say?"

"That's all. He didn't want to say more because he thought it might be traced back to him. He's already worried about losing his job if Ratek takes control," she said nervously.

"Why did he want you to tell me?"

"Not specifically you. I'm not sure that he knows that we're friends. He knows that I've got friends in the press and he wanted it to get out to the media that Ratek and Webster were working together." She paused and then went on. "Now that I think about it, he knows that we worked at the *Washington Post* and may have thought that I'd go to you with the story."

"Will he talk to me? I've always protected my sources."

"No way. He's too nervous about anyone knowing who he is," she fidgeted.

"What was this about someone tailing you?"

"There are already rumors floating around the company that Owens' accident may not have been an accident. There were two explosions heard before the car went over the bridge," she said uneasily.

"That doesn't surprise me. There have been several suspicious deaths during takeover battles involving Ratek."

"What are you going to do?"

"Have you told anyone else what you told me?"

"No," she replied.

"Good. Let's keep this conversation between us. And you're sure that you can trust the reliability of his information?"

"Without question. He'd never lie to me."

"I think it's time for me to make a trip to New York and pay a surprise visit to Mr. Max Ratek. I want to see the look on his face when I confront him and tell him that I'm doing a story about his collusion with Webster. This picture is going to be worth a thousand words!" Emerson grinned.

"Emerson, be careful. You don't need to become another one of those suspicious deaths!" Lynn cautioned.

"Don't worry about me. I'm careful. I'd better go. Got to catch a flight to New York from Cleveland tonight!"

Emerson excused himself and left Lynn to finish her coffee. On the drive to Cleveland's airport, Emerson tried to figure out who told Lynn about the conversation. He guessed it was Oakes. In any event, he was committed to making sure that nothing was tied back to Oakes, or Lynn, for that matter.

Birkman Investments
New York City
The Next Morning

Emerson stood in the crowded entrance lobby of the building in front of the bank of elevators waiting for one to take him to the floor housing Birkman Investments. As the elevator door opened in front of him, he joined the surge of bodies fighting to occupy it.

He was wedged in the middle of the crowded elevator when his mind transitioned from a subconscious observation to a conscious observation.

He realized that he had smelled Giorgio perfume while waiting for the elevator. The same perfume that the elusive and beautiful Martine had worn. Emerson peered quickly into the lobby and caught sight of a tall woman with a red tint to her hair. It looked like Martine!

Emerson cried out, "Martine!" She apparently didn't hear him and he tried to fight his way to the front of the elevator doors.

"I've got to get out!" he shouted as the doors closed in front of him. The elevator stopped on the next floor and Emerson was the first to exit. He rushed along the elevator bank looking for an elevator going down. They were all going up or on the first floor.

He found the stairs and raced down to the first floor, taking the stairs two at a time. He saw Martine entering the last elevator in the bank and charged through the crowd and wedged himself into the elevator. He turned to look warmly at Martine. It wasn't her. The redhead gave him a cold stare as he slowly turned around, embarrassed by his antics.

As much as he tried to put her out of his mind, he couldn't. He would often think of their fun-filled days on the islands and their sails together. He could still taste the goodbye kisses in front of Magruder Hospital in Port Clinton, the last time that he saw her. Her son, Austin, would be a year older now. Great kid, Emerson thought to himself. He hoped that her husband was continuing to treat her better, but on the other hand—and he knew that he was wrong for thinking it—he wondered if her husband had gone back to his old ways. The last communication that he had from her was the note he received on the day he accepted his Pulitzer Prize. It was postmarked New Orleans, he recalled wistfully.

The elevator reached the 20th floor and Emerson stepped out and walked to Birkman Investments' office.

The receptionist looked up from her desk as Emerson entered the opulent offices.

"May I help you?"

"Yes, I don't have an appointment, but it's a rather urgent matter that I need to address with Mr. Ratek concerning the Fallsview Tire situation," Emerson said as he handed her one of his business cards.

"I'll see if he's available to meet with you. Please take a seat," she instructed him.

"I'd rather stand, if you don't mind." Emerson leaned on the counter as she dialed Ratek's number.

"Mr. Ratek, I've got a Mr. Emerson Moore from *The Washington Post* here to see you," she said as she read from the business card. "He said that he doesn't have an appointment, but that it's urgent for him to see you about Fallsview Tire."

She paused as Ratek replied to her. She disconnected the call and looked up at Emerson. "Mr. Ratek said that he has a rather full day of appointments and will not be able to squeeze you in. He said that he might have some time at the end of next week."

Emerson saw right through the dodge. "Could you get him on the phone again and tell him that I'm running a story tomorrow about the relationship he has with Fallsview's interim CEO." That should get his attention, Emerson thought to himself.

"Mr. Moore, I shouldn't interrupt him again."

"Miss, this could be very embarrassing to Mr. Ratek if I don't have my story correct. Could you please convey my message?" Emerson urged.

With great reluctance, the receptionist called Ratek again. "I'm sorry to bother you again, Mr. Ratek. But this gentleman is persistent and said that he plans to run a story tomorrow about the relationship you have with a Mr. Webster."

She listened to Ratek's response and disconnected. "Please have a seat. He's going to try to clear some time for you on his schedule so that he can see you."

Emerson took a seat in the lobby as he glanced at the lobby clock which read 9:37 A.M.

Ratek's Office
New York City

~

Ratek fumed as he hung up the phone and looked out his huge windows toward the New York Stock Exchange. What did that nosy *Washington Post* reporter have on him and Webster? He spun around in his chair and called Webster.

"Hello, Max," Webster started as he took the call.

Ratek ignored any pleasantries and cut to the chase.

"I've got that *Washington Post* reporter, Moore, in my lobby and he's saying that he's going to do a story on our relationship. Now you tell me how in the world he would know that you and I have a relationship!" Ratek demanded.

"I wouldn't know. I haven't said anything to anyone," Webster responded with surprise. "No one here has any idea that we know each other. Let me get to the bottom of this. I'll call you right back."

Webster hung up and thought about his phone conversation with Ratek the prior day. He then realized that he hadn't shut his office door while he talked to Ratek. Perhaps Weimar or Oakes overheard him talking with Ratek. He couldn't confront them outright, because if they didn't know, why should he inform them now? He dialed Weimar. "Joe, I want you and Oakes in my office right now!" he ordered.

A few minutes later, they both arrived in his office.

"Shut the door!" he directed.

Weimar and Oakes could see that Webster was deeply agitated about something.

"Have either of you had any inappropriate discussions about me with that *Washington Post* reporter who's been snooping around here since the annual meeting?"

Weimar looked at Oakes closely, as Oakes was the first to reply. "I haven't talked to him in a few days, and when I did, I certainly didn't say anything inappropriate about you!"

"Don't give me any of your public relations bullshit! You talk to reporters all the time. Did you say anything to him that would cause me embarrassment or that you wouldn't say to my face? Answer me."

"No, I didn't say anything to him of that nature," Oakes responded a bit nervously Weimar thought as he observed the exchange. Oakes, Weimar thought to himself, you followed through on what we talked about yesterday morning.

Webster turned on Weimar, "And what about you?"

"Excuse me? Not only do I do my best to stay away from reporters, I have a duty not to disclose confidential company information."

"If I find out that either of you leaked any confidential information about this company or me, I will personally see that you are fired and will make sure that the media has the full story about your illegal activities."

"Phil, I'm not sure that you should throw around the term 'illegal activities' without proof. You need to be a bit more circumspect," Weimar started.

"Shut up! Now, both of you get out of here!"

Weimar and Oakes didn't talk until they were in the building's hallway.

Weimar was the first to speak. "He's apparently very distraught about this supposed leak."

"About that leak...," Oakes started.

Weimar interrupted him. "Jay, if you did this, you need to tell me."

"I have nothing to say." Oakes wheeled around in his scooter and headed to his own office. He didn't think that Weimar understood his intentions.

Ratek's Office
New York City

~

Ratek was on the phone listening to Webster who had called to report the results of his confrontation with Weimar and Oakes.

"I don't trust either of them. You'll need to keep a tight rein on them both," Ratek counseled.

"I intend to. I'll bring in outside attorneys and use my own public relations people if I need to," Webster replied.

"Careful on that, too. You'll want to give a perception that there are no problems at the top management level so that we can get this deal done. Afterwards, they're gone anyways."

"I agree."

"I'll let you know what I find out from this reporter," Ratek said as he concluded the phone conversation. He then picked up some papers and began working on another project.

Birkman Investments' Lobby
New York City

~

The clock on the wall read 11:15 A.M. Emerson had been waiting patiently since 9:37. He stood up and approached the receptionist.

"It's been some time now since he said he would see me. Could you check to see if we are still going to meet?"

The receptionist was very much aware of the length of time that Emerson had been waiting. It was a tactic that she had seen Ratek use often over her years as a receptionist.

She responded to Emerson's request, "Mr. Ratek is very much aware of your presence, I assure you. He indicated originally that he had a full schedule today and would try to clear some time for you. Please be patient."

Emerson took his seat, set up his laptop and began the initial draft of his story for the next day's *Post*.

Time had flown by as Emerson's hands flew across the keyboard. He was aware that the receptionist had gone and returned from her lunch as he worked on the story. His focus was interrupted by the receptionist's voice.

"Mr. Ratek will see you now."

Emerson glanced at the clock on the lobby wall. It read 2:10 P.M. Emerson's stomach growled and reminded him that he should have had a larger breakfast than the bowl of fruit he had at the Grand Hyatt that morning. He closed down his laptop and followed the receptionist to Ratek's office.

Ratek was seated in a chair behind his massive desk. He looked very serious and somewhat intimidating to Emerson as he plopped down in one of the visitor chairs in front of the desk.

"Thank you for taking time to see me on such short notice," Emerson opened the conversation as he handed one of his business cards to Ratek.

"Now, what's this about some preposterous story about Webster and me?" Ratek asked with disdain.

Emerson took a few literary liberties as he stretched what he actually knew. He was going to throw out a number of assumptions and read Ratek's reactions.

"I have a source that has indicated to me that you and Webster have a relationship going back some time. You both are in collusion to turn the company over to you."

Ratek wondered exactly how much Emerson knew. He was concerned that Emerson was aware of the dinner meeting in Cleveland with Webster. Ratek knew that he would have to be careful in the manner in which he responded.

"I categorically deny any relationship with Webster. This source of yours, is the source inside or outside of the company?"

That clinched it for Emerson. The fact that Ratek was trying to identify where the source was made it more likely that there was a relationship.

"I can't disclose that to you. Interesting that you're curious about the source's whereabouts when you say that there is no relationship." Emerson threw this last comment out to see what effect it would have on Ratek.

"Don't read anything into that," Ratek warned.

"We seem to have a disconnect as to whether or not there's a relationship between you and Webster. I'm going to go with my source and release the story in tomorrow's *Post*," Emerson advised.

"Do that and you will be hearing from my attorneys," Ratek admonished.

"Won't be the first time that I've heard from someone's attorney. I have full confidence in my source and the credibility of what they have divulged to me," Emerson stated firmly.

Ratek's plan had been to maintain his composure during the meeting with Emerson. He had been successful even though he was seething with anger.

"I would suggest that you proceed cautiously, Mr. Moore," Ratek said in a tone that conveyed danger.

"Are you threatening me?" Emerson probed.

"No, I'm just suggesting that you better know your facts. Good day, Mr. Moore." Ratek rose from his chair signaling the end to their meeting. Emerson picked up his laptop and walked through the office door, past the receptionist and into the outer hallway.

Grimes walked into Ratek's office.

"Did you hear the entire conversation?" Ratek asked as he disconnected his open phone line on the speakerphone. Grimes had been in the adjoining office and listening to the exchange between Emerson and Ratek.

"Yes."

Ratek was looking at Emerson's business card. "Ever been to Put-in-Bay, Simon?"

"Put-in-where?" Grimes queried.

"Put-in-Bay. Somewhere in Ohio, on Lake Erie." Ratek explained based on what little he knew about the island.

"No, never been there," Grimes replied.

"I think that you're about due for a little vacation. I think you should go there and pay a visit to our reporter friend. The same kind of visit that you paid Owens. I want you to emasculate him!"

Grimes smiled evilly. "I'll look forward to it."

"You can take the jet, but don't have it land on the island. See what's available in the area, and whatever you do, keep a low profile on this," Ratek cautioned.

"I always do. No one connects anything to me or to you. That's my track record."

"I know. You are very efficient!" Ratek knew that he could count on Grimes to accomplish delicate tasks that were necessary from time to time.

Grimes stepped out of the office to make his travel plans as Ratek reached for the phone to call Webster.

"Hello, Max," Webster said as he took the call.

"You definitely have a leak in your organization. Moore knows that we're in collusion and there's going to be a story in tomorrow's *Post*. I can't determine whether he knows about our meeting in Cleveland. Have you talked with anyone about it?" Ratek asked brusquely.

"No, I haven't mentioned a thing."

"I want to uncover his source and here's how you're going to do it: I want you to selectively provide information to your key staff members. If it comes back to us, then we will know which one of them leaked it."

"What if they share the information with each other? Then, we can't be sure."

What an idiot, Ratek thought to himself. "When you share the information, just tell them that it's between the two of you."

"I see. Great idea. I'll give it a try!"

"Make sure you pick up a copy of the *Post* in the morning so that we can see what's in the story. This could be bad for both of us," Ratek warned.

"Will do."

"I'll talk to you tomorrow." Webster disconnected.

Ratek sat back and fretted about the story and began to develop a number of alternatives to overcome the bad press. He picked up his phone and called his proxy vote solicitor and takeover consultant, Peter Barkley from Wilton Partners, to set up a late afternoon appointment.

In the Air
Between New York City and Cleveland

After the meeting with Ratek, Emerson rushed to LaGuardia Airport and was able to catch a 5:00 P.M. flight to Cleveland. Settled into his seat, Emerson gazed out the small window as the plane taxied and took off. Emerson never tired of the aerial view of New York City.

The plane would arrive in Cleveland at 6:30 P.M. It would take Emerson 90 minutes to be on his aunt's doorstep.

Emerson had talked with John Sedler, his editor, while he waited at LaGuardia Airport, and then completed his story for the next day's paper. He linked into a phone portal and e-mailed the story to Sedler.

Sedler had been excited about being the first to break the news of the alliance between Ratek and Webster. He was always excited when the *Post* was the lead paper on breaking news.

Carl R. Keller Airport
Port Clinton, Ohio

It was about 6:15 P.M. when Ratek's corporate jet touched down on the small airport's 5,000-foot runway. The airport was three miles east of Port Clinton. The jet taxied near the administration building and shut down its engines.

The jet's door swung open to reveal Grimes carrying a small overnight bag and standing in the doorway talking with the pilot.

"I agree. It's better for you to fly to Cleveland and overnight there. I'll connect with you on your cell tomorrow and tell you where to pick me up."

The pilot had provided Grimes with a map which had the airports in northeast Ohio identified so that Grimes could instruct him where to go. Grimes wasn't sure how his plans would develop over the next 24 hours and needed to have flexibility.

He descended the stairs to the tarmac and walked through the administrative office to the front parking lot where he was able to catch a cab that had just unloaded two riders. He instructed the cabby to take him to the Island House Inn in downtown Port

Clinton. As the cab pulled out of the airport parking lot, Grimes saw Ratek's jet taking off and heading toward Cleveland. He smiled to himself at how well things were starting off.

The ride to Port Clinton was a short one and took Grimes past the public beach on the south shore of the lake. Grimes felt himself being pulled in by the lake's allure. Past the water plant and the park, the cab continued along East Perry Street into town and turned left onto Madison. The cab turned a sharp right into a parking space in front of the Island House Inn.

Grimes paid the driver, stepped out of the cab, and paused to take in the beauty of the classic three-story, brick building trimmed out in white.

Grimes entered the Victorian style lobby and stopped to read a plaque listing some of the celebrities who had stayed at the inn. The names included Clark Gable, Spencer Tracy, Lauren Bacall, Humphrey Bogart, Desi Arnaz, Lucille Ball, Gene Autry, Ray Milland, Joe Dimaggio, Yogi Berra, and Whitey Ford.

Below the plaque was a stand with Lake Erie vacationland brochures and maps. Grimes picked up several to review later that evening.

Grimes walked over to the desk, and quickly reading the nametag worn by the man at the front desk, said, "Dave, I believe you have reservations for Grimes."

Dave looked through his list of reservations and smiled as he said, "Yes, we do. We've got you in the corner room overlooking the lake. It's room 132 on the second floor, the room that Humphrey Bogart and Lauren Bacall stayed in."

"Interesting," Grimes commented.

"If you don't have dinner plans you may want to check out our Italian restaurant, Anthony's, and its massive, mirrored bar," Dave added. He pointed to the restaurant on his left which fronted Perry Street.

"Or, if you're hungry for steak, you can try our Conrad's Steakhouse." He pointed toward the other side of the hotel.

As he took his key, Grimes responded, "I'll try the Italian."

Grimes, still carrying his overnight bag, walked into Anthony's. As the waitress walked him to his table next to a window on Perry Street, he took in the restaurant's huge oak 1896 bar with tall oak pilasters that framed the oversized mirror and the vintage tin ceiling. He sighed momentarily as he read the menu and thought briefly about the following day.

Birkman Investments
New York City

~

"This will change our plans somewhat," Ratek chafed as he talked with Webster the next morning about Emerson's story in the *Post*.

The short article stated that the *Post* had discussions with sources close to Fallsview Tire. The article said that it appeared that Fallsview Tire's CEO Webster and Birkman Investments' Ratek had a prior relationship and were in collusion to turn control of the company over to Ratek. The article continued to say that the Post was working on a number of additional sources to further substantiate the allegation.

Like sharks in a feeding frenzy, the other news services picked up the story and it was on many of the morning TV news programs.

The phones at Fallsview Tire and Birkman Investments had been ringing all morning.

"It looks like the cat's out of the bag," Webster said angrily.

"You need to confront your people again and make sure that there are no more leaks. I want your strategies buttoned up. No more leaks!" Ratek raged.

"I'll handle it," Webster assured Ratek. "I'm having my personal public relations representative talk to reporters and tell them that it's not our policy to comment on rumors. That will put an end to these inquiries this morning. We're just going to lock down and not talk to the press other than that. Do you see any problem from your side as far as the support you have built up with the other pension funds?"

"No, but I don't want to risk losing that support and their votes. We need to expedite the change in control and call the special shareholder meeting to put my board in place. Since you've got to set up the meeting, you should have P. Dayton Ford and Jimmy Malloy find a way to hold it as quickly as possible so we can start formally soliciting votes for my slate of directors," Ratek directed. "Then, I'll control the company with my directors!"

"I'll get right on it," Webster responded as the call ended.

Webster called Weimar, Oakes and Dansen into his office and screamed at them again about the leaks to the press as Polly the Parrott, Webster's public relations guy, watched. He also directed them to expedite calling the special shareholders' meeting and have Ford and Malloy find a way to make it happen.

The crowning blow for Oakes was when Webster had Polly the Parrot hand him the press release that Polly had drafted, and instructed him to issue it as written. Weimar, Dansen and a defeated-looking Oakes left Webster's office to comply with the instructions that they had been given.

∾

The next morning Grimes entered the small restaurant on Perry Street, just steps away from the Jet Express dock. He took a seat at the counter and ordered coffee from the cheerful blonde waitress with an effervescent smile. Her nametag read "Char."

Looking through the menu as he sipped his coffee and Char waited, he selected an omelet.

"Like to try our fresh-made doughnuts? We've got a reputation over the years for having the best homemade doughnuts around," Char beamed.

"Do you have chocolate doughnuts?" Grimes replied as he looked at the attractive waitress.

"Yes, we do."

"I'll take two. I love chocolate doughnuts," Grimes ordered as he thought quickly of the code name for the Fallsview Tire takeover and grinned to himself.

She left to place his order and Grimes focused on the map of Put-in-Bay. He had marked the area where Emerson resided and studied the streets on the island for possible escape routes should things not go as planned.

Char returned with the omelet and the two chocolate doughnuts. The huge omelet hung over the large plate.

"This is amazing!" Grimes stated in awe.

Char just grinned, refilled his coffee and returned to her other customers.

Grimes couldn't finish the huge omelet, probably because he wolfed down the two doughnuts. He paid his bill and walked to the rear of the restaurant where he found its trash bin. He opened his small bag and threw a smaller bag containing his shaving gear into the bin.

He then continued the short walk to the Jet Express dock, where he purchased his tickets for the ride to South Bass Island and downtown Put-in-Bay. He took a seat as he waited and watched the drawbridge open to allow a number of sailboats to motor through as they made their way the short distance on the Portage River to Lake Erie.

He didn't have to wait long until it was time to board one of the fastest jet-powered catamaran ferries in the world. The ride lasted about 22 minutes and took the riders along the west side of the island, around Peach Point, past Gibraltar Island which guarded the entrance to Put-in-Bay's harbor, and then to its dockage at the harbor's east end.

Grimes had been watching for Perry's Monument to appear and saw it as the Jet Express rounded Gibraltar Island. Grimes looked at the tall structure and noted the scaffolding that hung just below the top of the observation deck. They must be cleaning the monument, Grimes thought to himself. The monument would play an important role in his plan to eliminate Emerson.

Departing with the rest of the passengers, Grimes walked through the maze of golf cart rentals, bike rentals and cabs to cross Bayview Avenue and enter DeRivera Park which offered a quiet respite from the streets surrounding the park on three sides and their bars, restaurants and gift shops. The fourth side, fronted the harbor.

Grimes entered the park's bathhouse and swiftly stepped into one of the shower stalls with an attached changing booth. He opened his bag and began exchanging his long sleeved dress shirt and wool slacks for a light blue Tee shirt and a pair of khaki shorts. He slipped off his shoes and socks and replaced them with a pair of sneakers. On top of the Tee shirt, he added a garish Hawaiian shirt which he buttoned up. He then pulled out of the bag a large straw hat and oversized sunglasses which he placed on his head.

No one can miss me in this loud outfit he thought. He wanted to make sure that people would notice him.

He pulled out of the bag a small knapsack and threw it over his shoulder. He then stuffed the shoes and other items that he had taken off back into the bag and closed it. He walked out of the shower area and nonchalantly dropped the bag into a large trashcan.

A moment later, a member of the park's cleaning crew entered the bathhouse and began emptying the trashcans into the large trash bin next to the bathhouse. It was trash pick-up day for the island's garbage company.

Looking like a harmless day-tripper, Grimes strolled toward the 352-foot high Perry's Monument, which was about four blocks northeast of the park. He climbed the stone stairs to the monument's base and entered it. There, he climbed 37 steps and paid the fee to ride the elevator to the open-air observation platform, which was 317 feet above the lake, according to the U.S. park ranger who was operating the elevator and providing a brief history of the monument. Grimes noted that the name on the park ranger's badge read "Travis."

"Perry's Monument is the third tallest monument in the United

States and commemorates Oliver Hazard Perry's American victory in the Battle of Lake Erie during the War of 1812. Interred beneath the rotunda floor are the remains of three American and three British officers who were killed during the battle. Construction of Perry's Victory and International Peace Monument was completed in June 1915 at a cost of $480,000. It's comprised of 78 courses of pink granite from Milford, Massachusetts and topped with an 11-ton bronze urn. You'll be able to see it when you look at the top of the monument." Travis continued to drone with a historical overview for the rest of the ride.

Reaching the top of the monument, Grimes stepped out of the elevator along with two other tourists and began to walk around the open-air observation deck. The view of the harbor and the island was noteworthy, Grimes thought, as he looked around the island from his high vantage point. Seeing where the top of the cables was secured to the monument, he leaned over to see if he could see the scaffold itself. It was dangling just a few feet below the observation deck.

Grimes spotted a waste container near the elevator's entrance and decided that would serve his purpose. He waited until the tourists on the observation deck stepped back into the elevator and left the deck abandoned of everyone but him.

Grimes quickly reached into his knapsack and pulled out the Semtex that he had been carrying. He inserted a remote detonator in the Semtex and then buried the Semtex in the bottom of the plastic bag-lined trash container. He arranged the trash over the Semtex to make sure that no one would see the explosive and moved quickly away from the overflowing container as the elevator returned to the top level.

"Ready to return to earth?" the bearded Travis asked cheerily as he picked up a discarded cigarette butt and tossed it into the full trash container. "Some people are just so messy."

"Yes. That would be fine," Grimes responded as he ignored the messy comment and stepped into the elevator for the ride to ground level with the talkative ranger.

Grimes quickly walked away from the monument and walked to the Dairy Queen next to the Jet Express dock. He inserted a coin in the pay phone and dialed the number that he had for Emerson.

Emerson answered his cell phone on the second ring. "Hello?"

"Is this Emerson Moore from *The Washington Post*?" Grimes inquired.

"Yes, it is. Who's this?"

"It's not important who I am. But I have some inside information on some rather interesting developments at Fallsview Tire. Are you interested?"

Emerson reached for a pad of paper and a pen. "Yes, I am very interested. Who is this?"

"As I said, it's not important. I'd like to meet you to give you some files that I have. They deal with Webster and Ratek's strategy to take over the company together," Grimes baited.

Emerson's interest level soared.

"Where would you like to meet? I can be in Cuyahoga Falls within three hours."

"You don't have to come to me. I'm here in Put-in-Bay."

Emerson became suspicious. Informants didn't usually go out of their way like this to make the trek to the reporter.

"Where and when would you like to meet?" Emerson asked cautiously.

"I will meet you on the observation deck of Perry's Monument in 15 minutes. In front of the elevator doors."

"How will I know you?" Emerson quizzed.

"Oh, don't worry about that. I know what you look like," Grimes replied.

Emerson thought quickly and then asked, "Do you think that you've been followed?"

"Now why would I think that?" Grimes wondered.

Emerson nodded his head to himself. If the caller wasn't worried about being followed, he must be the follower. This could be risky he thought.

"Okay, I'll be there in 15 minutes."

Grimes hung up and smiled slyly. He walked to Ladd's Restaurant which was just east of the Dairy Queen and on the east end of the harbor. He asked for an outside table which provided an unrestricted view of the monument and ordered a cup of black coffee. He checked his knapsack to make sure that the radio control remote for the detonator was in place.

He didn't have to wait long before he saw Emerson striding from his aunt's house on East Point to Perry's Monument. Emerson disappeared inside the base of the monument.

Grimes took another sip from his coffee and waited calmly for Emerson to appear on the observation deck. He didn't have to wait long before he saw Emerson walking around the observation deck and then return to the area in front of the elevator.

Grimes grinned as he depressed the remote.

The quiet morning was interrupted by the sound of the explosion thundering in the air. A number of screams pierced the air amidst the confusion caused by this sudden intrusion into the island's early morning tranquility.

Smoke and flames emerged from the remains of the park's central trash bin near the Visitor Center which was about a block away from the monument on the park's 25-acre site. Fortunately, no one had been near the bin when it exploded; however, a few nearby-parked cars had been damaged.

Grimes looked from the undamaged observation deck to the burning trash bin in disbelief. He left money on the table and ran back to the Dairy Queen to use the phone as the sirens from the fire trucks and police cars filled the air.

Emerson had jumped at the explosion and then stared at the flames.

When Grimes reached the pay phone, two young college girls were using it. Grimes reached around in front of them, grabbed the phone and hung it up. "My turn!" he growled from behind his oversized sunglasses. The two girls looked aghast and scampered away from the eerie intruder.

Grimes dialed Emerson's cell.

Emerson's cell phone rang as he looked into the empty trash container next to him.

"Hello?"

"I'm running late. I'll be right there," the edgy voice responded.

To Emerson, the voice sounded like someone was flustered and less controlled than in the prior conversation. It sounded like someone who just had his plans go awry.

"I'll wait," Emerson replied although he wanted to say more. He wondered if that explosion, in some way, was meant for him. He leaned over the edge of the observation deck's wall and tried to guess which of the people approaching the monument was his informant.

Grimes climbed the steps to the elevator again and paid his fee. He made his way to the waiting elevator.

"Say there, you must really be interested in this monument to come back a second time this morning," Travis remarked proudly as he closed the door and the elevator began to ascend. "Would you like to hear the historical overview again?"

Grimes looked at him and winced. "Not really. Can you tell me if there is anyone else on the deck now?"

"Only one. He's a local. The rest cleared out when they heard that explosion over by the Visitor Center. Yesiree, can't be too careful these days," Travis chimed with his singsong voice.

"One other thing that you can answer. It may seem a bit odd, but I'm curious. I noticed that the trash container on the deck was almost filled to the brim. Did you empty it? It seemed on the verge of overflowing."

"Yesiree, can't have a mess here at the monument, can we?" Travis replied with pride at his own diligence. "Whatever was in there is probably gone now. Whoosh! All smithereens!" he said as he used his hands to mimic an explosion.

"Thank you," Grimes said with exasperation as he realized that the happy ranger had sidetracked his plans. He resolved to deal with Emerson personally.

The elevator door opened to allow Grimes to exit and then shut as the ranger returned the car to the monument's base.

Emerson was waiting for him when he walked off the elevator. "Are you my mysterious caller?" Emerson asked carefully.

"One moment, please," Grimes walked around the entire deck to confirm that no one else was present. "I need to be careful."

Emerson began to relax as it appeared that he was concerned about being followed. But Emerson was wrong. Grimes' concern was to make sure that there were no witnesses.

"Who are you?" Emerson inquired.

"I'm the angel of death!" Grimes rushed at Emerson and grappled with him as he tried to position Emerson closer to the wall so that he could push him over to his death. "You should have stayed away from Fallsview Tire!"

Emerson was able to slither out of his grasp and ran around the deck with Grimes in pursuit. Emerson pressed the elevator call button as he ran by the elevator doors. The second time he passed the elevator's gated doors, Emerson stopped and began to climb up the steel grid of the doors to the urn perched on top of the monument.

Grimes realized that Emerson was trying to buy time as he heard the elevator ascending. He reached up and began to pull on Emerson's foot to prevent Emerson from climbing higher and in hopes of pulling him back to the observation deck floor.

Suddenly, the elevator door opened and Grimes was staring directly into the face of Travis and a full load of tourists as he gripped Emerson's foot.

"Here, here. What's going on?" Travis' voice raised in consternation. "We'll have no horseplay on this deck, boys!"

Grimes let go as the doors opened and raced to the edge of the observation deck. He jumped over the side of the deck and onto the adjustable suspension scaffold that workers had been using to clean the monument's granite sides. He operated its electrical motor and began lowering himself to the ground.

Grimes was about ten feet away from the ground when the scaffold stopped its descent and began to ascend. He peered upward and saw Travis, with Emerson at his side, operating the scaffold's auxiliary control.

Grimes looked down, made the decision and jumped. He landed on both feet and rolled forward on the hard surface, bruising himself. He bounced quickly to his feet and ran to the golf cart parking area in front of the monument where he overpowered a tourist driving a golf cart and drove toward town. He looked over his shoulder and saw Travis on his radio, probably calling the police or other park rangers who were gathered around the burning trash bin.

It was going to be tight as the road curved close to the Visitor Center and the damaged bin on its far side. Grimes just had to make it past them and he would have a chance.

His luck held. Before they could react, Grimes had parked the stolen golf cart in front of the Boathouse Bar and hurried across DeRivera Park to the bathhouse.

He slipped into one of the shower stalls and took off his glasses, hat and Hawaiian shirt. He then stuffed them in the knapsack with the remote detonator and tossed them into one of the large trash containers as he walked out wearing a pair of more stylish sunglasses that he had produced from his pocket. He caught a cab and headed toward Miller Ferry at the opposite end of the island.

As the cab pulled out, he saw a number of police cars and rangers beginning a sweep of the area. They were looking for someone wearing a straw hat, oversized dark sunglasses and a loud Hawaiian shirt.

Grimes smiled to himself as he sat back in the cab for the short ride to the ferry dock. He rubbed his left arm which had taken the brunt of his tumble after jumping from the scaffolding. He realized that he made a mistake in trying to deal with Emerson face to face. He should have waited for another opportunity to kill him remotely.

Weimar's Office
Fallsview Tire & Rubber Company

~

"That was a rough meeting," Carli remarked as she recalled the expletives Webster used. "Imagine him thinking that one of us leaked information. I can't believe that he would think such a thing!"

"Imagine that!" Weimar said as he looked at the emotionally beaten Oakes. "Jay, are you okay? That had to be a real blow to you when he had Polly the Parrot prepare the press release."

"I feel like he cut the wheels right out from under me!" Oakes responded. "I'll be okay. I just don't like the way things are headed with Webster on board."

"I don't think any of us do. Wouldn't you agree, Carli?" Weimar asked.

"Most certainly. I need to get back to my office. Gentlemen, if you'll excuse me?" Carli asked as she stood up and left.

"Joe, about the leak...," Oakes started.

"If you have something to confess, then do it," Weimar cautioned, "because you shouldn't lose any time in issuing that press release."

"You're right." Oakes wheeled around and returned to his office. A few minutes later, Oakes' phone rang. It was the lobby calling to announce that the mayor had stopped by to see Webster. Oakes rode down to the lobby and greeted the mayor and a small contingent of city officials.

"Mr. Trabor, did you have a meeting scheduled with Mr. Webster?"

"No, we didn't. When Owens was around, he was always able to squeeze a little time in for me," Mayor Trabor said proudly.

"I remember that. But unfortunately, Mr. Webster isn't of the same ilk," Oakes warned. "I'm not sure if he'll see you."

"Let's take our chances." Pointing to the contingent with him, he said, "I've got most of the city council members here and several of the key members of my staff. We just want to convey to him that we'll do everything that we can to support Fallsview Tire. You're our largest corporate citizen and important to us all."

"I understand Mayor, and we appreciate your support. If you're willing, we can give it a try," Oakes said with an air of concern.

"Let's do it!" the mayor beamed confidently.

They squeezed into the elevator and rode it to the executive offices. A few minutes later, they were standing in front of Webster's assistant.

"Lita, we'd like to see Webster for a moment. They were ready to take a chance to see if he had a minute to talk," Oakes explained.

Lita looked with anxiety at Oakes, then, at the visitors. She knew that Owens and the mayor had a very good relationship, but also thought that Webster would not be willing to take the time to visit with him.

"Mr. Mayor, please let me check with him," she offered as she stood and walked into Webster's office.

"Thank you, Lita," the mayor said as he clasped his hands behind his back and waited expectantly.

They easily heard Webster's reaction.

"I don't care if it's the man in the moon. I don't want to be interrupted. Is that clear? Now, get out of here and shut my damn door!"

Lita closed the door quickly behind her as she exited Webster's office.

"I'm so sorry, gentlemen. He's tied up right now. Why don't I call your office later and see if we can't clear some time up on his calendar?" she asked, ever the diplomat.

"That would be fine, Lita," the mayor said as the group turned and headed for the elevator.

At the elevator, Oakes looked apologetically at the mayor and said, "I'm so sorry about this. As you can tell, we all miss Owens."

"Yes, I can see that. I wish you luck in dealing with your new boss. You've got your hands full."

"In more ways than one," Oakes agreed.

The elevator arrived and the contingent left as a dejected Oakes rolled to his office.

The Police Chief's Blazer
Put-in-Bay, Ohio

∼

The sweat rolled down Emerson's face as he realized how close he had come to being killed. He and Put-in-Bay Police Chief Chet Wilkens were riding to DeRivera Park where the stolen golf cart had been discovered on Hartford Street in front of the park.

Wilkens and another policeman had interviewed Emerson and the park ranger, Travis. Based on Travis' comments about the assailant's unusual interest in the trash container on the observation deck, Wilkens had deduced that the trash bin explosion was meant to have happened on the observation deck and to have killed Emerson.

Emerson was unable to identify the assailant because of the straw hat and oversized dark sunglasses. Based on the assailant's comment about Fallsview Tire, he was able to link the attack to his involvement with the Fallsview Tire takeover battle.

The Blazer parked on Hartford, about 75 feet south of the intersection with Bayview. A policeman was standing next to the golf cart as several others fanned out through the park and the downtown area looking for the assailant based on the description that had been broadcast.

"Anyone see where he went after parking the cart?" Wilkens asked the policeman.

"Nothing yet, Chet," the policeman replied.

"It shouldn't be too hard to spot that guy the way he was dressed," Emerson offered.

"I wouldn't be too sure about that!" a voice commented from behind the three of them.

They turned and saw the bearded Tom and his assistant, Chuck, from the DeRivera Park's administrative team approaching.

"How's that, Tom?" Chief Wilkens asked.

"We heard the explosion and ran out of the office to see where in the world it came from and we saw the smoke coming from near the Visitor center. We went right in and turned on the police scanner. We heard you folks were running over there and listened in as you took control of the fire."

"At first, and before we ran out, we though it might have been a boat exploding east of the monument," Chuck added.

"We listened in and then later heard you guys broadcast a description of a guy that you wanted to question. That's when I thought that I saw someone fitting that description enter the bathhouse, but I didn't see him come out. Chuck and I walked over to the bathhouse to see if this guy was still there. Other than a couple of guys at the urinals, it was empty. We thought it was strange and began looking around," Tom said helpfully.

Wilkens and Emerson listened attentively.

"Take a look inside of this." Tom handed Wilkens a knapsack. "Found it lying right on top of some trash in one of the trash cans."

Wilkens carefully opened the knapsack wide enough for he and Emerson to peek in.

"That's the shirt and hat he wore," Emerson confirmed as his eyes widened at the knapsack's contents.

Wilkens opened it wider to reveal a pair of dark, oversized sunglasses and a remote detonator.

"Thanks, Tom. This does change things," Wilkens said.

"Sorry, we couldn't help you more." Tom and Chuck turned and walked back to the park's office.

"Anything else about him that you can describe?" Wilkens asked Emerson.

"He wore khaki or cream shorts," Emerson offered weakly.

Wilkens' eyes swept the park, the public marina, the Jet Express dock and the downtown area on the three sides of the park. It seemed that everywhere he looked, he saw a sea of khaki or cream shorts.

"That's not going to help much. Come on back to the Blazer. We'll cruise around town and look for anyone acting suspiciously."

They returned to the Blazer with the knapsack which the chief would forward to a lab for DNA analysis. The chief radioed the new development to his police officers and had the station contact the Jet Express and Miller Ferry to be watchful for anyone wearing khaki shorts and acting suspicious. Odds were slim, but it was worth a try.

Webster's Office
Cuyahoga Falls, Ohio

~

It had been three days since Webster had given his specific instructions to Weimar and Oakes about having Malloy and P. Dayton Ford find a way to accelerate the special meeting of shareholders. They had been successful and the meeting would be held within two weeks. Webster was in the process of informing Ratek.

"Good. Now that that's handled, fire Ford and Malloy! You don't need them around anymore!" Ratek dictated.

"Fire them?" Webster questioned in disbelief.

"There's no additional value that they can bring to the transaction now. Get rid of them," Ratek directed again.

Webster had noted that Ratek seemed to be in a foul mood over the last few days. Every one of their conversations had been somewhat strained.

Ratek had been simmering about Grimes' failure to eliminate Emerson from the fray. He was also upset about the poor judgment that Grimes had shown by personally confronting Emerson rather than stepping back from the first attempt and planning another. Ratek had instructed Grimes to maintain a low profile, especially with Emerson. When the takeover was completed, Grimes could go after Emerson again.

"I'll see that they're both fired!" Webster responded uneasily.

They ended their phone conversation and Webster called Weimar and Oakes to meet with him. They joined him in minutes.

As he walked into the office, Weimar noted that Webster had not added any photos or personal possessions to his office. The signal was clear and to the point, Webster was definitely not in this for the long haul.

"Tell Ford and Malloy that they did a good job and that we won't be needing their services any longer. Also, get rid of that public relations firm in Cleveland that you're using. We can handle whatever we need to with you, Jay, and my public relations guy," Webster said slowly as he relished each word.

Weimar and Oakes had looks of surprise on their faces. This did mean that Fallsview Tire was going to roll over and allow the change in Board control to take place when the special shareholders' meeting was held in two weeks.

Webster continued, "I can tell by the look in your eyes that you both are confused. I feel that it's in the best interests of all shareholders that we allow Birkman Investments to take control. They're better suited to enhance the stock price and will come into this with no emotional attachments."

Oakes began to comment, but stopped when Weimar raised his hand. Weimar said formally, "But of course, it's your call as Chairman of the Board."

"Yes, it is, isn't it?" Webster growled. "That'll be all for now."

Weimar and Oakes stepped into the outer hallway where Weimar turned to Oakes and said, "I didn't want to do this to him in front of you. I'm going back in and fix this bad haircut."

Weimar reentered Webster's office. "Phil, do you have a moment?" he asked with his deep voice.

Webster looked up from the papers he was reviewing and

answered, "Sure, Joe, what is it?"

"About this nonsense regarding dismissing Ford and Malloy..." Weimar started.

Webster could feel his blood pressure beginning to rise as Weimar continued, "We may find it opportune from time to time to have Ford as an outside securities counsel available to provide us with additional guidance as we go through the maze of regulatory guidelines. We need to make sure that we are protecting the company. The same would hold true for Malloy, as far as providing counsel to us."

Weimar wanted to have them ready at his fingertips should a crisis develop and Webster change his mind about moving forward.

Webster first unleashed a volley of expletives at Weimar before calming down. "We can use Ratek's attorney and he's working with Peter Barkley and Wilton Partners to handle the vote accumulation for the change in control. Now, get out of here!"

Weimar left and almost walked into Oakes, who was waiting patiently in the outer hallway.

"How did it go?" Oakes asked anxiously.

"Funny thing. I went in to fix a bad haircut and walked out with a virtual lobotomy. His decision on Ford and Malloy is final. I wouldn't bring it up again. Going in there is like a trip to Disneyworld. I'd call Webster's office Fantasyland! And for us, the problem is that there's no Tomorrowland!" Weimar quipped.

Weimar left Oakes and returned to his office to make the unpleasant call to Ford to terminate his services to Fallsview Tire.

〜

Emerson put the phone down and furrowed his brow with concern. Based on his just-ended conversation with Lynn Arruda, it sounded like Webster was doing everything that he could do to derail the efforts of his team and make it easier for Ratek. The only reason someone would fire their top advisors during a takeover battle would be if they were rolling over and allowing the takeover to happen.

Emerson thought for a moment and then dialed Bob Welch at Kent State.

"Bob, it's Emerson Moore."

"Hello, Emerson. Still following the Fallsview Tire story?" Welch asked eagerly.

"Yes. Are you?"

"Do you think I could ignore this here in my own backyard?" Welch teased.

"How would you like to come up here to the island for a visit tomorrow? You could spend the night and I'd take you sailing. I've got a small catboat, but a fellow up here has a 34-foot Hunter that we can sail on. We'll sail, talk and have a nice dinner," Emerson suggested.

"Sounds like a great idea. How do I turn down an invitation to sail? I'll need to change a couple of meetings, but that shouldn't be a problem," he said.

They went over the travel arrangements and directions and

ended the call.

Emerson dialed Barry Hayen at the *Gazette* to let him know about their visitor and to have him set up the sailing trip. Hayen loved to sail too.

Putting the phone down, Emerson turned to his laptop and began typing another story about the continuing saga at Fallsview Tire. He'd e-mail it to the *Post* that afternoon so that they could run the story in the morning.

Webster's Office
Cuyahoga Falls, Ohio

~

"I don't care what you have to do! Find out who is leaking the information and fire them. This is embarrassing to both of us!" Ratek screamed into the phone as his eyes scanned the headline in the *Post* the next day. It read: *Fallsview Tire Blow Out! Fires Two Key Advisors!*

"But, Max...," Webster started.

Ratek was incensed about the leaks and interrupted Webster in mid-sentence. "This is unheard of. Somebody on the inside is responsible for this. I'll bet it's that Oakes or Weimar! You get to the bottom of this!"

"But there could be legal problems if I don't have proof. I need to conduct an investigation!" Webster pleaded.

"Do what you have to do, but get it done now!" Ratek said as he slammed the phone down.

Webster sat back in his chair for a moment before looking up a number. He picked up the phone and dialed Fallsview Tire's head of security. "Jenkins, I want to see you in my office right now."

A few minutes later Jenkins entered Webster's office.

"Close the door," Webster ordered.

Jenkins closed the door and took a seat in front of Webster.

"What I am about to request is very confidential. You are not to disclose this to any other person in this company or I will fire you and take legal action against you. Do you understand?"

An ashen-faced Jenkins nodded his head.

"I want you to bug Oakes and Weimar's phones. Someone is leaking confidential information to the press and I want to find which one of them is doing it."

"This is pretty serious," Jenkins began nervously.

"Yes, it is. Can you do it?"

"Yes sir," Jenkins responded reluctantly.

"Get it done tonight when no one is around."

Jenkins nodded his head and left Webster's office.

The Jet Express
Put-in-Bay Dock

~

The fresh morning island air greeted Bob Welch as he

disembarked with a boatload of passengers from the Jet Express onto the dock in Put-in-Bay. He walked through the crowd of golf cart and bicycle rental vendors to Emerson who was parked along Bayview in the Model A truck.

"Nice ride!" he said as he greeted Emerson.

"It's my aunt's, but I get to drive it and care for it," Emerson explained as Welch threw his small overnight bag in the truck's bed and climbed in next to Emerson.

"This is beautiful. The Jet Express ride was breathtaking and the view after you round Gibraltar Island and see Put-in-Bay for the first time is absolutely overwhelming!" Welch gushed.

"Now you know why I live here. I wake up every morning and experience this little island paradise!" Emerson stated proudly as he eased the truck into gear and then headed west on Bayview toward the Put-in-Bay Yacht Club. "I'll give you a tour of the island later. We'll head down to the yacht club, where we'll meet our sailing captain as well as a good friend of mine here on the island. His name is Barry Hayen. He's the publisher of the *Put-in-Bay Gazette*," Emerson explained.

A few minutes later, they parked the little truck next to the yacht club and were greeted by two men who looked like they were ready to go for a sail.

"Time's a wasting! We've got a good wind from the west," called one of the men whom Emerson introduced as their captain. The other was Barry Hayen.

"We're ready," Emerson said enthusiastically as they crossed the street and walked out on the dock to a 37-foot Hunter.

"There she be, the Huntress," the captain stated proudly.

A horn blew from a passing truck and Emerson turned to see Mr. Cassidy pulling to the side of the road.

"You boys going out in that fiberglass tub?" he asked jokingly.

"Sure are, Mr. Cassidy," Emerson called back.

"You boys need to go in a wooden power boat like mine. If God wanted us to have fiberglass boats, he would have made trees out of fiberglass," Mr. Cassidy teased.

"That's my aunt's boyfriend," Emerson offered as an explanation to a bewildered Welch.

"The most fun that I have is when I race parallel to a sailboat, wave at you sailors then watch as the mast sways back and forth. I just get the biggest kick out it," Mr. Cassidy chuckled.

"Now, that's not nice Cassidy," Hayen said as he pushed back at Mr. Cassidy.

"I'll be listening on the radio just in case the wind dies and you boys need a tow back into the harbor. I make more money from towing people! Got to run!" he called as he shifted the truck in gear and pulled onto Bayview to continue his errand.

"What a character!" Welch said as he let out a deep breath.

"Oh, we have all kinds of characters on this island," the captain said. "We better be going," he urged.

The Huntress seemed to strain at her lines as the wind teased her to put out into the lake.

"Nice looking boat," Welch commented as they boarded and the captain began to issue commands to ready her to sail. Within a few minutes, they were motoring away from the dock and northeastward through the harbor and then east of the island.

They ran the sails up and set the spinnaker to run with the brisk wind toward Cleveland. They filled the afternoon with sandwiches and a few glasses of wine purchased from Heineman's Winery on South Bass Island and the Mon Ami Winery on Catawba. The four sailors also chattered about the Fallsview Tire takeover battle and the idyllic life on Put-in-Bay.

Late that afternoon, they decided it was time to tack back to Put-in-Bay. They raised a small jib inside the spinnaker and, in a very smooth maneuver, they came about and dropped the spinnaker. Hayen and Emerson scrambled to stuff the spinnaker in its bag.

The captain brought the jib close to the wind and sailed close haul back in the general direction of Put-in-Bay. As they neared the mouth of Put-in-Bay's harbor, the Huntress came about. They dropped the sails and started the engine so they could motor in to the dock at the Put-in-Bay Yacht Club.

After freshening up at the yacht club's facilities, the foursome strolled up Bayview to the Crew's Nest for dinner. They were able to secure one of the tables with a green umbrella. Their table was next to the white picket fence lining Bayview and overlooked the west end of the harbor.

"To a fine day of sailing," Welch toasted as he raised his wine glass to his sailing buddies. He downed a quarter of his glass and set it on the table as he eyes roamed the enticing waterfront. "This has been just a delightful experience!"

"Must have been the company," Emerson teased.

"We're glad that you joined us today," Hayen addressed Bob Welch.

"Wouldn't have missed it for the world!"

They placed their orders and talked about life on the islands until the succulent perch and walleye dinners were served.

"Have you been running any models on the Fallsview Tire financials?" the captain, a savvy investor, asked between mouthfuls of fish.

"No. I've thought about it. Why do you ask?" Welch asked.

"There's a bunch of us up here that are always looking for a good investment. I wished that I had jumped in when their stock had bottomed and been able to ride it up. I could use a few shekels to augment my retirement income," the captain explained. "If you ever decide to take a look at it, I'd be real interested in your results. If they're going to fold, then, of course, I wouldn't want to risk it. Emerson, Barry, you interested in buying a little stock?"

"I'd like to, but I'm precluded since I'm writing a story about them. It's the paper's policy."

"I'll buy it for you. Who'd know?" the captain asked.

Hayen looked over his glass carefully at his friend, Emerson.

"Can't do it, Captain. It's one of those ethics things, you know," Emerson responded responsibly.

"Just what I hoped you would say. Barry, I like this guy," the captain said as he referred to Emerson.

"I'd better pass too," Hayen said. "I may do a story on the takeover attempt for the *Gazette*."

"Who's getting a makeover? You sound like a bunch of

women!" the voice from the sidewalk along Bayview interrupted their conversation. They looked around and saw Mr. Cassidy walking with Aunt Anne. Mr. Cassidy was occasionally running his tongue along his lips as he smiled at the group.

After brief introductions, Emerson explained, "Not makeover, Mr. Cassidy. We were talking about the Fallsview Tire takeover battle."

"Don't know nothing about takeover battles, gentlemen. How did your sail go today? Anybody get sick?" he asked mischievously with a raised eyebrow.

"Not this time," the captain replied to one of the island's biggest characters.

"Do you know why you have to give a sail boater the right of way?" Mr. Cassidy asked and continued quickly as he didn't wait for a response, "It's because they don't know how to handle a tiller!" He chuckled at his joke as the others groaned.

"James, I think that we're interrupting the gentlemen's dinner. We should be going along," Aunt Anne urged.

"I was just getting warmed up, Annie," Mr. Cassidy chortled.

"That's what I was afraid of," she responded. "Let's go, my little storyteller," she said as she tugged on his arm.

"Sorry to have to run off, boys, but when you've got charisma like me, women just don't leave you alone," he winked as he allowed himself to be pulled away.

"He's the unofficial island storyteller," Hayen explained to Welch.

"A real lovable guy. If he wasn't, I wouldn't let him hang with my aunt," Emerson added.

They finished their drinks and left with Welch promising the captain that he'd let Emerson know if he decided to run any financial models on Fallsview Tire. They walked the short distance to the Put-in-Bay Yacht Club and retrieved the truck.

"I'll take you for an evening tour of the island. We've got about 20 minutes until sunset," Emerson offered as they drove the truck downtown. He drove down Bayview and right onto Catawba then made a quick left at Delaware. Emerson drove slowly past the gift shops, restaurants and bars on Delaware and then turned right onto Toledo to Langram and out to the airport and Miller Ferry dock. He quickly made his way to the west side of the island and down West Shore to Peach Point where he parked the truck to watch the sunset.

"Listen!" he said as he cocked his head to the side. The bagpiper on Peach Point began piping the sunset to signal another day's end on Put-in-Bay, and also the official beginning of party time at the bars. The bagpipe's music carried across the harbor toward the Boardwalk and the mass of people gathered on its outdoor deck watching the sunset.

"What an end to a day!" Welch stated. "In all my days in New York City, there was nothing to compare to the magnificence of this evening."

"Ready to call it a night, or would you like to hit the Beer Barrel?" Emerson asked as he raised his foot from the brake and accelerated toward town and his aunt's house on the other side of Perry's Monument.

"Let's call it a night. I think it was the fresh air that did me in."

"I'm sure that the wine didn't have anything to do with it," Emerson kidded as they drove past Oak Point.

"Check out that old yellow car," Welch noted as they drove by.

"That's a 1939 Packard street rod. The guy who owns it thinks he's a writer. I met him once. He likes to sit there on Oak Point and write. See there. He's sitting at that table pounding away at his keyboard, trying to come up with another novel."

The writer wannabe waved as he recognized the old truck from the Sunday parades.

Emerson returned the wave. "He likes old cars and trucks and spending time on the island. We think one of these days he'll buy a place up here."

"Another potential island character?"

"Definitely!" Emerson responded.

As the truck came parallel to DeRivera Park, Welch changed his mind. "Let's stop in that Beer Barrel for one quick brew."

"Great. Pat Dailey is playing tonight," Emerson said enthusiastically as he realized that Welch would have a chance to hear the island's number one performer.

They parked the truck along the street and cut through the park to the sidewalk across from the Beer Barrel.

"If it gets too crowded later tonight, the police will shut down one of the lanes as people spill over the sidewalk and walk in the street," Emerson explained as they stopped to take in the lighted, artificial palm trees lining the front of the Beer Barrel's outside patio area.

They crossed the street and joined the crowd pushing to enter the island's fun palace where the singing of Pat Dailey drifted out from the inside of the building.

"They've got the world's longest bar in here," Emerson shouted above the noise to Welch as they found a table inside and ordered their beers.

"Is it always packed like this?" Welch yelled.

"Usually, but especially when Pat plays," Emerson yelled back as the waitress appeared with their beers.

The two turned their heads toward the stage where the bearded songster, wearing a cream ball cap and orange Put-in-Bay Tee shirt, sang his third song of the evening.

An hour later, they left the bar and returned to the truck for the short drive to Aunt Anne's house.

The next morning they slept a little later than they planned and missed breakfast with Aunt Anne, who had taken the golf cart to a meeting at the library. Emerson opted to drive Welch to Pasquale's on Delaware for a big breakfast.

"This is one of my favorite places for breakfast," Emerson told Welch as they walked through the crowded restaurant to sit at the counter.

"Packed!" Welch observed.

"Always. They've got some of the best breakfast choices on the island. You've got to try the ham and cheese omelet. It's exceptional," Emerson urged.

They ordered the omelets and wolfed them down. Then they polished it off with two large cups of Pasquale's secret roasted coffee.

"This is the best!" Welch exclaimed as he sat back and patted his stomach.

"What time do you have now?" Emerson asked as he realized that he forgot to wear his watch.

"Almost Jet Express time," Welch noted as he glanced at his watch. "I've got to be back for a noon luncheon. Couldn't cancel it," he said as they crossed the street and climbed into the old truck.

"At least, you got a break from that campus life!" Emerson mused.

"Enjoyed this tremendously," Welch replied as the truck turned right onto Catawba and then took another right onto Bayview. It moved rapidly down the street to the Jet Express dock.

"Let me know if you decide to run a financial model on Fallsview Tire. The captain sure is interested," Emerson reminded Welch.

"I'll do that. Thanks again." Welch stepped out of the truck and walked down the dock to the waiting Jet Express. He had already decided to run the model to see what it would show him.

Emerson put the truck into gear and continued eastward on Bayview to return to his aunt's house and a day full of chores that she had asked him the prior day to complete for her.

The Front Street Mall
Cuyahoga Falls, Ohio

∿

Ten days had passed since Emerson had been visited by

Welch. He had been busy with phone calls with Welch, several related meetings and two more tips from Lynn Arruda—and had placed another story in the *Post* about the continued decline of Fallsview Tire.

Emerson had driven again to Cuyahoga Falls and had checked into a room at the Sheraton Suites. He was enjoying a stroll in the late afternoon sun along the Front Street Mall. Tomorrow was the special shareholders' meeting of Fallsview Tire. But this afternoon was the start of the Crooked River Festival which included a special concert by Put-in-Bay's Pat Dailey. When Emerson heard that Pat was going to be at the festival, he had called him to let him know that he would be in town and would stop by. Pat, in turn, had invited Emerson to help him pass out trophies for the winners of the car show which would take place before the start of the concert.

Emerson walked down the long row of highly polished cars and admired each one for its uniqueness.

"Hey Emerson! Don't you love us anymore?" cried a familiar voice.

Emerson spun around and saw Jimmy from Jimmy's Café standing next to his gleaming show car.

"Sure I do," he responded as he laughed at the gregarious Jimmy. You just couldn't help but like the affable café owner.

"I thought I had you hooked on my Jimmy Specials!" Jimmy kidded. "Where have you been?"

"Stranded. It was just supposed to be a three-hour cruise," Emerson kidded.

"Come over here. I want you to meet a couple of friends of mine." Jimmy grabbed Emerson's arm and dragged him over to the DJ and a man seated in a nearby booth. "Meet two of the car show's sponsors. Aloha Phil spins the music and this is John Shapiro who publishes *Cruisin' Times*, the northeast Ohio hot rod magazine."

"Hi Phil. Cool tunes," Emerson commented.

"Nothing like good old rock and roll. Isn't that right, John?" Phil asked Shapiro.

"Usually, but tonight Phil's got that one speaker aimed right at my right ear. I'll be deaf before the night is over," the wily Shapiro responded.

"Nice ride," Emerson observed as his eyes ran carefully over the 1955 Chevy sedan delivery with an orange top and a grey pearl bottom, chrome bumpers and chrome five-spoke Astro Supreme wheels.

"It's one of only 8,000 made and great for marketing," Shapiro responded over the loud music.

"Listen guys. After the concert tonight, you're invited over to the café for Jimmy Specials, okay?" Jimmy offered.

"If you don't mind me wearing my aloha shirt," Phil teased.

"No problem, my man," Jimmy said with a huge smile.

"As long as you're buying!" Shapiro kidded.

"Okay, okay!" Jimmy winced in feigned pain.

They agreed to meet later, although Emerson indicated that he needed to make it an early night due to the meeting in the morning. He wanted to be fully alert for the next day's events.

Jimmy and Emerson walked down the mall to check out the remaining cars on display. They ran into Pat Dailey who was helping with the judging and Emerson reaffirmed his assistance in distributing the trophies. There were nearly 100 cars parked on the mall for the show.

Emerson left Jimmy with some of his other friends and returned to the outdoor amphitheater where he had an iced tea and listened as Jack Bishop's New Flames band played their set of oldies but goodies. What a lovely setting, Emerson thought as he looked around at the Front Street mall, the amphitheater, the river in the background and the towering offices of Fallsview Tire. He imagined that Webster's team was working late in order to be prepared for the next day's meeting. He wondered how prepared they would be. He also wondered how they could concentrate with the music from the band.

The New Flames finished with one of the old Meters tunes and cleared the stage. Workers hurried to ready the stage for Pat Dailey and the trophy presentations. As the car owners began taking seats, and eager fans of Pat's sought good seats, Emerson stood and walked down to the front of the stage where Mayor Trabor was talking with Pat. They both greeted Emerson as he approached them.

"Gentlemen," Emerson acknowledged in return.

"Good crowd tonight," the mayor said as he surveyed the ever-growing group of fans scrambling for seats. Every seat had been taken and people were congregating behind the last row so that they could hear Pat. "Standing room only, just like the last time you were here, Pat."

"Glad to be back, Mr. Mayor. We'll have them all standing in no time," he grinned as he ran his hand through his beard and adjusted the bill of his cap.

"Planning on attending tomorrow's meeting?" Emerson asked the mayor.

"Wouldn't miss it! I'm still hoping for a miracle. Fallsview Tire has been a cornerstone for our community," the mayor spoke with hope.

"I'll be there, too!" Emerson said. "After the stunts Fallsview pulled on Ratek last time, it'll be interesting to see what happens tomorrow."

"But the big difference is that Ratek has his own man in their now, according to your stories," the mayor noted.

"True, but you never know," Emerson said mysteriously.

"You have the inside track on what's going on in there, don't you? You know something that you want to share with me?" the mayor asked eagerly.

"Can't do that. Got to protect my sources," Emerson said cryptically.

"Here's the trophy list. Come on, Emerson, you can pass them out as I announce the winners," Pat interrupted as he turned with the list in his hand.

The mayor walked to the stage and gave Pat a warm welcome to the Crooked River Festival. It took about 10 minutes for the roguish Pat to joke through the awards as he made ribald comments about each of the owners while Emerson handed out the trophies.

Finished with the trophies, Pat picked up his guitar and sat on a stool in front of the microphone.

"Ever been to Put-in-Bay?" he asked the large crowd.

They roared back in affirmation.

"Close your eyes then, and I'll take you right back there!" Dailey said mischievously as he launched into *Great American Saturday Nite.*

Fallsview Tire & Rubber Company
Cuyahoga Falls, Ohio

~

From his office window on the top floor, Weimar watched the crowd's antics below as they moved to Pat Dailey's music. He'd prefer to be with them rather than working late this evening. Webster had ordered him to review all of the proxy material and voting regulations one more time to make sure that Weimar understood every nuance. It appeared to be meant more as punishment for Weimar and a parting shot from Webster since he had been unable to identify the leak. The events of the next day with Ratek would release Webster from his responsibility as CEO of Fallsview Tire and any further dealings with Weimar and Oakes.

Weimar sensed that the takeover was a *fait accompli.* They would be going through the motions tomorrow to bring Ratek's attempted takeover to a successful conclusion.

He turned as he heard a noise at his doorway. He saw that it was Oakes on his scooter. Their relationship had been strained as Weimar internally wrestled with his ethics about reporting Oakes as the source of the leaks. He had done his best to stay at arms-length from his co-worker.

"Long day," Oakes said with a weary voice.

Weimar was sympathetic to the emotional drain that the stress and MS played on Oakes.

"Yes, but longer tomorrow," Weimar stated forlornly.

Hearing the music, Oakes noted, "At least some people are having a bit of fun tonight."

Weimar nodded. "How are you holding up?"

Oakes recognized that Weimar was referring to his health. "I'm hanging in there. The worst moments for me and dealing with my MS were in the first few months, when women who were older than me started opening doors for me."

Weimar chuckled softly. He would miss the close relationship that the two of them had. Weimar shut down his laptop. "Time to go. Like to walk out together one last time?"

"Sure!"

The two made their way down the hall and to the parking garage with the ominous cloud of the next day's event hanging over them.

Sheraton Suites
Cuyahoga Falls, Ohio

∼

The private celebratory dinner in Max Ratek's penthouse suite on the top floor was ending. Ratek had looked around the room at the people who were responsible for his successful takeover of the tire company, which would be accomplished the next day and smiled in appreciation of their efforts. Seated at the round table were Peter Barkley from Wilton Partners, Michael Searle, Simon

Grimes, a rather tense Judith Beckwith and Phil Webster.

The champagne had flowed freely that evening as they looked forward to the culmination of their sly strategies. Ratek raised his glass and the room quieted again for another toast by the dominating host.

Ratek turned to look at Webster.

"And to our esteemed Chairman & CEO of Fallsview Tire, who so fortuitously moved into his new position where he could so brilliantly engineer tomorrow's outcome!"

Webster nodded his head in acknowledgement of the accolade as Ratek continued to feed his insatiable ego up through the last minute. Ratek wanted to be sure that there would be no last minute hitches.

At the comment about fortuitously moving into the position, Grimes smirked evilly as he recalled his effectiveness in eliminating the former chairman so that Webster could maneuver himself into the driver's seat, so to speak. Grimes had been keeping a low profile since the Put-in-Bay debacle with Emerson.

The effects of too much champagne were causing Grimes to become a bit woozy and romantic. He had been playfully grabbing Beckwith's thigh under the table where no one could see. He had grinned as she brushed his roving hand away several times before reluctantly giving in so as not to cause a stir.

Beckwith was infuriated with Grimes' boldness. She vowed to repay him in a manner that he would never forget.

"Thank you, Max," Webster replied before turning to address the entire table. "I'd also like to thank each of you for the role that you played in setting up tomorrow as a very good payday for all of us."

Webster prattled on as Peter Barkley watched and thought how Ratek played Webster like a violin. He had seen Ratek do this before. So had everyone at the table.

As Webster ended his ego trip, Ratek brought the dinner to a close. "We've got a big day ahead of us tomorrow. Shall we call it a day?"

Everyone understood that Ratek was telling them that it was time to return to their individual rooms. Beckwith was relieved to stand and move away from Grimes.

"Phil? Could you step in here a moment?" Ratek asked Webster as he stepped into the bedroom portion of the suite.

"Sure. What is it, Max?"

"Now, I want to be absolutely positive that there will be no surprises tomorrow."

Ratek looked menacingly at Webster.

Webster sensed the dangerous tone.

"No. I've met with everyone at Fallsview Tire. There shouldn't be any problems. I've got them all under my thumb," he said as he tried to muster a confident smile.

"What about that Weimar and Oakes? Expect them to try anything at the last minute?" Ratek asked as he thought about what could go wrong.

"No, I've got them under control. And tomorrow, remember that I'm running that shareholders' meeting from the podium. I can control events from there."

"I've asked Barkley to sit with me in the event that anything happens at the last minute. Just adjourn the meeting for a few minutes if you feel that we need to talk."

"I'll do that. We've got all bases covered," Webster said reassuringly.

"I'm counting on it," Ratek said sternly.

"I'll see you at the meeting, then," Ratek said as he dismissed Webster.

Webster left the suite as Ratek picked up the phone and dialed one of the other suites.

After walking out of the suite and into the hallway, Beckwith felt someone grope her bottom. She turned quickly to see Grimes grinning stupidly at her.

"Did you enjoy that?" she asked warmly as she moved closer to Grimes.

Grimes in his semi-drunk stupor thought that the ice queen was finally going to succumb to his advances as he anticipated kissing her. "Yes, nice and firm like your thighs."

"You enjoyed squeezing them tonight when I couldn't do anything, didn't you?" she smiled seductively.

"Yes and now I'm ready to make your dreams come true," Grimes responded inanely as he began to lift his arms to hold her.

"And I'm going to give you a dream that you'll never forget," she cooed captivatingly. "It's called a nightmare."

Grimes was caught completely off guard and didn't see her large purse swing up. It connected heavily under his chin, knocking him off his feet.

"You bitch...," he began as he tried to get up. In his drunken haze, he didn't see her foot with a pointed toe coming hard at him. It connected squarely at his crotch and he rolled over on the floor in pain.

"Dream about that you S.O.B.!" Judith said as she walked away.

Webster stepped into the hallway and, seeing Grimes doubled over on the floor, asked, "Is there a problem out here?"

"We just carried our celebrating a bit too far. Didn't we, Simon?" she asked coldly as she looked at the contorted, groaning figure on the floor and walked to her room.

Webster stepped into the glass elevator and took it to the first floor.

Grimes stopped groaning for a moment as he thought to himself that the bitch would pay for tonight. A nightmare would be nothing in comparison to what he was capable of doing. Revenge would be sweet, he thought.

Webster walked quickly through the large lobby and under the huge portico in front of the hotel. His car was parked in the hotel parking lot next to the Front Street sidewalk. As he walked to his car, he thought that he saw someone familiar-looking enter the hotel. He paused for a moment and then put it aside as a figment of his imagination.

After one too many glasses of champagne, he was not relishing the drive home to Cleveland and the early drive back to the office and hotel for the shareholders' meeting. He wished that he had thought ahead and spent the night at the hotel.

Oh well, he thought, after tomorrow, his mission would be

completed and he could return fulltime to his real estate business in Cleveland. He pulled out of the parking lot onto Front Street and right onto Broad. He shuddered as he drove over the bridge where Owens had been killed, and turned left onto Route 8, accelerating as he drove up the ramp.

Ratek's Room
Sheraton Suites

$\sim$

"Hello" the voice answered.

"Peter?"

"Yes?"

"It's Max."

"I just walked into my room."

"What did you think about our dinner tonight?"

"What a vain person that Webster is!" Barkley responded. "He makes me want to toss my cookies. I couldn't believe his self-conceited babbling."

"He's been that way the whole time," Ratek commented knowingly.

And at times, like you, Barkley thought to himself. "You played him well," Barkley complimented Ratek.

"He's my puppet. I pull the string and he twitches," Ratek smiled with malice. "Wouldn't it be nice if life were so simple?"

"Yes, but it's not, is it?"

"No. The reason I called is that I want to be sure again that we have all of the votes locked in tomorrow for our slate of new directors." Ratek didn't want to take any chances.

"When I checked at five o'clock, we had them. With Fallsview Tire rolling over and not trying to fight, we didn't have any problem in getting the vote for our new Board members. By late morning tomorrow, you and your new Board members will be in control of the company," Barkley replied confidently. "I've got two of my people jetting in, first thing. They'll be setting up a remote vote tabulation center in one of the conference rooms off the ballroom so that they can monitor and report the total votes for the meeting."

"Good. Well, I'll see you in the morning." Ratek hung up and walked over to the sidebar where he poured himself another glass of champagne. He stepped to the sliding glass doors, slid them open and walked onto the balcony.

It was a warm July night as he first looked down at the water rushing through the rapids and then to his left at the brightly lit headquarters building of Fallsview Tire.

He raised his glass toward the tire company and downed his champagne. Tomorrow, you're all mine, he thought as he leaned against the balcony's railing and listened to the sounds of the night.

Special Shareholders' Meeting
Sheraton Suites

～

The early morning sun cast a warm glow on the leaves of the maple trees growing precariously along the far bank of the river.

Even with the water racing through the rapids, there was a strong sense of peace along the river. Quite the opposite of what was transpiring in the hotel perched on the other side of the bank.

Tension and high energy levels seemed to grip the small army of people getting ready for the special shareholders' meeting. Like army ants, each was working diligently in their respective area of responsibility. There were levels of high activity on two floors—the main level and the floor below.

In the lobby area outside of the ballroom, Weimar caught Oakes' eye and motioned him aside. "Today's the big day," he lamented.

A TV crew hustled by with a cart brimming with equipment.

"The beginning of the end," Oakes said sadly as he thought about the potential break-up of the company.

"That actually started when Ratek made his first purchase." Weimar paused, then continued, "No, that's not correct either. It started when Owens prematurely was promoted to the CEO position and pushed through that Millington Trucking Company deal."

"You're probably right," Oakes agreed as he glanced at his watch. "It's almost 9 o'clock. I need to run. Two guys from Wilton Partners are setting up their laptops in the Boardroom Conference room so that they can monitor and tabulate the final vote today."

"I've got to check and make sure that security is set up and then check my notes at the front of the room." Weimar, as he did at the last shareholder meeting, would be sitting on the raised dais as the company's chief legal officer and secretary to assist Webster with running the company's final meeting of shareholders.

Weimar walked over to the Fallsview Tire's head of Security as Oakes opened the throttle on his scooter and raced to the conference room.

"What in the hell happened to you?" Ratek screamed when he saw Grimes enter his suite to join the team for breakfast and a last minute discussion.

Grimes rubbed the black and blue mark under his chin and looked at Beckwith who was sitting so coolly at the table, ignoring him as she spooned another piece of fruit into her inviting mouth. Still smug and superior aren't you, Grimes thought, as he looked at how she ignored him. You'll regret last night, he vowed to himself.

"Afraid that I had a bit too much to drink last night and I took a tumble when I got to my room," Grimes explained.

Ratek had noticed the look that Grimes had given the well-coiffured Beckwith and the lack of reaction on her part. He was suspicious.

"Are you sure that was all that happened?" he probed.

"Yes, that's it. What do we have for breakfast here?" Grimes asked as he tried to stop Ratek's questioning and gazed at the small buffet breakfast which had been served.

They concluded their breakfast and went over their plans for the shareholders' meeting.

∽

Weimar was standing on the raised dais and looking through his thick notebook of parliamentary rules and procedures when Webster appeared at his side.

"All set, Joe?" Webster asked as he glanced around the room to see it quickly filling. The excitement promised by this event had attracted a high request for admission tickets and a large turnout was expected.

"Yes," Weimar responded as he waved briefly at Cuyahoga Falls Mayor Trabor and his contingent from the city. They were very concerned about the financial impact that any break-up of the company would have on the local economy and its citizens. "In some ways, Phil, this reminds me of the Alamo, but the big difference was that they fought to the bitter end."

Webster's eyes narrowed. "That's enough of that shit, Joe! Just do your job!"

Webster stormed off to greet Ratek and his legions of attendees, and to personally escort them to their reserved seats in the front row. Ratek's contingent included Peter Barkley from Wilton Partners, Michael Searle, Judith Beckwith, Simon Grimes and the 10 new Board members who would be elected to their terms that day. Webster had reserved seats for the old Board members in the last row of the ballroom. He wanted them out of the way.

"Good morning, Max!" Webster beamed as he greeted his comrade in arms.

"Morning. Everything under control?" Ratek asked with concern.

"Without a doubt!" Webster replied confidently as he smiled at the attractive, but aloof Beckwith. Everything had been coming together as they had planned. "I should get up to the podium and start the last rites," he laughed at his reference to the meeting and walked to the front of the ballroom.

Fallsview Tire's security team began to close the doors to the ballroom when a furtive figure slipped through and was able to find one seat in the last row.

Webster stepped to the podium which had the name "Phil Webster" in large letters on the front. The Fallsview Tire & Rubber Company name was not in evidence. Just another ego trip on Webster's part.

"Good morning. I would like to call this momentous meeting into session. When I took over this position unexpectedly a few weeks ago, I promised to deliver a return to our shareholders and today I am delivering on that promise." Webster paused and smiled in self-aggrandizement. "I would like to introduce to each of our shareholders your new Board members who will take decisive action to deliver a high return on your investment."

Oakes winced from the back of the room as Webster introduced Ratek and the rest of his sycophants. He had been nursing his wounded pride when Webster excluded him in preparing his final speech to shareholders. Oakes sat in the back of the room with a sense of resignation.

"Seated on my right is our company general counsel and secretary, Joseph C. Weimar. Mr. Weimar would you kindly provide our shareholders with the formal report of the results of our proxy tabulation?" Webster asked as he followed his script.

Weimar gritted his teeth and responded. "Yes, Mr. Chairman. The preliminary results of the vote tabulation show that 63 percent of the votes from shareholders have been tabulated and indicate that the incumbent Board members have been replaced by the slate of directors proposed by Birkman Investments. As we have done in the past, the polls will remain open for another 15 minutes."

Weimar sat back in his chair and looked at Webster.

Webster began a 15-minute speech which highlighted his accomplishments over the last few weeks—another show of his vanity. Displays of the new Jupiter tire and banners lined the room.

Boardroom Conference Room
Sheraton Suites

~

Steve Graham and Rob Wilson from Wilton Partners had been monitoring the vote tabulation on their laptop. Graham would have to run the final vote in to Weimar at the close of the polls which would happen in another 14 minutes. The final vote would affect the formal transfer of power to Ratek.

Graham had been staring out the window at the view of the river when he heard Wilson exclaim.

"Oh, oh."

Graham turned as Wilson screamed, "Look at this!"

Graham raced to Wilson's side to look at the laptop's large screen.

"They're flipping their votes! They're voting against Ratek's new Board! They can't do that!" Wilson moaned.

"I'll call Institutional Voting Services," Graham said frantically as he looked at his watch. Only minutes to go before they had to report the vote tally.

With all of the corporate governance issues and voting liability issues, Institutional Voting Services had emerged as a third-party organization to review proxy material and cast votes on behalf of its member pension funds, which consisted of 98 percent of the funds in existence. The pension funds had abdicated their right to vote to Institutional Voting Services.

Graham was quickly connected to his contact at IVS.

"Brian, it's Steve Graham. What's going on with the IVS vote on Fallsview Tire this morning? Is this aberration being caused by a computer problem? We're minutes away from closing the polls!" Graham's deluge of questions swamped Brian at the other end of the phone.

"Plain and simple, Steve. IVS is changing its vote," Brian replied.

"But why?" Graham pleaded as he sought to understand why.

"IVS now believes that it would be in the best interest of shareholders to maintain the incumbent Board."

"And that idiot, Webster?" Graham asked. Barkley had filled him in on how egocentric Webster was.

"That's all that I can say," Brian said.

"There's more to this than what you're telling me!" Graham said with growing suspicion.

"I've said all that I can say. Got to run." The phone line went dead.

"What are we going to do?" Wilson asked as he watched the vote change in favor of the incumbent Board.

"I'll call Barkley. You need to write the final tabulation as we see it."

Graham called Barkley on his cell phone with no response. Graham didn't realize that Barkley had reached into his pocket to switch his cell phone from ring to vibrate and had accidentally turned the phone off.

"No answer!" a panicked Graham told his assistant as he grabbed the final tally and began to run it down to the ballroom.

Ballroom
Sheraton Suites

∽

A frazzled-looking Graham entered the ballroom and made his way down the far aisle to the raised dais whereupon he handed the final vote tabulation to Weimar.

As he entered the room the furtive figure in the last row slipped out of the ballroom to make a quick cell phone call and quickly reentered the ballroom to retake his seat in the rear.

Webster, Ratek and Barkley watched Graham as he walked down the far aisle and handed the tally to Weimar. Barkley and Ratek were concerned by the frantic look on Graham's face.

"Better go find out what that's about," Ratek said as he leaned over to Barkley. Barkley stood and walked to the rear of the room and out into the hallway where he met Graham.

Weimar's eyes widened in amazement as he opened the

envelope and read the surprising results.

"Mr. Weimar, do you have the final results of the vote tabulation?" a concerned Webster asked from the podium.

"Yes, I do. Yes, I do," Weimar repeated with a huge smile.

"Could you please disclose the results to our shareholders?" Webster pushed anxiously.

"The voting polls are now officially closed. The proposal to elect the slate of new Board members has been defeated by an overwhelming vote of 78 percent against."

Weimar's eyes sought out Oakes at the rear of the ballroom and he shot Oakes a huge grin.

Screams of excitement and shock filled the ballroom and mixed with applause from the employees in attendance and the city government officials. Webster slumped over the podium in utter disbelief. Ratek's face was flushed with anger at this totally unexpected turn of events.

Before Ratek or Webster could say anything, the doors at the rear of the ballroom burst open and a contingent of visitors led by former Fallsview Tire CEO Steve Walent entered the room. The contingent included ousted CFO Cliff Bronson, P. Dayton Ford, Jimmy Malloy, Gary Welson, Bob Welch and Emerson Moore. They stopped next to the last row where they were joined by the incumbent Board members and the furtive figure who had been seated in the last row. It was Emerson's friend, Barry Hayen, from the *Put-in-Bay Gazette*.

The contingent walked to the front of the room amidst the flash of cameras capturing the moment and, with the exception of Emerson and Hayen, stepped on the dais. Emerson and Hayen found two unoccupied seats in the front row from where they could take notes for their story. Walent stepped to the podium and took control of it from the shocked Webster.

He looked at Weimar and started, "Mr. Weimar, as a result of the voting tabulation, the incumbent Board members have retained their seats and have elected me, effective immediately, as Chairman of the Board and Chief Executive Officer, my prior position with the company. Do you see any legal issues with this action?"

Weimar looked behind Walent and at the cherubic, smiling P. Dayton Ford and back to Walent. He responded enthusiastically, "No sir. And welcome back, Mr. Walent."

Weimar sat back in his chair to watch what would happen next. He had a feeling that he was going to enjoy the next few minutes.

"Thank you, Joe. With that behind us, Mr. Webster, I would kindly ask you to remove yourself from this dais and take a seat next to your good friend, Mr. Max Ratek. I'll be conducting this meeting from this point forward. Ladies and gentlemen, this has been a long and trying time for many of us. I'd like you to make yourselves comfortable as I share some of the events of the last weeks and our plan to turn around Fallsview Tire."

The 60-year-old CEO continued, "As many of you know, I resigned from this position two years ago to take care of my Emily in her last days. She had been so supportive of me in my career, it was my turn to support her with my undivided attention. That, I did.

"A few weeks ago, I received an interesting phone call from one of my good friends, Barry Hayen." Walent turned and grinned at Barry in the front row before continuing. "Barry's the publisher of the *Put-in-Bay Gazette*. I've got a cottage on Peach Point on South Bass Island. He wanted me to meet with a reporter from the

Washington Post regarding a story that he was developing about the attempted takeover of Fallsview Tire." He paused to glance at Emerson seated next to Hayen.

From their seats in the front row, on the other side of the aisle, Ratek and Webster glared at Emerson.

"I had been following the takeover attempt and initially met with Emerson to give him some background information on the company. The more that we talked, the more that I realized how much I missed the fray and leading the company. It was something that actually evolved over the last few weeks.

"Emerson, Barry and I met with Bob Welch from Kent State University when he was invited up to the island to see Emerson and take a sail on my boat, the Huntress. Bob, for those of you who don't know, runs the Masters of Science Program in Financial Engineering and a mock trading floor in the school of business. He also headed one of the major investment houses on Wall Street before his move to Kent. It turned out that Bob had been following developments at Fallsview Tire for some time.

"After we talked, Bob went back to the university and ran several business models. Using mathematics, computer science, statistics and economics, he created several simulations. The simulations helped us develop a wide range of potential financial solutions to this mess that Fallsview Tire is in. He also worked with Cliff Bronson, who was my right-hand man as CFO when I was here before. Cliff was released prematurely by the company. I'll discuss the turnaround strategy in a few moments."

Grimes was fidgeting in his seat as he watched the impact that Emerson had had on spinning this out of control for Ratek. If only he had been successful in killing Emerson, he thought.

"When our friend, Mr. Webster, decided to cut loose several key advisors—which absolutely astonished me—we contacted them. We invited P. Dayton Ford, one of Wall Street's leading takeover attorneys; Jimmy Malloy, the proxy vote expert; and Gary Welson from Cleveland's public relations and investor relations firm, Dunhill & Easton, to meet with us and join the team I was putting together to thwart Mr. Ratek at the eleventh hour. Funny thing, it's not too hard to pull together a meeting when you invite people to meet at your cottage on an island, especially when it's in Put-in-Bay!"

The crowded ballroom tittered at this last comment.

"We put together a strategy that involved split-second timing this morning and the utmost secrecy. People were brought in on a limited need-to-know basis. Last night, we met in a conference room below this floor and went over our strategy. Malloy had arranged to have representatives from Institutional Voting Services arrive at the office early this morning. The proposed turnaround strategy was e-mailed to them this morning and we had a teleconference with them shortly after they received it. They liked the turnaround plan that we developed with Kent State's system, knew my past history in successfully leading this company and saw that the long term potential for a greater return would be realized from my team and not Mr. Ratek's team. Shortly after 10 o'clock this morning they began flipping their vote to support the incumbent Board members."

Ratek was outraged by the sheer audacity of their approach. He glared vehemently at Webster who had slid lower in his chair.

Ed Madigan, one of Jimmy Malloy's staff, entered the ballroom and walked to the podium where he handed a piece of paper to Walent. Walent looked at the paper and then announced proudly to the room, "Hold onto your hats everyone. It looks like Fallsview Tire is in for a record day in trading volume. The stock is already up three dollars a share on the news of what's transpired here today. I'd like to thank Mr. Emerson Moore for the story he put on the wire this morning about what was happening!"

Emerson nodded in acknowledgement. He had written as much as he could and e-mailed it before they had entered the ballroom. Malloy's team had also been monitoring the voting tabulation on their laptop and had provided Walent and Emerson with the vote tally. To make sure that the contingent knew when to enter the room and to take notes of what was transpiring before they entered, Emerson had arranged for Hayen from the *Put-in-Bay Gazette* to sit in the rear of the room and to step out of the meeting to call them so they'd know it was time to make their dramatic entrance.

Ratek quickly calculated what the increased stock price meant to his investment and smiled. Maybe he wouldn't lose financially on the deal. He'd walk away with a bruised and battered ego. Although, that still didn't sit well with him.

The door at the rear of the ballroom opened and a tall, well-dressed gentleman entered.

"I'd like to introduce to you another key player in this turnaround strategy. He just entered the room. Louis, don't sit down. Folks meet Louis Barnhill, the president of Millington Trucking. Millington Trucking, you will recall, caused a number of major problems for Fallsview Tire. I talked with Louis last night and told him about our plans for today. During that conversation, we agreed to spin off Millington Trucking and will be assisting them in their return as a public company.

"Some of you may recall that their pension is over funded. We have agreed to a pension reversion which will allow us to guarantee the pension benefit for his employees and allow both companies to share equally in the amount of the over funding. We will use that amount to pay for the takeover battle fees and our plans to restore profitability."

Weimar was quickly calculating the impact all of this would have on the value of the company stock in his company 401k plan and what it would do for the other employees. He found it difficult to contain his glee.

"I'm also announcing plans to offer stock options to every employee of Fallsview Tire. By golly, we're in this together and we will win together. Their stock options will be priced at market value. If the board decides, and I hope you do," Walent glanced at his standing Board members, "to grant me a stock option, I'd like it set at an amount 20 percent higher than our employees. I want them to win first and our shareholders to win before I win. And by the way, Board members, I'd recommend you, too, set your stock options at a 20 percent premium over the daily average stock price."

Walent went on another 20 minutes before concluding the meeting as he detailed his innovative, values-based plans to create a positive workplace and deliver shareholder value. He then adjourned the meeting.

The podium was swamped by well-wishers as the crowd surged to welcome Walent back to the helm.

Ratek stood and looked at Webster, "You nauseate me. Why don't you just slink back to Cleveland?"

Webster didn't respond. He couldn't. For one of the first times in his life, he was speechless. He retrieved his briefcase from the podium area and left the building, ignoring reporters' pleas for an interview.

Ratek next turned on Grimes. He leaned in close to him and said, "None of this. None of this would have happened if you had done your job with that nosy reporter. He pulled this off!"

Grimes cowered under his boss' berating.

"Let's go." Ratek turned and started for the door followed closely by his demoralized team. They were not looking forward to the drive to the airport or the flight back to New York.

A number of reporters tried to stop Ratek to interview him, but he barged right through them as if they didn't exist.

Weimar and Oakes met halfway in the far aisle.

"Who would have guessed this happening!" Oakes exclaimed.

"Quite a surprise," Weimar agreed. "Now, you can relax about this leaking inside information stuff. But, as your legal counselor, I'd suggest that you cease and desist."

Oakes looked at Weimar in surprise. "I didn't leak anything. I thought it was you."

"Me? Oh come now. I couldn't do something like that. It's absolutely unethical. If you didn't leak it, who did?" Weimar asked in a quandary.

They were both surprised when a voice interrupted their thoughts.

"Joe and Jay, I'd like you to meet my niece."

Weimar and Oakes turned around to see Lita standing with a blonde haired woman. "This is Lynn Arruda."

Lynn extended her hand and was shaking their hands when she suddenly squealed in surprise. She had been hugged from behind by Emerson Moore.

"Hi Lynn. It's been quite a morning, hasn't it?" Emerson asked.

Weimar's and Oakes' eyes went from Emerson to Lynn to Lita.

"Emerson, this is my aunt whom I've been telling you about. She's been the CEO's executive assistant for years."

"So you're the one I've heard so much about!" Emerson said as he realized who was the source of the leaked information. Emerson leaned close to Lynn and whispered, "I thought your source was a male."

"I couldn't tell you everything," she said as she winked.

"Lita!" Weimar and Oakes cried virtually in unison.

"What? What?" she asked with a mischievous look.

"Have you been a bad girl lately?" Weimar asked cryptically.

"Nothing that I can tell you about. You're the company's head legal beagle. However, what I can tell you is that whatever you're alluding to is now in the past and won't happen again," she said as suggestively as a 61-year-old female could say.

"Promise?" Weimar asked as he interpreted that she would not leak confidential information again.

"Promise," she responded.

"You two have a thing going or what?" Emerson asked perplexed by the cryptic nature of the exchange.

"Nothing that we can tell you about, my dear," Lita grinned wickedly.

"Aunt Lita!" Lynn teased.

Oakes and Weimar exchanged looks and the tension between the two over the last few weeks evaporated.

Changing the subject, Oakes stated as he looked at Emerson, "So you've been a very busy boy behind the scenes."

"More than I had planned," Emerson replied. "Originally, I was tracking down information for my story. You can imagine my surprise when I visit some guy in his cottage on Peach Point and learn that he's the retired CEO of Fallsview Tire!"

"I thought you'd be surprised," a voice spoke from behind Emerson. Emerson whirled around to see Barry Hayen from the *Put-in-Bay Gazette* approaching. Emerson quickly introduced everyone.

"I didn't say anything to Emerson up front about Walent being the former CEO. I didn't want to get his hopes up and then crush them if Walent wouldn't meet with him," Hayen explained.

"Sounds like you have a lot of interesting people on that island," Weimar concluded as he thought about Hayen's comment and what he knew about Emerson.

"Oh, we have a lot of interesting people on the island. Don't we, Emerson?" Hayen asked.

"I agree!"

"Our islanders work hard in the summer and then have the multiple talents and skills to survive the brutal winters when we become extremely self-sufficient. We're virtually cut off from the mainland," Hayen said.

"Anyhow, back to the story. We brought Bob Welch in from Kent State and the next thing we know, they're working on a turnaround," Emerson offered.

"Fascinating. Absolutely fascinating. It's too bad that Jay and I couldn't have been intimately involved in this adventure of yours. I would have relished it," Weimar said with feigned despair.

"So, will you two be sharing the next Pulitzer Prize award?" Oakes asked as he looked at Emerson and Hayen.

Emerson laughed. "I certainly don't expect another award to come my way. Because we worked together on this, we are sharing the byline in the final story."

Hayen grinned at the comment.

Carli Dansen now approached the group. "Hey everybody, there's an early appreciation luncheon downstairs in the Reflections Lounge. Walent has invited us all to attend." Seeing Lita and Lynn start to walk away, Carli continued, "And Lita, you can bring your guest with you."

Oakes saw that Walent was surrounded by a phalanx of reporters and that Welson was helping manage the impromptu press conference. "I need to excuse myself and get involved with that interview. I'll see you all downstairs."

The group watched as Oakes scootered over to Walent and observed that the company's Board members, P. Dayton Ford and Jimmy Malloy were beginning to head to the luncheon. They decided to join them.

Weimer thought as he walked, that the afternoon—and the next several weeks, for that matter, were going to be extremely busy and yet energizing for the senior management team—and the rest of the company's employees. He smiled to himself about the new sense of vitality which he was feeling.

Ratek's Jet
Over Pennsylvania

~

The limo ride to the Akron-Canton Airport and the early stages of the flight were conducted in a cold silence as Ratek continued to brood about the last-minute and unexpected resistance which rebuffed his control of Fallsview Tire. He was extremely anxious about the call he would have to place to Hollingsworth. He expected that Hollingsworth had already seen the breaking news on the failed takeover attempt and knew that Ratek had been outsmarted.

Ratek looked around the aircraft at his cowering team— Michael Searle, Judith Beckwith and Simon Grimes. He thought to himself how Peter Barkley had conveniently found an excuse to stay with his team to wrap up the reporting and escape his wrath on the plane. It was a good move on Barkley's part as Ratek was going to have his head for not ensuring that a vote flip wouldn't happen. They had never incurred this type of twist in the past, but Barkley should have anticipated it.

Ratek needed to vent. He unleashed a torrent of expletives at each of the plane's occupants. After 20 minutes of tongue-lashing, he felt his anger beginning to somewhat subside. He asked Beckwith and Searle to take seats at the rear of the plane so that he could talk privately with Grimes.

Grimes looked concerned as Ratek motioned for him to come closer.

"Kill that *Post* reporter! Do you understand me? You kill him! No if's, and's or but's. You kill him!" Ratek dictated harshly.

"I'll get it done. There won't...," Grimes started nervously.

"I don't want to hear it. Don't fail me!" Ratek interrupted angrily and forcibly.

The balance of the plane ride continued in icy silence with Searle and Beckwith electing to stay in the rear of the plane where they felt they were somewhat distanced from Ratek's rage.

Jimmy's Café
Cuyahoga Falls

∽

After lunch and a brief one-on-one interview with Walent and CFO Bronson, Emerson and Hayen had excused themselves to finalize their story for the next day's *Post*. Once it was completed, they had plans to meet with Lynn Arruda and her aunt at Jimmy's Café.

"Wow!" Hayen said as they approached the uniquely painted building. "Reminds me of New Orleans and Mardi Gras!"

"Sure does. Jimmy, the owner, lived a number of years in New Orleans! He's a very talented artist. So's his wife, Carla," Emerson responded as they entered the café.

Hayen devoured the New Orleans style décor and artfully painted walls of the astonishing café. The shelving units and wall paintings reminded Hayen of sights he had seen in New Orleans.

"Quite a sight!" Hayen said as he stepped to the coffee bar.

"Well, thank you!" said the female worker wearing the low-cut top which struggled to contain her rather large bosom.

Hayen's face turned red as he realized that she thought he was referring to her cleavage.

Emerson stepped in. "Hi, Natalie. We'll take two Jimmy Specials with extra chocolate syrup!"

"Okay, Emerson," she responded with a seductive smile. "Buffie, I'll take care of this one," she called back to her co-worker as she stepped away to prepare the two specials.

Still looking embarrassed by her misperception, Hayen said to Emerson, "I was talking about the paintings!"

"I know," Emerson grinned. "She was just funning you!"

The tall owner with the thick gray tousled hair walked into the order area. Upon seeing Emerson, he warmly welcomed him. "It's been a while, Emerson. You staying out of trouble, my friend? Don't want you getting into trouble, you know."

"I've been staying relatively out of trouble," he responded with a raised eyebrow. "Although, I can't say the same for my friend here. He's a bit embarrassed because Natalie mistook his admiring comment about the photos as a comment about her cleavage!" Emerson chuckled at his friend's predicament.

"Oh, you mean C.C.?" Jimmy asked.

"C.C.?" Emerson didn't understand.

"It's the new name that people here have given her. C.C. or Community Cleavage! She got a big kick out of it!"

Hayen and Emerson moaned.

He introduced Jimmy to Hayen, and then spying something in Jimmy's hand asked, "What do you have there?"

Excitedly, Jimmy answered. "It's my new poem. Would you like me to read it to you?"

"Yes! By all means," Emerson responded as Natalie returned with the coffee and Emerson paid the bill.

"It's called Pink Velvet Ladies," Jimmy explained enthusiastically as he started to read his poem in his soft, warm and friendly voice,

"Pink Velvet Ladies are spawned in all the right places
And debut on earth with velvety pink faces
Wrapped in the proper historical shawl
They never-the-less look baby small.

Pink Velvet Ladies coo on stretched satin sheets
Dressed in baby fashions from baby boutiques.

Pink Velvet Ladies are rocked with an African beat
While their cocoa-buttered mothers keep out of the heat
And Daddy writes cheques with black Indian ink.

Pink Velvet Ladies go to private places
Where they learn French and social graces
And gloss the lips of their pink velvet faces."

Jimmy ended the poem and was silent.

"Marvelous!" complimented Hayen.

"Jimmy, you're the best," Emerson added in wide-eye amazement. "You're one of the most talented people that I've ever met!"

"Thank you," Jimmy said with heartfelt modesty.

"We've got to get you to make a visit to Put-in-Bay sometime," Emerson commented.

"You'd fit right in with the folks on the island," Hayen mused.

"There's a talented lady up there who just completed a beautiful sculpture of *Winged Victory*. It's a statue that was displayed at the old Victory Hotel which burned to the ground years ago. You two would have a riot sharing stories and your talents!" Emerson added as he thought about his friend, Judy.

"I'd like that. Hey, kiddo!" he called as Lynn Arruda and her aunt walked into the café.

Lynn exchanged greetings, made introductions and placed their orders. "Let's sit on the patio," she suggested and they retreated to the front patio as Jimmy went back to his other customers.

"It's been quite a day!" Emerson remarked as they each took a seat under one of the tables shaded by green umbrellas.

"I gather that it has," Lynn responded.

"How are things going in the office?" Emerson asked Lita.

"Well, I need to be careful how I answer that. We have policies about leaking information!" she replied with an all-knowing smile.

"Aunt Lita! Certainly you can offer an overall comment about how the day went," Lynn urged.

"As long as it's off the record?" Lita said as she looked at the two newspapermen.

"Off the record," Emerson agreed.

"Ditto!" Hayen said.

"It was like a breath of fresh air. We've been running so long. We had the wind knocked out of us. Today, there was a sense of renewal spreading through the whole company and a lot of excitement about all of us getting stock options!"

"What a beautiful quote! And we can't use it!" Emerson moaned. Looking at Lynn, he commented, "I still can't get over that you misdirected me by telling me that it was a guy friend of yours leaking the information."

"I didn't want to get Aunt Lita in trouble. Forgive me, Emerson, please!" Lynn looked at Emerson with her deep blue eyes.

"How could I ever say no to you, Lynn? Of course, you're forgiven," Emerson stated easily.

They talked for another hour before wrapping up their conversation with promises from the two ladies to make the trek to visit them in Put-in-Bay. Emerson and Hayen walked over to Emerson's car for the drive back to Put-in-Bay.

Ratek's Office
New York City

~

The sky over lower Manhattan was darkened by the ominous clouds rolling in. Thunderstorms had been predicted for late afternoon.

Ratek had been pacing in his office for the last half hour as he strategized how he would open his conversation with Hollingsworth. He glanced at his watch as the skies opened and a torrential downpour made the disappointing day even more dreary. He reached for the phone and called.

"Yes?" the voice on the other end answered.

"Sir Edward, it's Max," he started with feigned confidence.

"I know who it is. I recognized the voice. I've been expecting your call all day. What's taken you so long to call?" Sir Edward asked with a formal, muted tone.

"I didn't have a chance to get to a phone where we could talk privately," he said as he provided a very lame excuse.

"I see," Sir Edward responded with apparent disdain and a perception that Ratek was not telling the truth. "Rather messy day, wasn't it?"

"That would be an understatement," Ratek said nervously.

"Indeed it would," Sir Edward retorted firmly. "What do you have to say for yourself?"

Trying to shift blame, Ratek started, "It was Peter Barkley at Wilton Partners who didn't foresee the potentiality of their move."

"Max, who has ultimate responsibility?" Sir Edward quizzed stoically.

"I do."

"Then don't try to bullshit me with excuses. You're usually the vanquisher. Today you were vanquished. It was an overwhelming defeat for our dear Michelangelo of Wall Street and wrought, no less, by a reporter. Tsk. Tsk, Max," Sir Edward said mockingly.

Ratek was quiet. His usual swagger had evaporated.

"Nonetheless, I'll still expect the agreed upon minimum return on my investment," Sir Edward stated somberly.

"Of course," Ratek agreed as he quickly calculated in his mind the gain on the stock price, the return on investment to Sir Edward and the costs of this ill-fated escapade. He frowned as he realized that overall, he had lost money on the hapless attempt.

"I'll expect it within the week. Goodbye."

The phone line went dead. Sir Edward had never hung up on Ratek before. In fact, no one hung up on Ratek.

"Max?" the voice on the intercom asked.

"Yes."

"We're in the conference room. We've pulled together the financials on Zeus in Chicago," Searle's voice announced as he used the code name for the next takeover attempt. Ratek smiled that his team hadn't wasted any time in pulling themselves up by their bootstraps and digging into the next target. That was one of the traits of Birkman Investments—always targeting companies to take ownership positions and turn them around or break them up.

"I'll be right there," Ratek replied as a burst of energy, stimulated by going into the next hunt, surged through him. He replayed in his mind the initial strategy that had been drafted for the Zeus takeover as he walked to the conference room.

He swung open the door and saw Searle, Beckwith, Grimes and two junior analysts in the room poring through documents. He noticed that Beckwith was seated away from Grimes and smiled. Grimes didn't understand the signals from Beckwith that she was not interested in being romantically involved with Grimes. Ratek had been watching the interplay for the last few months and enjoyed the conflict between the two. He felt that it helped create an edginess and creative tension amongst the team members.

He settled into a chair and opened the files placed in front of him.

"Looks like this one is ripe for raping and pillaging," Grimes said as he reviewed the files. Beckwith threw him a look of utter disgust and looked back at her documents.

"We're back in the hunt!" Ratek said as he began to review the next target's financials. Hopefully, this one would be easier than today's debacle, he thought.

He joined the others in a focused detailed review of the documents which was interrupted at 7 P.M. with the delivery of sandwiches, appetizers and an ice bucket filled with ice.

Searle opened the cabinet at the end of the conference room and began to mix drinks for the attendees. Beckwith joined him to help with the drinks and started breaking up the ice in the bucket with an ice pick.

Grimes allowed his eyes to rove over Beckwith's figure as she stood with her back toward him. Her tight, light blue suit with the thigh-high skirt was especially appealing to Grimes.

Once the drinks were prepared, Beckwith volunteered to serve them. When she approached Grimes, and without anyone being able to see what he was doing, Grimes ran his hand up her calf. Without a moment's hesitation, Beckwith dumped the drink-laden tray on Grimes' lap, soaking and staining his slacks.

Grimes swore as Beckwith apologized, "I am so sorry. I just get so clumsy at times! I'll fix new drinks for everyone."

Grimes took charge. "I'll fix the drinks!"

Beckwith turned to look at Grimes and gave him an indifferent stare as he began to mix the drinks. Grimes was careful to make the drinks for himself and Beckwith extra strong. Once finished, he walked around the table and served everyone. He tossed the tray on the cabinet top and grabbed his drink.

Grimes slowly raised his glass to his lips and slyly looked over the rim of the glass to watch Beckwith take her usual big first gulp. He watched with glee as the look in her eyes showed her surprise at how strong the drink was. No one else noticed Beckwith's initial reaction.

Beckwith glared at Grimes, then picked up the drink and downed the rest of it in one huge gulp. Grimes was impressed that she wasn't going to show any weakness.

Beckwith stood and pronounced, "You guys need to try to keep up with me! Who's ready for another?"

Grimes finished his drink and rose to her challenge, "I'll take another."

Ratek and Searle had not been paying attention to their antics, but were more focused on continuing the review of the documents. They echoed that they didn't need another round.

Beckwith stood, broke up the ice and mixed drinks. She made hers a double and Grimes a triple shot. She smiled to herself as she thought about the surprise in store for Grimes when he took his drink. She served the drinks and sat down to stonily watch Grimes.

Grimes expected that she'd pull some sort of stunt and was very careful as he took his first sip. He saw her watching him closely for his reaction. The drink was strong, very strong. He took a deep breath and tossed it down in virtually one large gulp and then stared at her with a sly smile as if to challenge her. Bring it on, baby, he thought to himself.

Beckwith tossed hers down also in a display of machismo and stared defiantly back at Grimes and smiled. She felt the effects of the liquor impacting her and was glad when Ratek looked up from his files and spoke.

"I think it's time to call it a night. It's almost 10 o'clock."

Searle concurred, "Sounds good to me." He started picking up the files.

Grimes felt a bit woozy from the evening's drinking. He stood and wobbled.

Ratek noticed and asked, "Too much to drink tonight, Simon?"

Grimes grabbed the back of the chair to steady himself. "Maybe, just a bit too much. I'm heading for home," he slurred. Grimes walked unsteadily out of the conference room as Beckwith watched with an aloof smile.

Ratek, Searle and Beckwith finished gathering the documents and Beckwith helped Searle carry them to his office where they would be secure. Ratek stopped by Searle's office as he was leaving.

"Anyone need a ride? It's still raining outside."

Searle grabbed his briefcase "Sure. I'll catch a ride with you."

"Judith, care for a ride?" Ratek asked his attractive employee.

"No. I'm going to put the bottles away in the cabinet, then head for home," she replied.

"We can wait for you," Ratek offered.

"No. No. Just go ahead. I'll catch a cab."

"Okay, it's your decision," Ratek said as he and Searle headed for the outer office door.

Beckwith returned to the conference room and began to clean up. She was bending over to place a whiskey bottle on one of the lower shelves when two arms encircled her waist. She stood up quickly and whirled around to come face to face with a very drunk Grimes. She thought that he had left the office and hadn't heard him re-enter the conference room.

"Waiting for me, my dear?" he asked with his foul breath.

"Only in your nightmares," she retorted. "Now, let me go," she demanded as she struggled to loosen herself from his arms.

Grimes held her tighter and pulled her closer. "We are really meant for each other. We're both strong individuals," he slurred.

Beckwith reached her right hand behind her for leverage on the cabinet. Her hand brushed the eight-inch ice pick with the wooden handle. She didn't realize it at first, but recalled what it was when Grimes started to slobber kisses on her neck.

Beckwith's hand closed around the ice pick's handle and she started to raise it.

Grimes wasn't so drunk that his self-preservation defense was off. He had learned a lesson from her in the hallway of the Sheraton Suites and knew he had to keep an eye on her. Seeing through his drunken haze that her arm was rising with the ice pick, he pulled back and slapped her hard across the right cheek and then across the left cheek. The ice pick dropped to the floor and rolled under the edge of the cabinet.

"Nice try, my little bitch. Were you going to use that on me? I'll teach you what pain is." Filled with fury and pumped with adrenaline, Grimes threw Beckwith to the floor, tearing off her suit jacket as she fell.

Her blonde hair spread out on the floor. She turned over and got on all fours and tried to crawl away, but Grimes grabbed her by one foot and abruptly jerked her back to him as he kneeled on the floor.

"I'm going to make you scream like you've never screamed," Grimes shrieked as he lowered his body on top of hers.

"No man makes me scream," she roared as her right hand found the fallen ice pick and grasped it firmly. She swung it up as Grimes readied to slap her again. With hair in her eyes, she struck blindly. The ice pick struck something soft and she continued to push it in deeper without knowing where it was.

Grimes' eyes bulged in pain and his inhuman cry filled the air with a guttural scream. His head jerked back with the ice pick deeply imbedded in the left side of his neck. It had pierced his carotid artery.

Beckwith shook her hair out of her eyes and saw the ice pick protruding from his neck. She pulled it out and struck again. The blood pumped out of the side of his neck and gushed down his body.

The sudden interruption of blood flow to the brain triggered a stroke and his right side, his dominant side, went numb. Grimes continued to struggle with her as best as he could with his left hand, but he was unable to overcome her as he weakened from the loss of blood. Within minutes, he was dead.

Beckwith struggled to her feet and leaned against the cabinet to regain her breath. She was drained by the wrestling match with Grimes. Her blouse and skirt were stained with Grimes' blood. She picked up her suit jacket and sat down in one of the conference room chairs. As her strength and senses returned to her, she stood and slowly walked to the conference room door. She opened it and walked through, closing it behind her.

A moment later, the door reopened and Beckwith stuck her head in. She spoke deliberately and haughtily to Grimes' dead body. "I told you, no man makes me scream!"

The ice queen closed the door and put on her suit jacket as she walked down to her office to call the police with her story of self-defense.

Ratek's Residence
New York City

~

Ratek heard the phone ringing as he approached the door of his townhouse. He quickly inserted the key and unlocked the door, then ran to the phone.

"Hello?"

"Max?" the cool voice asked.

"Judith? Is everything all right? You seem a bit distant." Ratek knew Judith well enough and read an undertone in her voice.

"It's Simon, Max." Beckwith paused for a moment. "He's dead," she said matter-of-factly.

"What? What do you mean he's dead? What happened? Where?" Ratek pummeled her with a torrent of questions.

"Here. In the conference room. He had too much to drink, as you know, and came back after you left. He assaulted me and I defended myself. I didn't mean to do it, but I killed him," she said nonchalantly.

"You killed him!" Ratek exclaimed in disbelief.

"Not intentionally. I was just defending myself," she responded coolly.

"Are you okay?" Ratek probed.

"Sure. After I called the police, I walked back into the conference room to pour myself a drink. I had to step over his body to get to the cabinet. Then, I came back here to my office to call you and let you know."

Ratek was convinced that she had ice running through her veins. To be able to walk back into that room, step across the body and pour herself a drink just amazed Ratek.

"I'll be right down," Ratek stated.

"No need to. The police should be here any minute," she replied abjectly.

Ignoring her comment, Ratek asserted, "I'm coming down to the office. There'll be a lot of questions to answer about tonight's events."

"Suit yourself," Beckwith said with indifference.

Ratek called for a car and walked out to stand underneath the portico until it arrived. Grimes is gone, he thought to himself. He should have made a comment to the two of them about how much they both were drinking tonight. He was sure some of it was a result of morning's disastrous events at the special shareholders' meeting. They both must have been stretched to the breaking point and their restrained antagonism for each other erupted tonight. He was going to miss Grimes after all of these years of working together. He was especially going to miss the dirty deeds that Grimes committed for him.

The car pulled up in front of the townhouse and he dodged the raindrops as he took a seat in the rear. He bitterly retraced the events of the day and one name seemed to continually rise to the forefront as the reason for the day's debacle and triggering the ensuing death of his good friend. That name was Emerson Moore.

Ratek took a personal oath to repay Mr. Moore in kind for his friend's death. He turned his face to look blankly through the rain-streaked window as the car drove quickly down the West Highway toward lower Manhattan. An evil smile crossed Ratek's emotionally drained face as he smashed a fist into the side of the car's door.

Aunt Anne's House
Put-in-Bay

~

Emerson had just parked the golf cart in the garage as he returned from dropping his aunt off at a sick friend's home. He heard the phone ringing in the house as he entered the house.

"Hello?"

"Emerson, it's Barry," the *Put-in-Bay Gazette* publisher said as he identified himself.

"Hi Barry. What's up?" Emerson asked.

"Did you see the wire stories today about the takeover battle yesterday?"

"Just briefly. As soon as I got up, I had to run Aunt Anne over to a sick friend's house right away. I planned on looking at them when I returned. Why, is there anything of particular interest?"

"Yes. It seems that two of Ratek's people were involved in a bit of a fracas in their New York office last night. One ended up dead."

"Which ones?"

"Beckwith, the pretty blonde, and Grimes. Grimes is dead. It appears that he accosted her and she killed him in self-defense."

"Interesting. I didn't like that Grimes. He gave me the creeps." Emerson shivered briefly.

"I'll let Chet Wilkins at the police department know in the event they want to run a DNA match on him and the hair sample from your assailant at the monument."

"Thanks. I'd be very interested in the results. If it turns out to be Grimes, I may want to make a visit to New York to see Ratek," Emerson contemplated.

"Be careful. Let the police handle it if it turns out to be a match," Hayen cautioned.

"I'm always careful. I'd just like to be able to write the final chapter in this story with Birkman Investments. I don't think it's over yet."

"Just be sure that it's you writing the final chapter and not me. I don't want to be writing your obituary!" Hayen admonished.

"All right! You're starting to sound just like my Aunt Anne. I'm going to run and take a closer look at the stories. Let me know if you hear anything and I'll keep you in the loop too." Emerson ended the call and took the stairs two at a time as he ran up to the second floor and his laptop.

Emerson logged on and scrolled through the stories and the story about Grimes' "accidental death," as it was being called.

How ironic that one of the takeover battles that Birkman Investments was involved in has now resulted in the death of one of its key people, Emerson thought to himself.

His phone rang and he answered it. It was John Sedler, his editor at the *Post*.

"Hi John. Bet you're calling about the death at Birkman Investments," Emerson guessed.

"You saw it then?" Sedler asked crisply.

"Just saw it on-line. Incredible."

"I think you need to hop a plane and see if you can get an interview with them," Sedler strongly suggested.

"Fat chance. I'm probably the last person that the Birkman people want to see," Emerson replied as he wondered how he could convince them to see him.

"Find a way. You're pretty good at that."

"Okay. It may take a day or two. But I'll try," Emerson promised.

Three days later, Emerson was driving the golf cart along Bayview in front of the public docks when he pulled over to talk to Tom and Chuck from DeRivera Park.

"Nice evening," he said as he watched the growing darkness

and looked towards the boats crowding the public docks. The partyers had started several hours earlier and were beginning to go in full swing. Several of the boats had sound systems rocking and strings of colored lights glowing to add to the festive atmosphere.

"Warm night. Clear skies," Tom commented as his ever watchful eyes patrolled the docks looking to head off any potential problems. "It's early and they're partying tonight!"

"I was just out on the dock by that 40-footer at the end. They've got the music booming and dancing on the dock and on the boats. There's a group of them that have got their own version of the wave. But they're not standing up like at the football games and waving their hands. Use your imagination and you'll figure out what they're waving," he said with a mischievous grin as he stroked his beard.

"Maybe, I'll have to take a walk out there myself," Emerson teased. "You've got to clear up a rumor for me that I heard, though."

Tom and Chuck looked at him.

"Which ones are the wildest partyers? Toledo police or Toledo firefighters?"

"Hard to say," Tom said thoughtfully. "With all the pressure on those guys, they need to be cut a little slack to blow off some steam."

They smiled and turned as the Put-in-Bay police chief's Blazer pulled up behind Emerson's golf cart with its lights flashing. Chief Chet Wilkens stepped out of the Blazer with a pad of tickets in his hand. "You know that you're illegally parked on this side of the road?" He pointed to the no parking sign that Chuck was leaning against.

"Oh no, you're not going to give me a ticket are you, Chet?"

Emerson moaned.

"Nope, I was just giving you a hard time," Chet said as he slid the pad of tickets into his back pocket. "But, I'll probably run out of tickets by the end of the evening."

"Well, we better be moving on, Chief," Tom said as he and Chuck began to walk out on the docks for their evening patrol.

"Good. I wanted to talk with you alone anyhow," Wilkens said.

"About?"

"Emerson, we got the results on that DNA sample from the lab. It was a match with the guy that wound up dead in New York at that investment firm you told me about that other day," the chief said seriously.

"Grimes!" Emerson exclaimed.

"Right. Grimes was the name. We've passed along our report of your assault to the New York City police. One of the detectives is supposed to give me a call tomorrow."

"Interesting. I apparently was getting a little too close for comfort on the story I was doing."

"Sounds like they just wanted you out of the way. And from what I heard, you're responsible for upsetting their entire applecart. They might still want to pay you back for that," Wilkens warned.

"Think they're still fretting about what I did, huh?" Emerson asked.

"Wouldn't you if you lost millions? All I can say is that it's a good thing that you don't have plans to go to New York. Stay here on the island and try to keep a low profile. Okay?"

"Okay." Emerson decided not to tell him that he had indeed planned on visiting New York. And now, even more so. He wanted to confront Ratek with the DNA evidence and read his reaction.

The chief's radio called for him to join several of the police officers in the park opposite the Beer Barrel.

"Got to run. You take care of yourself, Emerson."

"That I'll do," Emerson said tongue in cheek.

For the next two days, Emerson contemplated how he was going to approach Ratek. He picked up the phone and called Oakes at his office.

"Oakes speaking."

"Hi there Jaybird! It's Emerson Moore."

"Hello Emerson. How's our extra special takeover writer doing today? You know that we're thinking about having a bust of you placed in our lobby?" he teased.

"Yeah, yeah. So, how's life in the aftermath? Everything coming together?" Emerson questioned.

"Very good. Walent's jumped right back into the saddle and is getting up to speed quickly. The company's been revitalized under him. It so refreshing to see the positive changes that he's bringing. I'd heard a lot about him when I joined the company, and everything they said about him seems to be right on the button. His winning ways are the foundation for this company's rebirth," Oakes said proudly as he eased over to the window to look out at the rushing river.

"Heard anything more from that scalawag, Ratek?"

"Off the record?"

"Sure. Off the record."

"He's selling his stock back to the company. We're working through the documents and filings right now," Oakes said eagerly. "I'm doing something special though."

"What's that?" Emerson asked.

"I'll be delivering the check to Ratek in his office at Birkman Investments. Walent doesn't want to do a wire transfer of the funds. He wants the check personally delivered. I think he wants to rub Ratek's nose in it one more time as a parting shot," Oakes said proudly.

"How exciting! I'm coming along!" Emerson surprised Oakes by his statement.

"You're coming along? What do you mean you're coming along?"

"Just what I said. I need to bring full closure to my story," Emerson pushed.

"I can't agree to that," Oakes deferred.

"Go ask Weimar. Better yet, ask Walent. He'll agree that I should be present for the check turnover," Emerson pushed again.

"I don't know," Oakes muttered with concern.

"Check with them and let me know. I'll be here all day. You've got my number."

Weimar's Office
Fallsview Tire & Rubber Company

～

"He wants to do what?" Weimar asked Oakes incredulously after Oakes relayed Emerson's request.

"I know, I know. It sounds unreasonable to me too," Oakes replied to his friend.

"Not for one second will I support this. This is highly irregular!" Weimar protested.

"He wants us to talk to Walent. If we don't, I have a sense that he'll pick up the phone and call Walent directly," Oakes cautioned.

"Okay. Let's go see Walent," Weimar said, with his mind set against permitting Emerson to make the trip with Oakes.

A few minutes later, they were in front of Walent, and Oakes had just finished relaying the request from Emerson.

"Steve, this is an extraordinary and unusual request from an outsider. I'm not comfortable with an outsider, albeit a supporter like Moore, going with Jay to deliver the check to Ratek," Weimar stated with concern. "Highly unusual."

"Joe, are you worried about him stealing the check?" Walent asked with a mischievous look in his eyes.

"No. I'm concerned about his unnecessary presence at

Birkman Investments' office as the check is delivered."

"Jay, tell me about your security plans," Walent directed.

"Very simple. I'm taking the corporate jet to Teterboro Airport where I'll be met by one of the limo services we've used in the past. Then, I'll be driven directly to Ratek's office building. My only exposure will be the gap of time that I'm traveling from the limo and up to his office. But, who's going to think that some guy in a wheelchair is carrying such a large check? They won't give me a second look," Oakes explained.

"Wheelchair? You're not taking that scooter you're on?" Walent asked with surprise.

"It's my standby and travels a little easier than the scooter." Oakes smiled at Weimar as he recalled the incident in the New York restaurant a few weeks earlier when he couldn't go up the stairs to use the restroom and had to surprise the waiter by turning the patio area into an outside urinal. Weimar returned the smile as he also recalled the incident.

"It'll add to my deception," Oakes continued.

"Joe, sounds like we don't have a security issue. In fact, Moore's presence adds to our security," Walent noted.

"But Steve...," Weimar began to protest.

"No buts about it. We owe Moore for his role in getting me involved. If he hadn't contacted me, we wouldn't have this company today," Walent said firmly. He looked around his familiar office. "I didn't realize how much I missed being a part of the company. It's really good to be back."

Weimar smiled at his old boss.

"It's good to have you back, Steve!" he said with deep gratitude. Weimar hadn't cared that much for Owens and dramatically less for that sleaze bag Webster who was still keeping a low profile in Cleveland.

"Jay, call Moore and tell him that he's welcome to accompany you to the devil's lair."

Oakes and Weimar left Walent's office, walking past a beaming and rejuvenated Lita who was humming happily as she typed a memo on her desktop computer for Walent to sign.

As they entered the outer hallway, Oakes spun his scooter in a tight turn in a show of exuberance at having won the discussion.

"Careful there. You're going to kill someone or hurt yourself," Weimar said with mock caution to his co-worker. "You're enjoying this way too much!"

"I'm not telling Ratek that Moore is coming with me. We'll let it be a big surprise. Can you imagine the look on Ratek's face?" Oakes said in glee as he spun his scooter around again.

"Yes, but this is way too unprofessional for me!" Weimar chided Oakes.

"I need to call Emerson." Oakes wheeled around and made a straight drive to his office as Weimar muttered under his breath about having to pull another prank on Oakes. Maybe he'd disconnect the battery to his scooter when he wasn't looking. That would rain on his parade, Weimer mused.

As he entered his office Oakes turned abruptly and narrowly missed the sharp, pointed desk corner in his haste to make the call to Moore. He quickly called the number and Emerson answered on the second ring.

"Hello?"

"Emerson, it's the Jaybird!"

"Well, don't you sound chipper!" Emerson exclaimed at the excitement in Oakes' voice.

"You're going to New York with me!" Oakes blurted.

Emerson's face broke into a large smile as he contemplated confronting Ratek with the DNA evidence.

"Good. Where do I meet you?"

"At the Put-in-Bay Airport and hopefully tomorrow. I've got the corporate jet and we'll fly in and pick you up as soon as I can make the arrangements with Ratek. I'll call you as soon as I talk to him."

"Great. I'll be here."

They concluded their call and Oakes called Ratek's office.

In the Sky
Approaching Put-in-Bay

~

Thin and wispy cirrus clouds had formed at 20,000 feet and were moving eastward over South Bass Island as they marked the high-altitude front of an approaching depression with rain. The pilot of Fallsview Tire's corporate jet was thankful that they would be making a brief stop to pick up one passenger and then be quickly airborne. He wanted to avoid the bad weather any time that he could.

He approached the island from the south and dropped altitude so that he was a few hundred feet above the lake's choppy water. He flew over Miller Ferry, which was also approaching the island and pointed the sleek aircraft at the fast approaching runway.

Within a few minutes, the jet was taxiing toward the administration building on the airport's west side.

"Look at that!" the pilot exclaimed as he pulled abreast of the planes belonging to Dairy Air. His eyes swept over the Holstein cow markings painted on the fuselage of the six-passenger, grey and blue Cessna 207 and the one-passenger, white and red Cessna 152.

"That's different!" he yelled back to Oakes who was seated in the first row.

"Quite unique," Oakes agreed as the co-pilot opened the door and swung the ladder down to the tarmac where their passenger waited.

Emerson climbed up the stairs and took a seat across from Oakes as the co-pilot secured the door and joined the pilot in the cockpit.

"Beautiful day!" Oakes said as he greeted his comrade in arms.

"Every day on Put-in-Bay is a beautiful day!" Emerson stated proudly about his newly adopted home.

"I've never been here before. What a view as we flew in," Oakes noted.

The plane gained momentum as it rolled down the runway and began to lift over the trees at the runway's end.

"You haven't seen anything. Watch for the monument and the bay as we fly by," Emerson urged.

"Breathtaking," Oakes agreed as he took in a bird's eye view of the island.

Teterboro Airport
Teterboro, New Jersey

∾

"Need a hand?" Emerson asked as he stood up in the aisle and the co-pilot began to open the plane's door.

"Sure. These legs of mine are a bit unsteady," Oakes said as he slowly stood in the aisle and held unto the seat back.

Supporting Oakes with one arm, Emerson helped Oakes slowly, but deliberately walk down the aisle to the open doorway. Carefully, Oakes grasped the railing and taking a step at a time made his way down the stairs to the ground where the co-pilot had unloaded Oakes' wheelchair.

Seeing it, Emerson asked as he continued to help Oakes, "Where's your scooter?"

"Left it at home. The last time I was in New York, I couldn't get to the restaurant's second floor restroom because the lift wasn't working. I didn't want to chance another problem so I brought this one. It's pretty slick," Oakes said as he reached for a remote control on his belt and used it to maneuver the chair five feet to the bottom of the stairs. "Faster than the scooter and believe it or not, has four-wheel drive so you can drive it up hills."

"Who'd ever think of a wheelchair with four-wheel drive? So you just put it in four-wheel and climb stairs?" Emerson asked with interest as he watched Oakes lower himself into the chair.

"In a manner of speaking. It has gyroscopes and sensors that allow it to climb stairs by allowing the four wheels to rotate up and over each to go up or down stairs. Once it climbs the stairs, it returns to four wheels and full power. I can actually use this to zip across a tennis court and play tennis. I can also raise and balance on two wheels so that I'm at full height. Makes it easier to get food off the shelf at the grocery store or look someone directly in the eye when you're talking to them."

"Amazing," Emerson said in awe. "Why didn't you use it to exit the plane and come down the stairs?"

Oakes paused before answering.

"It's an issue of pride, I guess. I'm not quite ready to give in to the MS. In fact, I don't think that I'll ever give in. I fight it every chance I get," Oakes said with determination.

The co-pilot approached Oakes and said, as he pointed to the edge of the tarmac, "There's your car, Jay."

"Thanks, let's go." Oakes grabbed the joystick and pushed it forward to zip off quickly to the waiting limo for the late afternoon ride into lower Manhattan.

"That chair flies," Emerson observed as he began to hurry after Oakes.

"It should," the co-pilot called after him. "It's running on Fallsview Tires!" he teased.

Emerson chuckled to himself and increased his pace.

Birkman Investments
New York City

~

The doors of the elevator opened to allow Emerson and Oakes to exit onto the 20th floor and then closed to continue its journey to the top floor.

Emerson and Oakes went down the long hallway which overlooked the huge, open atrium on one side. At the end of the hallway, they were greeted by the massive oak doors and sign announcing the offices of Birkman Investments. Max Ratek's name as Chairman and CEO was prominently displayed on the signage.

Entering the office, they were greeted by the receptionist who recoiled with concern when she saw Emerson. She quickly recalled the testiness of his last visit.

"Jay Oakes from Fallsview Tire to see Mr. Ratek," Oakes said as he raised his chair to a standing position. "This is an associate of the company's, Emerson Moore."

"I'll let him know that you're here. If you'll just take a seat in the conference room to your right," she directed nervously.

Oakes lowered his chair and the two entered the conference room where Emerson seated himself next to Oakes, who positioned himself at the end of the long table.

Looking around the room, Emerson noticed that the carpeting had been replaced. He wondered if it had anything to do with Grimes' death.

Ratek's Office
New York City

～

The receptionist's message had been a surprise to Ratek. He stood up from his chair and began to pace his office as he sorted out the significance of Emerson's presence.

His mind quickly worked through several scenarios. Perhaps Fallsview Tire wanted a witness to the transfer of funds. He dismissed that thought as they could have sent one of their own, perhaps that attorney of theirs, Weimar. It must be a bone that they threw to Emerson since he had connected the parties to help defeat Ratek. That sounded more logical he decided.

Ratek loved to play chess. He loved the strategy and the anticipation of his opponent's moves. When he didn't like the way a game was going, he'd been known to dump the pieces from the board and start over. He had been playing in the back of his mind ways in which he could make another run at Fallsview Tire in the next few years. He planned to watch and wait until an opportunity presented itself and then, like the phoenix rising from the ashes, take control of Fallsview Tire.

As for Mr. Emerson Moore, Ratek still seethed over their past confrontations. With Grimes gone, he would have to find someone else to carry out his more nefarious tasks. One of the first would be to eliminate Emerson from the face of the earth.

Ratek resolved to play a game of cat-and-mouse carefully with this wily reporter. He would ooze civility and prohibit Oakes and Emerson from seeing any disappointment in him as a result of the takeover defeat. Ratek marched confidently across the office and opened his door to join his two visitors in the conference room.

"Gentlemen," Ratek greeted Oakes and Emerson as he entered the conference room and took a seat.

"Mr. Ratek," Oakes acknowledged.

Emerson nodded his head in greeting. He had his portfolio open and a pen in hand, ready to take notes.

"I trust that you had a safe flight in?"

"No problems. I hope you don't mind that I've had Mr. Moore accompany me. He's wrapping up his story about the attempted takeover and wanted to be here for its conclusion," Oakes offered as an explanation for Emerson's presence.

Turning to look directly at Emerson, Ratek declared, "Quite alright with me. Over this summer, you've seemed to be very adroit in securing more information than what I would have liked to see in the public eye, Mr. Moore. I commend you on your ability." Ratek was playing to Moore to keep him off guard.

"Thank you. There's one thing that I've been curious about since the beginning of all this," Emerson stated.

"And that is?" Ratek asked inquisitively.

Emerson continued to press the edge. "Why the stupid code name, chocolate doughnut? I heard you use that on the flight from Cleveland to LaGuardia."

Ratek remained emotionless on the outside while his inner being stormed.

"Mr. Moore, I would tell you that you and I have now found our first point of agreement. I thought it was stupid also. My deceased associate, Mr. Grimes, happened to have a weakness for chocolate doughnuts and suggested the name. We used the code name to placate him. I assure you that it would not be a name that I'd select."

Hearing Grimes' name, Emerson noted, "I see that you have new carpet in here. Didn't like the previous color?" Emerson wanted to jab with a comment about blood red, but held back.

Ratek, for a moment, glared at Emerson and then recaptured his self-control. He clearly understood the shot that Emerson had just taken.

"Carpet needs to be replaced from time to time," Ratek casually dismissed the question. Turning to Oakes, he asked, "You brought the check?"

"Yes," Oakes responded as he patted his suit coat breast pocket.

The door opened and the receptionist stuck her head in. "Excuse me, Mr. Ratek. I've shut down the switchboard and am getting ready to leave. Is there anything you need from me?"

Ratek glanced at the clock on the wall and saw that it was nearly 5:30 P.M. He recalled that his key team members were visiting customers or out gathering information on other acquisitions.

"Anyone else around?" he asked.

"No sir. Friday night, everyone tries to get out a bit earlier," she explained, hoping that he wouldn't want her to stay later. She had plans for an early dinner date.

"I won't be needing you. Have a good weekend," Ratek smiled at his pretty receptionist.

"One more thing. There's an invoice on your desk for approval on the upstairs construction. Good night." She closed the door and hurried to her date.

"Increasing office space?" Emerson asked. It might be a signal as to how well the firm was doing.

"Yes, I am. We're expanding to the floor above us. Care to see it?" Ratek asked as he saw an opportunity to spin the story to the overall successful track record of his firm in providing higher than average returns to his clients. Looking at Oakes and his wheelchair, he added, "I'm afraid that you won't be able to accompany us on the internal stairwell. The elevator entrance to that floor is being remodeled."

Oakes grinned. "No problem. Show me to the stairs and I'll show you how easily I can navigate them."

The three of them covered the short distance to the interior stairwell where Oakes positioned his chair at the bottom of the first step. He quickly manipulated the controls and two wheels of the chair rotated over the other two wheels as the chair began to climb the stairs. Oakes deftly handled the joystick and controls to the top of the stairs where he returned the chair to rest on four wheels.

"Quite a contraption, you've got there!" Ratek said with genuine interest.

"It does get me over obstacles," Oakes responded as he glanced at the dust covered floor littered with pieces of sheetrock, metal and lumber.

On the one side of the hallway clear plastic sheets were hung from the ceiling to the half wall, which had been framed in and overlooked the atrium. The sheets were meant to contain the construction dust to the immediate area and offered little protection to a contractor falling through it to the floor 21 stories below. Carpentry tools and sharp edged electric saws were scattered around the area, which was a maze of offices under construction. At the end of the hallway, the elevator doors yawned open dangerously, although guarded by an OSHA mandated barrier able to withstand 200 pounds of direct pressure.

"You'll need to watch where you're going up here," Ratek warned as he kicked aside a steel rod.

"We'll be careful," Oakes said as he carefully eased over a piece of scrap lumber.

"Let me tell you what we're doing here," Ratek began his PR pitch. "We're increasing our staff by 30% in order to serve our growing list of clients."

Emerson halted him with a question. "What's causing your client base growth?"

"Our track record of successes. We're continuing to outperform other investment houses in the return on investment that we are able to provide our clients," Ratek boasted grandiosely.

"And how do you think your clients will feel when they read this?" Emerson decided to move in for the kill and handed Ratek a document that he had pulled from his jacket's inner pocket.

"What's this?" Ratek asked as he unfolded the document and began to read it. He scanned over it and fought to control his initial angry feelings. He looked up emotionlessly at Emerson. "And what does this have to do with me or Birkman Investments?"

Emerson smiled. "Jay, the document that I handed Mr. Ratek is a copy of a police report, which I was able to obtain, on an initial DNA match. It indicates that the attempt to murder me in Put-in-Bay at the monument was made by Mr. Ratek's associate, Mr. Grimes."

Oakes' eyes widened. His job was to deliver a check to Ratek and not to get in the middle of attempted murder.

"Conjecture. Pure conjecture!" Ratek stormed as he began to lose his self-control.

"Even more important is that the explosives used to try to kill me have been identified as Semtex. Coincidently, the same explosive that was used in Owens' death," Emerson said to Oakes as he carefully evaluated Ratek's reaction.

"That still doesn't mean a thing!" Ratek roared.

Oakes turned his head to also observe Ratek.

"Furthermore, there have been a number of incidents of suspicious deaths of key people at companies that Mr. Ratek was taking over. All caused by explosions. All caused by Semtex. Coincidental? I don't think so. Earlier today, I turned all of my notes over to the authorities. I'm sure that you will be hearing from them shortly and then you will have an opportunity to talk about my conjecturing," Emerson said with a firm resolve.

Ratek saw the end in sight. His world would crumble. He'd lose his reputation as the Michelangelo of Wall Street. He'd lose his clients. He'd lose his independence. Without another thought to controlling his emotions, Ratek exploded at Emerson, "You've been a thorn in my side a little too long, Moore! You started my downfall with your nosing around where you shouldn't have! It's about time that you learned a lesson!"

Losing control, Ratek picked up the steel rod and swung at

Emerson. Emerson dodged the powerful swing and moved in close to grapple with Ratek. Ratek's good conditioning and his weight advantage allowed him to better Emerson and he cast Emerson to the floor. Emerson's head struck the corner of a table saw leg, momentarily dazing him.

As Ratek approached Emerson to strike a blow with the steel rod, he was knocked to the side by the footrest of Oakes' wheelchair. Oakes had driven the chair hard at Ratek.

"You, too!" Ratek exclaimed in astonishment. "You weakling. You stay out of this!"

Ratek violently pulled Oakes out of his wheelchair and threw him to the dusty floor.

"I'll make sure that you don't interfere again!" Ratek took a quick look at Emerson and saw that he had pulled himself to a sitting position. Ratek pushed the wheelchair to the head of the stairs and shoved it. He laughed sinisterly as he watched it bounce to the landing below.

Turning to see Emerson beginning to rise to his feet, Ratek rushed toward Emerson. Suddenly he felt himself stumble and fell to the floor. He looked around quickly and realized that he had tripped over a two-by-four that Oakes had skillfully aimed at his feet as he went by.

Ratek rolled over and grabbed the end of the two-by-four, snatching it from Oakes' grip and shouted at Oakes, "I told you to stay out of this!" He cast the two by four through the sheet of plastic, creating a gaping hole. The two-by-four fell 21 stories to the floor of the atrium.

Emerson had painfully pulled himself to his feet and leaned against a table saw. He saw Ratek charging him in a bull's rush and stepped aside at the last minute. Ratek missed Emerson and hit the partially completed, waist-high wall. Ratek lost his balance and leaned precariously into the plastic sheeting. He held tightly to the roughed-in wall to prevent himself from following the two-by-four to the atrium floor.

Emerson turned around. He saw Oakes trying to stand by clawing his way up one of the metal studs of an unfinished office. Emerson heard a noise to his right and whirled to see Ratek, with a menacing look, coming toward him. Ratek again had the steel rod in his hand.

Emerson looked down the hallway and the clutter which for the most part had been swept to one side. He spied a four-foot piece of two-by-four and rushed to pick it up, with Ratek on his heels. He scooped it up in one quick movement and spun around to meet Ratek face to face.

Ratek swung the bar with an overhand blow. Emerson parried as he swung the two-by-four upward. Ratek pulled back and swung again. This time, the force of Ratek's swing caused Emerson to lose his grip on the two-by-four. It flew out of his hands and through the plastic sheeting to the atrium floor below.

Ratek licked his lips in anticipation of Emerson's death. Without thinking, Emerson backed himself into a corner close to the gaping elevator doorway. He looked down the hall and saw that Oakes couldn't help him. Oakes was now standing on wobbly legs and grasping at his belt. It appeared to Emerson that Oakes was going for his cell phone to call for help. Emerson knew that he had to buy time.

Ratek jabbed at Emerson, playing with him as a cat plays with a mouse before the kill. Ratek feinted to the left and then struck quickly to the right and connected squarely with the side of Emerson's head. Emerson dropped to his knees and then onto to his side. He lay next to the elevator's barrier-protected, open doorway.

Ratek saw an 18-volt cordless circular saw with a 6-1/2 inch blade nearby. He made sure that Emerson was still woozy and walked over to the saw which was missing the guard on the blade. Turning it on, he listened as it whirred and smiled evilly. He turned it off, looked at Emerson again and turned it back on as he walked toward Emerson, gunning it as he walked. He thought momentarily that he heard the saw's whirring echo when he shut it off for those brief seconds, but ignored it as he stood over Emerson.

Emerson, with blood flowing from his head wound down his face, was having difficulty seeing. He heard the approaching danger, but was weak from the blow. He could barely move to try to save himself.

Ratek said sinisterly as he gunned the saw dangerously close to Emerson's face, "Good bye, Mr. Emerson Moore. You're going to pay dearly for what you have done to me!"

Emerson was too weak to move.

Ratek raised the saw high above his head in a display of macabre showmanship and began to lower it to kill Emerson.

Just then, something slammed into Ratek, and caused him to lose his balance. He fell and found himself sitting in Oakes' remotely controlled wheelchair which forcibly crashed through the elevator's protective barrier. Ratek screamed as the fast moving wheelchair propelled him into the open elevator shaft. The wheelchair fell away from him and bounced a few times on its way down the shaft, before crashing to the bottom.

Ratek's scream had suddenly stopped. As he was pitched through the opening, he been able to grab the elevator car's dangling cable. He was hanging by two hands to the 5/8-inch diameter loop of cable from the car above him. He knew that he couldn't hang on to the greasy cable for long and called to Emerson for help.

"Moore, throw me a line for God's sake! Don't let me fall!" Ratek screeched in terror.

Emerson slowly wiped the blood from his eyes with his shirt. He weakly rolled over onto his belly so that he could see into the elevator shaft. Hearing a noise behind him, he turned to see Oakes crawling along the floor to join him.

"Let me see what I can find," Emerson responded in an effort to help. But it was already too late.

Ratek's hands lost their grip on the slippery cable and the shaft was filled with his guttural screams as his body careened off the walls of the shaft as it fell. The thumps of his body striking the sides of the shaft carried to the ears of Oakes and Emerson.

Twenty feet above the shaft's bottom was the terminal motor device, a piece of angle iron set at an angle to act as an emergency brake for a descending elevator car. As Ratek struck it, his body was impaled and then broke away. It continued its fall to the bottom of the shaft where it was pierced by a series of two-inch thick steel buffers protruding 24 inches from the floor of the elevator pit.

Emerson and Oakes crawled to the edge of the shaft and looked down at Ratek's body and the crumbled wheelchair.

"I guess I won't be needing this anymore," Oakes said calmly as he tossed the wheelchair's remote control into the shaft. Minutes passed.

"Thanks, Jay," Emerson said gratefully. "I don't know what more to say."

"I'm just glad that I brought that chair on this trip. The gyro keeps it from falling on its side and it was easy to direct it up the steps. I just aimed it and pushed the throttle down. You should have seen the look on his face!" Oakes paused for a moment then continued. "He should never have called me a weakling! My manhood is not dependent on my physical abilities," Oakes stated with conviction, but with a pallor on his face.

"Are you okay, Jay?" Emerson asked with concern.

Oakes replied slowly and with remorse, "Yeah, I guess. The reality of what I did to Ratek is just hitting me."

"Well, I'm very appreciative of you coming to my rescue! Otherwise, it might have been you and me at the bottom of that elevator shaft."

"You're right," Oakes agreed.

Reaching for his cell phone, Emerson said, "I'll give the police a call, although with all the racket we made, I'd expect that someone else would have reported it. Looks like we'll be spending the night in town."

"I'll call the Waldorf and get us rooms—and me a rented wheelchair!" Oakes offered.

Shortly afterward, the police arrived and began their investigation of the evening's events. Oakes and Emerson were excused after two hours and Emerson assisted Oakes in one of the building's wheelchairs to a cab on Broad which they took to the Waldorf. While riding in the cab, Oakes called Steve Walent and Joe Weimar at their respective homes to let them know what had happened. Weimar had asked if Oakes still had the check and Oakes affirmed that he did and that they'd have to sort out to whom it should be delivered.

When they exited the cab at the Waldorf, the rented wheelchair was waiting for them.

Looking at the standard issue wheelchair, Oakes commented, "Not what I'm used to. This is a Model T!"

"I promise not to get us into any messes in the next 24 hours where you'll feel shortchanged because you didn't have your high performance ride," Emerson kidded.

They checked into their rooms, ordered shaving gear and a change of clothes for the next day, and then went to the Bull and Bear Restaurant on the Lexington Avenue side of the hotel for dinner. Emerson had been able to borrow a laptop and quickly wrote a story about their evening's escapade which he e-mailed to his editor, John Sedler, after first calling him.

Following dinner, they returned to their rooms and crashed for the night to recover from the evening's trying events. The next day held the promise of additional questioning by the police.

The next morning, there was a knock at Oakes' door. He wheeled himself over to the door where a grinning Emerson stood. "Take a peek out here."

Oakes wheeled into the hotel corridor and saw before him a new wheelchair, exactly like the one that he had the previous day. Standing behind the wheelchair was a uniformed driver. The identification on the shirt said Tom Ketcham—Federal Express Custom Critical.

"What's this all about?" Oakes questioned with surprise.

"When we returned to our rooms last night, I called Steve Walent and told him about your distress at the loss of your turbo-charged high-performance wheelchair—the chair that saved my bacon. He said that he'd call the local distributor and then follow up with a good friend of his who happens to be president of Federal Express Custom Critical. Overnight, they brought it right out for you," Emerson said with a big smile.

"This is a surprise," Oakes said with genuine gratitude.

The driver returned the rented wheelchair to the front desk and Oakes and Emerson re-entered their rooms to get ready for the day.

Later that day they returned to Teterboro Airport to meet the corporate jet for the flight to Akron-Canton Airport. As they were taxiing on the tarmac, Sir Edward Hollingsworth's corporate jet took off and headed for Sir Edward's island home on St. Martin. Sir Edward had decided that it might be beneficial for him to lay low for several months until the ugly mess with Ratek subsided.

Aunt Anne's House
Put-in-Bay

The ringing phone greeted Emerson as he walked into the house. He had just pulled the Model A out of the garage and was going to meet Barry Hayen for a day of sailing. There was a good breeze blowing in from the west.

"Hello?"

"Emerson?" the voice asked

Emerson recognized the voice as John Sedler's, his managing editor. They hadn't talked in seven days.

"Hi John, what's up?" he asked anxiously. He didn't want to spend time on the phone.

"I've got an idea for a story. Ever been to Key West?"

Coming in May 2005

When Rainbows Walk

The next book in the Emerson Moore series!

When Rainbows Walk starts in Israel, Spain, New York City and Put-in-Bay. It culminates in Key West and involves a terrorist, the Mafia and our Put-in-Bay investigative reporter, Emerson Moore. It promises to be an action-packed adventure filled with twists and turns.